ANARCHY

Hive Trilogy Book 2

By: Jaymin Eve and Leia Stone

Copyright © 2016 by Leia Stone and Jaymin Eve. All rights reserved.

No part of this publication may be reproduced. Stored in a retrieval system, or transmitted in any form or by any means, electronic, mechanical, photocopying, recording, or otherwise, without written permission of the author.

This is a work of fiction. Names, characters, places, and incidents either are the product of the author's imagination or are used fictitiously. Any resemblance to actual persons, live or dead are purely coincidental.

Stone, Leia
Eve, Jaymin
Anarchy

For information on reproducing sections of this book or sales of this book go to www.leiastone.com or www.Jaymineve.com

leiastonebooks@gmail.com

jaymineve@gmail.com

This book is dedicated to the artists, the dreamers, the writers, the musicians, the people that make life interesting.

Contents

Learn to speak Charlie 5
Chapter 1 6
Chapter 2 22
Chapter 3 42
Chapter 4 59
Chapter 5 76
Chapter 6 89
Chapter 7 108
Chapter 8 127
Chapter 9 133
Chapter 10 150
Chapter 11 169
Chapter 12 185
Chapter 13 201
Chapter 14 219

LEARN TO SPEAK CHARLIE

BAFF = Best Ash Friend Forever

FML = Fuck My Life

WTAF = What The Actual Fuck

YOLO = You Only Live Once

FOMO = Fear Of Missing Out

OMG = Oh My God

TOTES = Totally

Chapter 1

"Jayden!"

My scream sounded slightly hysterical at this point. I knew I needed to pull myself together. It was just a date, for freak's sake. Sure, it was a date with Ryder, who was probably the hottest ash on the planet, but it wasn't like I'd never been on a date before. I needed to pull my shit together immediately and there was no one better to help me with that than my BAFF. Best ash friend forever came with certain requirements, and first date help was at the top of the list.

Jayden's eyelashes entered the room first. Those luscious lashes were like a damn foot long, and my boy knew how to flutter them for full effect. Behind them were coal-black eyes, with a slight ring of silver. Ash eyes. Which looked hot as heck on the chocolate-skinned stunner who was my best friend. He ground to a halt a foot inside my room, hand dramatically slamming to his hips.

"Hell to the freaking no, Charlie. You will not leave the house in that! Over my dead, well-dressed body."

I sighed and somehow stopped myself from rolling my eyes at him. "Dude, I did not scream because I needed your help choosing—"

"You need more than my help, girl, you need a mutha-freaking intervention. Jeans, Converse, and a tank is not date material. It's Ryder. Did you forget that you were possibly going to have the chance to fuc–"

"Jayden!" My horrified snort of laughter cut him off this time. "I need you to help with my hair, just my hair."

He strode the rest of the way across and plonked himself down onto my bed, his muscled biceps looking even more prominent than usual. Someone had been doing more than just chasing Oliver through the weights room.

"Nope, no way in all hell. We make a deal right here and now. I will do your hair and makeup, have you looking like the second hottest ash bitch in this Hive, but I also get to choose three outfits for you, and you must wear one of the three."

This time my eyes were rolling, there was no way to stop them. He was so damned dramatic. I studied myself in the mirror, not really seeing what was so wrong with my outfit. I'd gone for sexy comfort, not knowing where we were going tonight. Besides, Ryder seemed to like me exactly the way I was, even with my Tomb Raider style of dress. It was just my hair, which was a freaking mess of weirdly shaped curls. I couldn't use a curling iron to save my life. Looked like I was going to have to compromise tonight.

I met Jayden's eyes in my mirror and gave him my best resting bitch face. "Okay, find your three outfits, and if you even mention nipple pasties this time, I will personally show Oliver that photo of you from when you were fourteen."

His eyes widened. "You wouldn't. I had acne and braces and weird lanky arms and legs. That's the shittiest best friend move ever."

I shrugged. "You've given me no choice but to play hardball."

The slightest of grins tipped up his lips. "You win this round. I will choose three Charlie-approved outfits for you, then we can work on that horror hair you have going on there. Shit, girl, I hope I have enough time. How long until your date?"

Ryder was taking me out at midnight. We were on Hive time, which was geared toward awake at night and asleep for a lot of the daylight hours. "Two hours," I said to Jayden.

He was suddenly up, and in a flurry of energy stormed to my closet and started flicking through the hangers and drawers. I remained where I was. I'd seen him like this many a time; he was on a fashion warpath and it was safer to stay on the sidelines until he was ready for me. My stomach clenched in anticipation then. It really didn't matter what I wore, I was so ready for this date tonight.

One hour and forty-five minutes later I gave myself one last look in the mirror. Jayden had out-freaking-done himself tonight. There were no nipple pasties and I was really happy with my outfit: skintight black jeans that had to have been custom made, they hugged my legs and cupped my butt perfectly, Jayden was probably creeping in my bedroom at night and taking my measurements or something. But I was not going to complain. The jeans were topped off with a deep, rich purple top hanging dangerously low off one shoulder, exposing my black bra and draping across my figure nicely. It was tight enough to be fitted, but loose enough that I didn't feel uncomfortable or exposed. Black ankle boots added three inches to my five-feet-seven. Team that with the bottle of O-negative blood I drank and I was ready for a date.

A knock at the door sent my stomach fluttering. Oh man, I had it bad. I inhaled deeply and smiled. Crossing the length of the living room, I rested my hand on the door knob and took another deep breath.

Date with Ryder, leader of the sexy six and ash enforcer. No big deal.

"Have fun, bitch. Wake me up to give me details," Jayden called out behind me.

Chuckling, I opened the door and in that moment all thoughts of my BAFF fled my brain.

Standing before me was the kind of guy you gawked at in magazines ... and he was carrying flowers. Ryder stood well over six feet tall, and every inch of him was toned muscle. Dark locks of hair hung wild, framing his chiseled jaw. He was wearing jeans tonight, soft and worn, and on top of that a dark gray, ribbed, long-sleeved Henley. It fit perfectly to his well-honed muscles. He looked every inch the warrior, and trust me, I'd seen him in action. He was a scary mutha when he was angry.

He handed me the flowers. The blooms looked extra delicate against all the masculinity of their backdrop.

"You look beautiful," he said, his low voice growly. I liked it.

As he stepped closer, towering over me even with my heels, I swallowed hard, hit all of a sudden with the memory of him in a towel. That was a good day. Not sure what else happened on that day in the Hive but the towel had definitely happened.

Clutching the yellow daisies closer, I couldn't halt my grin. "Thanks, I didn't think you were a flowers kind of guy."

Jayden popped up behind me. "I'll put them in some water," he said as he winked at the lead enforcer.

Ryder reached out and took my hand and just like that we were walking down the hall of the Hive, hand in hand like a ... a couple. Ah, if only it were that easy. Ryder was still dealing with the fact that he drained his fiancée Molly to death when he turned into an ash over thirty years ago. But for now this was more than enough. Got to start somewhere, and he was already hitting the right buttons.

After taking the elevator down to the main floor, we quickly made our way into the enforcer garage. Opening the door, I raised an eyebrow as I saw the rest of the sexy six leaning up against the blacked-out Humvee.

Oliver let loose with a catcall whistle: "Dayum, little unicorn, you sure do clean up well."

I grinned at Jayden's boyfriend.

"Crashing my date, boys?" I hollered back, only half joking. Seriously, were they coming? Surely Ryder could handle any minor threats.

Ryder turned to me and whispered so softly I could barely hear him. "After the attack from Sanctum and the other incident in the pit ... I can't take any chances."

Whoa. Date night had officially turned heavy. Of course, the Sanctum was certainly one big scary group of asshole killers to worry about, but the other incident, the one in the pit, was worse.

Just a week ago Ryder had released a vampire prisoner who had fed from me, only to find out he was human and I had somehow, with my magical unicorn blood, cured him of his vampirism. Ryder said he'd taken care of the body, and no one knew anything about me being the cure, but still, I hadn't slept well since that night. I didn't even want to think about what it all meant.

There was one thing I did know: if Ryder thought he needed the entire sexy six out to guard me on our date night, it sure as shit meant I was in trouble.

"We're going to India Palace," Ryder said to Kyle.

The huge jovial male, with his mop of dirty-blond hair, was Ryder's best friend, the one guy he trusted most with his secrets. Kyle was the only other one who knew about my blood being the cure. He had been there in the pit and was helping to cover it all up.

Kyle flicked me a grin before nodding at Ryder. Then he and the rest of the boys piled into the second Humvee. Ryder opened the passenger door of our car and ushered me in. As I slid into my seat, his arm grazed across my shirt, scraping the side of my right breast. I almost jumped out of my seat, and the tension in my body, which was already at its peak, shot up further. Was it actually possible to be so attracted to a guy that literally the slightest touch had me tied up with so many emotions?

Our gazes clashed for a moment and it took everything inside of me not to clench his shirt in my fists and pull him into me, to touch my lips to his, to taste that intoxicating spiciness which was all Ryder.

His full lips quirked at the corners and something dark rose in his ash eyes, the silver swirling in arcs. "Buckle yourself in," he finally said, pulling away, his body grazing mine again.

Pretty sure that time was deliberate.

He shut the door and I took a second to pull myself together. Holy hot day in hell, he was totally going to be the death of me.

As Ryder got into the other side, I forced my mind out of the gutter and back on the dinner ahead of us. Indian food. Ten points for Ryder. My inner food whore was officially drooling. Bring on the garlic naan and butter chicken.

An hour later I was having trouble breathing because I'd basically inhaled every menu item at India Palace. Ryder smiled, flashing one of his dimple-filled grins.

"I'll be honest. I've never seen a girl eat that much."

I shrugged. "Just wait until dessert."

One good thing about being an ash—increased metabolism and inability to get fat—I hoped anyway. I'd never seen a fat ash or vampire, so that had to mean something.

Ryder's grin widened, turning into a laugh. Goddamn, he had the best laugh. He was always so serious. And the way his eyes remained locked on me, like there was no one else in the room…

Which wasn't technically true, since there was a scattering of ash and vampires about, though I had no idea why the vamps were here, seeing they didn't really eat food. It did convey a sense of security, having the sexy six around us. The boys were keeping an eye on me and Ryder, and somehow managing to eat even more than I did. Except for Sam of course. The most serious of the sexy six was patrolling outside. Over-achiever, that one.

As Ryder's laughter died off, I fluttered my lashes, giving him a subtle wink. "Nice to see you can laugh. For a while there, right after I first met you, I was sure you had a Botox addiction and couldn't actually smile."

He chuckled again and let his eyes roam over me, landing on my lips. "I won't tell you what I thought when I first met you. Wouldn't be gentleman-like."

Well, hot damn.

I sat up straighter, and just as I was about to make another attempt at flirting, movement outside the wall of glass just beyond Ryder distracted me. The window looked out over downtown Portland, and until now the streets had been pretty quiet, which wasn't a huge surprise at this late hour. A shadow flashed again and I relaxed when I recognized Sam, decked out in a black trench coat. He was doing his best to fulfill every stereotype of our sire's kind—the old tall, dark, and deadly vampire.

Still, his outfit had a practical use. The rain was falling softly outside—Portland was always raining—and it was icy tonight with winter approaching. I hoped Sam was okay out there.

"How did you all meet?" I asked, turning back to Ryder. My curiosity about this tight-knit group of males was high. Ryder had been following my gaze, so he knew what I meant.

He flicked another glance back over his shoulder, eyes locked on the silent, patrolling enforcer, and the fierceness he wore so effortlessly softened just a little.

"You know the basics of Kyle and me. We were best friends from a young age, as were our mothers. My ash genetics kicked in first, but with everything that happened, I was lost for some time…"

He trailed off and I knew he would be caught in memories then, unpleasant ones of killing his fiancée. "So Kyle actually went through the culling first, and had a place in the Hive by the time it was my turn to fight to the death."

Obviously they'd both made it through that barbaric practice. Not a huge surprise. Even before I knew the boys so well, I'd have bet money on them surviving. They were both absolutely lethal. If they'd have been in my group, I'd never have made it through alive.

"Oliver came to our Hive about ten years after Kyle and me. The cullings weren't so organized then. Let's just say they were more of a total bloodbath, less sponsors and no rules. No one wanted to train a gay guy, no one wanted a gay guy to join the Hive period. This was in the nineties, when people weren't as accepting of that lifestyle."

I leaned forward on my elbows as his rich voice wove this tale around me.

Ryder shrugged. "I saw him practicing on his own. He was good, fast as hell, and powerful. I offered to train him and told everyone in the Hive that he was not to be harmed. He survived and is one of my best hand-to-hand combat fighters."

Could this guy get any more intriguing? And sexy? Because kindness was something I found utterly irresistible in this world filled with bullies and assholes.

"And Sam?" Sam was such a puzzle to me. Always silent. Totally deadly.

Something flashed across Ryder's face but then it was gone.

"Sam's been through a lot. He joined us about fifteen years ago. Found him when we were out on a call. We were alerted to the fact that a rogue ash was feeding on hikers up in Canada, leaving a trail of rumors and stories behind as he made his way into Oregon. We weren't sure if it was a true call in or not since there were never any bodies left, just reports of animal-type attacks. Still, I had a feeling, so we checked it out. Sure enough, we found Sam. He was near dead—hypothermia can be deadly to ash—and despite this he managed to half kill me before I could capture him. Took me an entire year to gain his trust. Never regretted my decision though, he's saved my life over a dozen times, is as loyal as they come, and surprisingly enough, wicked on a snowboard."

The last part startled me. Sam snowboarding? Who knew?

"Jared?" I asked next. I loved the way that Ryder's entire face changed when he talked about his best friends. I wanted more of this openness.

Ryder startled me with a bark of laughter. "That's a crazy story. Let's just say we met at an annual enforcer conference in Australia. I nearly lost my arm and Jared is no longer allowed in his home country."

I raised an eyebrow and nodded. Okay, I would need to hear the rest of that story another time.

"And lastly Markus, with his pretty little man bun." The Scottish enforcer was one of my favorites. He was a massive monster but funny as all hell. And kind. Most importantly he was kind.

Ryder leaned back a little, that damn half-smile on his face. I loved that smile. "Markus made it his life's mission to bring me down a few—"

He was cut off by the sound of glass shattering behind him.

The enforcers around me acted immediately, tables upturning and weapons drawn. Ryder was already out of his seat and had me yanked to the floor by the time a projectile flew through the smashed window and clanked against the hardwood floors. Chaos broke out, and the enforcers closed quarters around us. No more than a few seconds had passed as I leaned forward to see better. Was that a gas canister?

Just as I had that thought, we were moving. Two of the guys had me under each arm and were practically lifting me off the floor and floating me across the room. Seriously? Okay, I might have a little trouble taking orders, but there was no need to manhandle me. I was not some damsel that needed to be carried out by her brave knights. I had two freaking feet and I could use them just fine.

It was extra annoying that in the crazy chaos I couldn't even tell who was holding me. At least I could sense Ryder was close by. Smoke began filling the room, and as the vapor hit, my lungs burned and I started coughing and spluttering. What the fuck? We were in Portland, not exactly a war-torn city. Who was attacking us and where the hell had they gotten this type of weapon? It had to be Sanctum. It was too much of a coincidence that the very restaurant we were in just got randomly attacked.

My eyes were streaming tears as our group zipped through the restaurant and out into the back kitchen. Everyone was screaming and I could hear what sounded like gunshots outside—five or six pops in a row. Shit was getting serious now. As soon as we cleared out of the main room, I realized Ryder was on my right, pressed closely against me.

"Sanctum?" I shouted at him, before dissolving into another coughing fit.

We finally reached clear air near the open back door, but the longer we stood there the more the damn smoke followed us. Sucking in as much of the fresh Portland air as I could, my cough started to subside, but I could already feel the roar of pain in my throat. Ryder hadn't answered me yet, and before I could ask again he let me go and withdrew the gun he always carried.

"Stay here," he said, his tone firm. He turned, and with Kyle on the other side of him, the pair slid out the back door—probably checking to see if it was safe for us to leave.

I glanced back to find the smoke still billowing out of the main restaurant and surrounding our group. Had Ryder seriously warned me to stay put? I was so totally ignoring the bossy enforcer, because really, who the hell did he think he was ordering me to do anything? He could be in danger out there. It was that thought more than any other that propelled me forward.

Oliver, who had been standing beside me, made no real objections when I followed the rest of the enforcers into the alley. I noticed Ryder, Kyle, Markus, and Jared near the main street. The lights were filtering across their faces. Oliver and I strode closer.

As I neared the group I heard Jared call out. "It's the damn Bible thumpers again!"

Markus, who towered over the other men, was looking uncharacteristically serious as he turned to face Ryder. "They're gone. Sam went postal on them, shot up their vans."

"Bible thumpers?" I asked as I stepped into their inner circle. Ryder didn't seem overly surprised to see me, but still gave me a bit of a deadpan glance. He'd totally known I would not stay put, but still had to issue the demand. Men.

Before they could answer, my eyes were drawn to a nearby wall, which was plastered with government issued "Are you an ash?" posters, the ones which listed the symptoms and had the hotline number at the bottom. All of them were defaced with red spray paint, so fresh it still dripped from the posters. It took me a second in the dim light, but then I finally realized what had been tagged on them. One word: *Evil*. I shivered. Okay, now I was more than creeped out—standing here in the dark streets after having just been smoke-bombed out of my dinner date.

Some of the tension left Ryder as he holstered his weapon and gestured to the poster. "They're a pain in my ass. Call themselves 'Deliverance.' It's a religious group that think we're all evil and want to wipe us from the Earth, and since they have insane amounts of money, they have plenty of resources at their disposal. Their end game is to cure the world of vampirism."

A moment later Ryder and I froze as if a damn light bulb had gone off above both of our heads.

Holy shit.

Did they know about the pit? No! They couldn't, right? How could they know? Ryder would not have left any loose ends for them to find, that was for sure, but I guess there was still my blood work out there. The Hive had taken more than one sample from me, and who knew where those results ended up. Not to mention we were all pretty sure there was a mole in the Hive, maybe feeding information out into the human world. That was why we trusted no one outside of this core group. And Jayden.

With their hate-on for our kind, I didn't believe Deliverance was in bed with Sanctum, but the timing of the two attacks was hard to ignore. Was there a connection between the groups? Someone in our Hive? Or had we just been unlucky enough to be the only ash out on Deliverance's nightly "clean up the streets" vendetta? Either way, I knew my time was running out. Secrets always came out.

I must have made a noise, some sort of distressed whimper. Ryder's head shot up and we shared an intense look. From the corner of my eye I noticed the bewildered stares of the rest of the boys. Kyle was the one exception. He already had all the facts.

There was so much hidden emotion on Ryder's stony face. He seemed worried, like, for the first time he had no answers.

A Humvee peeled around the corner, distracting us all. Sam was at the wheel, his face alive and murderous. Shooting up the Deliverance was clearly his idea of a good time. He screeched to a halt, opening the door and tossing Ryder the keys.

"Four men packing deadly weapons. They intended to kill, or possibly capture," he said, in typical Sam style, using as few words as he could.

Ryder's hardened expression did not ease, although he let out a small huff, resigned.

"Boys, we need to talk." He motioned to the Hummer and in silence we all piled in.

I knew what was coming. We couldn't keep my secret forever, and if Ryder trusted the sexy six with my life, then I did too. We had to tell them so they knew just what we were up against.

No one spoke as we left the restaurant; the tension inside the vehicle was palpable. It was a tight squeeze in a single car. Guess they'd go back for the other Hummer later. After about ten minutes of silent driving, I realized Ryder was going in the opposite direction of the Hive. I was about to say something when I saw a familiar landmark. He was taking us to the lake, the place where he grew up. No doubt he was worried that the Humvee was bugged, and after the Sanctum attacks we weren't taking any chances. We needed to ferret out that mole in our Hive ASAP.

The other enforcers remained mute, staring out the window, following Ryder's lead. As we halted in a small section which was blocked off from the main road by a mass of trees, Ryder threw the car in park and we exited.

I snuggled tighter into my black jacket, pulling my hood over my head against the cold. Ryder maneuvered his way around to me, reached out and took my hand. Even in the darkness I could see the silver of his eyes as our gazes met.

His voice was calm, serious. "Do you trust me?"

"Yes." There was not an ounce of hesitation in my reply. I trusted Ryder to the same level as my mom and Tess. Family level. Sure, he had electrocuted me once, but I had pretty much let that go.

The hardness he'd been shrouded in since our date had been interrupted, finally started to ease. My trust meant something to him. His grip tightened as he pulled me close and turned to lead us through the trees. The rest of the guys flanked us as we walked for a few minutes away from the car and into a wooded green space. Portland was full of government-protected greenspace forests, which I loved; it felt like home when I was surrounded by nature.

As we crunched our way through the woods, I wondered how the rest of the sexy six would react to the fact that I was some sort of vampire cure. I was nervous. Even though I knew these guys deserved to know the truth when they had to risk their lives for me, I still wondered if we were doing the right thing spreading this information.

Eventually Ryder stopped and we all huddled in a circle. The rain had thankfully eased, but the cold was still prevalent. Ash genetics could only do so much to keep us warm.

Jared was the first to speak: "What's up, mate? Must be some serious sort of news to drag us out into the ass-end of the city?" I took a moment to appreciate the Australian enforcer's accent. Man, I was a sucker for accents, and we had a sexy mix of them in this group.

Ryder's voice was low but clear, and I took some reassurance in the way he seemed completely unworried.

"Charlie is more than just a female ash…"

My focus, as always, was on the lead enforcer, but for some reason I felt the scrutiny of one of the others. Sure enough, as I shifted my gaze, I realized Sam was eyeballing me. Hard. I shivered a little. He was the toughest of all the enforcers to read, and even an idiot would see he was filled to the brim with secrets.

"Remember that vamp in the club who bit her…?"

I realized that Ryder was still explaining, and unable to stand the tension any longer I had a brain-to-mouth-filter malfunction.

"I'm the cure for vampirism," I blurted.

There was dead silence for a few moments after that— wide eyes and slack jaws. Yep, that was not what most of them had expected the news to be.

Oliver, who was as manly as they came, decided now to channel his inner Jayden as he threw out a few flamboyant hand gestures. "Excuse me? What did you just say?"

I exhaled loudly. "Like Ryder was saying, that vamp asshole bit me at the club and then you all threw him in the pit..."

They nodded.

"We went down to free him," Kyle said, "as per Quorum orders, and imagine our surprise when he turned up as a human."

Most of the boys still looked shocked, but Sam's face was a mask of calm. I was getting a feeling about him, like he knew more than he was saying. Of course, before I could press him, the others distracted me with a bunch of curses and angry exclamations.

"Well, shit, looks like our little unicorn is dipped in gold," Markus finally said, his brogue deep and smooth. "What's the plan?"

Ryder took a moment. I could almost see the tumult of thoughts flashing through his mind. "I got rid of the human. No one knows about Charlie."

Sam's growl cut him off. "You can't know that." His voice was dark, ominous. The man of few words looked fired up, which had more alarm bells ringing in my head.

Ryder's brow furrowed at his mysterious best friend. "You're right. I don't know for absolute sure that this information is not in the community. And the timing of the Sanctum and Deliverance attacks are suspicious to say the least. The truth is, it's only a matter of time until someone comes for her again, so we have two options. Stay and play good boys at the Hive—use that time to tap into our resources and try to find the mole, try to find who hired the Sanctum, and see if we can discern any connection between Sanctum and Deliverance. Then when the shit hits the fan, I take Charlie and run." Clearly he'd had the same thoughts as me outside the restaurant. "Or … I can just take Charlie now and run."

Whoa. Run where? Survive how? The fact that Ryder was willing to drop everything and run away to protect me did crazy fluttery things to my insides. I understood why we had to run. Not even Ryder could take on the entire vampire population, yet I hated the thought that anyone would give up their life for me. This was bullshit, the entire thing.

"*We* run." Markus said with force.

"Huh?" I said, furrowing my brows.

Kyle nodded. "We stay in the Hive, gather information, and when the shit hits the fan, we run. Together."

He put his fist in the center of the circle, and each of the sexy six followed suit. After their macho fist bump, Ryder tucked me closer to his strong frame.

"I'll start planning for that day. Until then, we tell no one."

As we turned to start back to the car, Sam, who had still been staring at me the entire time, growled through clenched teeth: "This can never be mentioned inside the Hive. If her secret is found out by the humans, she will be experimented on and drained to distribute the cure and end the virus. If her secret is found out by the vampires, she will be decapitated and then burned for fear of her taking away all their power." Since he rarely spoke in full sentences, we all knew he felt strongly about this information.

Ryder reached out and placed a hand on his friend's shoulder. "That will never happen, brother. Not while I'm still alive to fight."

Sam's worried words brought it all home for me. He was right. No matter who found out about this, there was no happy ending for Charlie. Can I just say FML?

Chapter 2

The next morning I stumbled out to find Jayden sitting at the coffee table nursing a bottle of blood and giving me the evil eye.

"What?" I grumbled. I needed a bottle of half blood, half espresso right now. After returning from my date I had tossed and turned, thinking about all the drama in my life, worried and scared. I hated that feeling of being out of control, like I was sitting on a bomb and I had no idea how long until it exploded.

Jayden pointed a finger at me. "You didn't wake me to tell me about your date so I figured Ryder slept over and now I see your ass stumble out of your room alone. Tell me you at least made out with him?"

I smiled. Oh Jayden. Always making sure my sex life was legit. Where to start? "Well, there was a steamy kiss at my door."

He leaned forward, eyebrows raised, and I swear he even turned his ear in my direction like he didn't want to miss a word.

"But that was after we got attacked on our date by a religious group that thinks vampires are the devil incarnate."

The cheeky expression fell from his face. "Oh. I see. Kind of a mood killer."

I nodded. "Yep and that's not all."

If Ryder was telling the sexy six, I sure as hell was telling my bestie. I knew what Sam had said about never repeating my secret in the Hive was sound advice, but I wasn't planning on being inside these walls when I did.

Grabbing his hand, I tilted my head to indicate we needed to walk outside the apartment. Jayden looked confused for a second, but didn't hesitate to follow my lead as I slipped on my tennis shoes and grabbed a bottle of O-negative. There was no conversation as I led Jayden to the roof jogging track. It was empty this time of day. Bright with the light of the sun, no vampires would be up here. I also found great perspective staring out over the entire city.

Taking Jayden's hand, I led him as far from the entrance as possible, to the edge, staring down the sixty stories. My bestie was quiet, which was about as far removed from his personality as was possible. He no doubt had sensed the secrecy in my actions. Standing up on my tiptoes, I whispered into his ear.

"That guy that bit me at the club turned into a human. My blood is so tempting because it's the cure and we might need to leave the Hive at any moment because people are after me."

I popped back down on my flat feet and waited for his response. As our eyes locked, I could see his were wide and full of emotions. A lot of which looked like concern. He slipped his hand in mine and squeezed.

"Oliver knows?" he murmured.

I nodded. "As of last night."

His face became serious. "Don't you leave me here, bitch. No protecting me for my own good." I sucked in deeply, so relieved to know that even with this new information on my magic blood, nothing had changed between Jayden and I.

I grinned, punching him lightly on the arm. "Wouldn't dream of it, bitch."

Needing to relieve my inner tension, I took off running, Jayden at my heels. He could have easily overtaken me—he was descended from the second house, and they had an affinity for speed—but instead kept pace with me. Running was my drug now. As my feet pounded the track, the wind in my hair, I felt like I was running from all of my problems and it gave me a temporary reprieve from the insanity that had become my life.

After showering, I dragged myself down to my boring-ass job of answering phones in the enforcer call room. Stepping through the door, I stumbled a little to see Ryder sitting in my chair, his feet up at my desk. I often had an enforcer in here with me, but never the big bad leader of the crew.

I nudged his legs out of my way. "Excuse me, big day ahead. Important job of phone answering."

His heavy boots hit the floor. "Nope, sorry. You're fired."

I ground to a halt halfway into my chair. "What?"

Could he fire me? Was the Quorum involved? Maybe after last night they wanted me somewhere else. OMG please don't let it be washing dishes or some shit.

Ryder produced a sleek black gun from behind his back and a walkie-talkie. My eyebrows shot up as he handed them to me.

"Let's be honest, you're not a people person, and how am I going to keep an eye on you unless I make you an enforcer trainee?"

OMFG. "What? I'm an enforcer?" I jumped up and down like a teenager as Ryder's lips quirked into a smile.

"No. You're a trainee, a rookie who will watch and learn and never leave the car. Got it?"

I took the gun, sliding it into my belt, and clipped on the walkie-talkie. Fuck yeah. "Got it."

He nodded and walked away, motioning that I was to follow. I looked behind me and glanced one last time at my boring-ass desk and phone. Peace out, stupid job. Peace out.

Following Ryder into the enforcer locker room, I met the gaze of the sexy six and tried not to smirk in pride.

Kyle looked me up and down, his eyes resting on my walkie-talkie. "Well, well, what do we have here?"

Markus advanced towards me, inhaling deeply. "Smells like a rookie."

I rolled my eyes. First unicorn, now rookie. Oh hells no. Pick a nickname and stick with it.

"Rookie with a gun, boys," I joked, turning a full circle to show it tucked in my waist belt.

Oliver gave a half smile. "Perks of dating the boss. I didn't get a gun for months."

Slivers of heat filled my cheeks. I knew my face was probably a little red. Were we officially dating? I mean … we had been on a date. Still, there were no labels or titles attached to us yet. Ryder was all dark and mysterious; he probably beat labels up for fun in his spare time.

Ignoring the Latino enforcer, Ryder called the boys in closer. "Listen up, Lucas has approved Charlie to be an enforcer trainee. This gives her a weapon, an access badge, and clearance to leave the Hive grounds on official business."

The room was heavy, our silence saying everything as we all shared a look. This was a part of a greater plan, this was Ryder preparing for the possibility that we may one day leave the Hive. I swallowed hard, losing the thrill I'd initially felt at my new job.

The boys nodded curtly, which had me squaring my shoulders. I could do this, I was going to be trained and have a gun. Screw the Hive. Game on, bitches.

Ryder turned to me, handing me a keycard with my name on it. "Guard this with your life. Don't go sneaking around, and stay out of the medical ward. Every door you open with that gets logged into a database that the Quorum looks over daily. Be good."

I saluted him. "Yes, boss."

My curt reply was followed up with a sexy smoldering grin, all eyelashes and bedroom eyes. How far could I push him now that he was my boss and possible dating partner?

A few of the boys snickered.

Ryder quickly concealed his earlier charm into a mask of calm, not giving into my pushing of his buttons. "Your locker is number eleven. Uniform is inside."

I rolled my eyes. He was no fun. All work. I strode across the aisle and found number eleven quickly. There'd better be some cool black army fatigues inside, ones with small pockets so I could hide knives and shit. Pulling the lever, I opened the locker. A whoosh of air hit me first, and then in the next instant I was doused in a warm brown liquid. My breath caught as a startled scream ripped from my throat.

What. The. Actual. Fuck.

I blinked a few times in shock as the liquid ran down my face and dripped into my open mouth. The moment it hit my tongue I recognized the smooth, sugary flavor. Chocolate.

Those mutha … effing … asshole … freaking…

At the roar of laughter behind me, I swung around with my biggest baddest death glare. "Welcome to training, rookie," Jared choked out between laughs.

Even Sam was trying to contain his usual toughass façade.

I didn't utter a word, continuing to glare. They were just lucky I hadn't been wearing my favorite shoes. I would have actually shot them with my new gun if my ass-kicking boots had been ruined. Something in my expression must have finally sunk into the stupid six across from me.

Their laughter stopped.

Oliver gave Ryder a worried look. "Her gun isn't loaded, right?"

Ryder's smile was quickly lost. "Charlie, it's a joke. We've all been through it."

Usually his slightly pleading expression would soften me right up, but today I was covered from head to toe in a bucket of warm melty chocolate. Did I mention how hard this was going to be to get out of my hair? Not to mention how torn I was to not start licking this liquid orgasm off of my arm. I was a chocolate whore for sure, but I wouldn't tell them that.

I smiled sweetly. "Oh, totally, just a joke, right. Ha, ha." The words had barely left my mouth before I began stalking towards Ryder. All of the guys backed up, but unfortunately for them they'd caged themselves into the side of the locker room where there was no easy escape.

Ryder put his arms out. "Charlie…"

I was already across the room, but decided to tap into the heat at my center, which was the home for my levitation power. I hadn't used it since the culling, but thankfully everything seemed to still work the same. I leapt across the room and landed right on Ryder. He caught me and together we fell backwards.

Rubbing my chocolate hands on his face, I laughed.

Ryder gave me an amused glare. "Now we both have to shower."

I raised an eyebrow. "Is that an invitation?"

The silver of his eyes started swirling as I heard his low groan. Hah. Guys were easy. I was going to say that was round one to Charlie.

After showering—alone—and cleaning up, I went down to my scheduled feeding time, hoping to see Tessa. I had sent my human best friend a hundred emails begging her to come talk to me, but she was mad at me for crushing her dreams of wanting to be a vampire. She thought this was the answer to us being able to stay friends for the rest of eternity. I thought it was a direct path to her losing her soul. Vampires were cold-blooded assholes. Lucas was the only one I even liked. He was different for some reason.

Jayden was working at the front desk and I took a few minutes to excitedly tell him that I was now a rookie enforcer. My bestie was suitably thrilled for me, before handing me my bottle of O-negative. I glanced nervously down the hallway, where the rooms were. Jayden gave me the slightest shake of his head, telling me that Tessa wasn't here yet. I knew my face had fallen, and with a sad sigh I dragged myself to the private room.

I don't know why I bothered to keep waiting. I had all but decided that Tessa wasn't ever going to show up here again. Downing my blood, I bopped my leg as I waited. Then the door handle moved. I held my breath, only letting it out as my bestie walked in, platinum blond hair perfectly curled, make-up expertly painted, designer clothes exquisitely chosen.

"Tessa," I nearly choked. So much had happened since we last talked. I stood quickly, but as I tried to cross the room to hug her, she flipped up her hand in the universal sign for "halt the hell up." Her lips had that tight firm line they always got before I was about to get bitched out.

"Charlie, I need you to understand something because clearly this place has warped your brain." Her voice was all business. Ouch.

I just nodded.

She started pacing. "Thanksgiving is coming up, and then Christmas." My heart dropped when I saw where this was going. Tessa's family was rich. Her father died when she was little but her mother had inherited all the money—her mom who had no idea how to love Tessa properly, thinking buying her things would do it. Every holiday season her mother would jet off to Paris or some other exotic location with her current boyfriend and Tessa would spend those holidays with my mom and me.

"Are you going to be able to get an entire day off and come home and help cook with your mom and me?"

My hands flew to my hips, in what I hoped was a defiant pose. "Yes, I will." I had an all access pass now.

Tessa nodded, a bitter smile across her lips. "What about in twenty years? Fifty? Your mom will be dead and so will I. But you will remain young and strong and you'll stop coming to see us. You and I won't talk about boyfriends anymore. You have Jayden now."

She crossed her arms as tears welled in her eyes. Shit. Fuck. Fucking shit.

"No, Tessa!" I held her as the cries racked her body. Whoa … I had not spent much time around humans since I turned. She felt so warm and fragile in my hands. Everything came crushing down on me then—my old life. It was lost to me now.

Pushing her back, I made her face me, waiting until she stared directly into my eyes. "Getting old is a good thing. Being human is a good thing. You don't want to be in this shithole and be dependent on blood and deal with the politics and power struggles. You can't have children if you become infected and turn into a vampire. You can't have a lot of things." I pulled one of her bouncy curls and watched it spring back perfectly, just like I had a hundred times before.

Tessa's chuckle was low and strangled. "I can have you, my best friend. You don't get it! You clearly don't miss me like I miss you. Your life with Ryder and Jayden is fine and you're fine without me." She pulled back from me, turning away.

"That's not true. It kills me not to live with you anymore, to make sure you're up for class and you don't drink four-day old molding coffee or get roofied at a party."

A burst of laughter rang from her then and I smiled. The tension which had been plaguing my insides, pretty much since we'd had our last fight, started to ease.

"Withdraw the request to be changed, please," I begged.

Whatever mirth had been on her face faded away as her expression became a hundred percent serious. "It's not just for you, Charlie. I love Blake, and I have nothing holding me to the human world. I never wanted kids, you know that. I'm not withdrawing it."

Anger and fear lit up inside of me, and words fell from my lips before I could think them through. "Tessa! Don't be stupid. You don't understand this life at all!"

Tessa flinched back like I had slapped her. "Stupid?" she screamed. "Thanks for listening to my problems. Some best friend you are!"

She stormed out.

Dammit! I collapsed to the ground and dropped my head into my shaking hands. Way to go, Charlie. Piss off one of the few people in this world who love you. It had been going pretty well up to that point too. I just lost my mind whenever she mentioned becoming a vampire.

Since my time was up in this room, I couldn't wallow in my pain any longer. I stormed out and gave Jayden a little wave before leaving the feeding room. I just wanted to be alone. Maybe go outside, maybe run away on my own and leave everyone behind. Seriously, how the hell had my life gotten so intense and complicated? Opening the large double doors that led to the hallway I was taken aback. Sam was just standing there like a creepy sentinel, face completely void of emotion. We silently observed each other for a brief pause, before some of his statue-like pose eased.

"Outside," he said, jerking his head and beginning to walk.

Well, hello, once in a lifetime moment. Had tall, dark and silent actually sought me out and spoken directly to me? Like actual speaking? Okay, it was only one word, but for him that was practically a novel.

My eyebrows creased as I followed him into an open elevator. There was a vampire in there, so we both stood quietly as we made our way down to the ground level. The vampire inhaled deeply and I turned to see his eyes pulsing. For shit's sake, not this again. Sam turned hard eyes on the bloodsucker, all of us in a weird stare-off. The male vampire swallowed hard, and when the doors opened at level five he all but ran out. Then Sam and I were alone.

I had no idea what Sam was going to say to me. Was he fetching me for Ryder, or was this to do with that look he wore the other night in the forest? Surely he didn't want to talk about the weather or how insane the last episode of *Supernatural* was. If I knew anything, it was that this enforcer did not do the small talk thing. He hardly did the big talk.

When the doors opened at ground level, Sam strode out flashing the front desk ash his badge. Fumbling in my pocket I found my own special magic card and quickly did the same thing. No more signing in and out? Hells yeah!

Once we were outside, the sunlight and fresh air knocked into me with a welcome burst of energy. I should have mentioned this to Tessa—no more sunlight if she was changed. That girl was a big fan of Hawaii and the Caribbean, a beach baby through and through. After college we had planned on spending six months travelling through the islands. But as a vamp she would never suntan again.

The darkly handsome enforcer, with his few days of stubble on his jaw, looked menacing as he continued striding across the outdoor area. He didn't look back to see if I was following.

"Sam?" I said, stopping where I was.

He still didn't turn, just kept walking briskly, disappearing into the woods that dotted the front of the property. What the hell? This guy was all kinds of quirky. I debated whether to follow him, but in the end my curiosity was the strongest emotion. Groaning, I jogged to catch up with him, weaving through the woods to find him perched on a rock overlooking the creek. Damn he was fast.

I let out a big huff of air as I collapsed down next to him.

"Another rookie prank? Gonna throw me in the creek?"

He didn't smile, only looked sideways at me. "I'm going away for ten days on my bi-yearly fishing trip."

I gave him a deer in headlights look. "Okay … that's nice." First snowboarding and now fishing. Who knew?

Still, as interesting as that information was, why was he telling me this? As if he'd heard my thoughts he turned more fully toward me, his steely gaze penetrating. "Look, I think Ryder is blinded by his affection for you. I think this situation is much more serious than you know and you need to watch your back. Since I'm not going to be here to keep an eye on you, be extra vigilant."

"What the hell are you talking about?"

Sam leaned in and whispered: "You have no idea the power of the blood running through your veins, what it could mean for the world—a world caught in the grips of fear over a virus that is not curable."

It was true, the *Anima Mortem Virus* had changed the world. Vampires and ash. Dividing the world of humans even further.

I was in a bit of shock over how much Sam was saying. Today he was channeling the love child of Chatty Cathy and Debbie Downer, with all of his ominous news and crazy insight. This was beginning to scare me.

"You act like you know something, something I don't know…"

A flash of animation flickered across his face but it was replaced with a cold hard gaze. "I'm just looking out for you, little rookie. See you in ten days. Be safe."

He jumped up and was gone.

Sam was … seriously? He barely ever talked, and the one time he does speak he gives me vague and cryptic information on how much shit I was in and how scary my life was—information I already knew, so why bother? I could have sworn he wanted to say something more but had stopped.

Damn. I stayed a while and threw rocks into the creek, trying not to think about Sam's warning.

Eventually, I had to make my way back to the enforcer locker room. Ryder had only given me so much time to clean up and get blood. It was time for my first shift as trainee. Hells yeah. Screw Sam and his depressing drama. Screw Tessa and her vamp obsession. I was gonna shoot some shit today.

Two hours later, I sat on the bench with my head in my hands.

"Seriously? No calls?" I griped.

Ryder and Kyle were playing cards. "That's a good thing," Ryder reminded me.

Oliver was lifting some weights. He sat up and wiped a towel across his forehead.

"So what's up with Sam's lonely-guy fishing trip to Alaska twice a year? Think he has some hot human chick he shacks up with in a hotel?"

The boys chuckled, but I perked up at one detail I had not known. "Alaska? It's winter. Who fishes in the winter?"

Ryder looked at me, that intelligent gaze probing into my inner thoughts. "There's king salmon this time of year. He brings a bunch back." He directed the rest of the conversation at Oliver. "We all know Sam is a standoffish guy. Let him be."

Yeah, standoffish when he isn't scaring the shit out of you.

Markus distracted us all then with a subject change. "Just because there are no calls doesn't mean you don't have to train, Charlie. Ryder might be easing you in, but I'm not taking your cute unicorn ass out into the field until you have a little more training under your belt."

I kicked out my right leg then, shooting the chair across from me in his direction before jumping to my feet, a wicked grin on my face.

"Now we're talking."

Twenty minutes later I was standing at the end of a long firing lane, cold Glock in my hands. We were on level seventeen of the Hive. Apparently this place had more secrets I didn't know about, like this gun range for enforcer training only. We were alone. Markus stood to my right and pointed at the target.

"Bullets can disable and even kill an ash, but the only true kill spot is right here." He tapped the center of his forehead.

I nodded, flexing my hands across the grip. Guns didn't scare me, I had been training with them ever since the attack a year ago, when two random ash asshats almost had their way with me. Thankfully they'd been thwarted by some blond hottie Viking vamp. He'd saved my ass before disappearing, never to be seen again. I'd been keeping an eye out in the Hive, but no one even came close to looking like my memory of him.

I focused on my trainer again. "So headshots are the best for ash. Like zombies."

Markus cracked a small smile. "Not every day I get compared to a zombie."

"What about killing vampires?" I asked.

His face tightened with concern and he actually looked over his shoulder and up into the corner of the room. Following his gaze, I saw a small camera with a red light. WTF? Should have known we'd be under surveillance. Ash were not to be trusted, even though they were happy for us to do their dirty work.

"Generally we don't train in disabling or killing vampires, they don't like their weaknesses advertised. But the six of us have had to do some training. It's rare, but sometimes the vampires in rival Hives can be a concern to the Quorum. In that case, grenades work well."

My eyes bugged out. Grenades. That was a swift reminder that our official job title was protector of the Quorum and vampires. The other shit, bringing in new ash and policing stupid ash, seemed like PR work. Since vampires stayed away from ash as much as possible, it was easy to forget that they were the true power in our world. They used ash for their own gains; we were nothing to them.

"Right, so no need to worry about killing vamps." I nodded, and said no more.

I understood that we couldn't really speak freely with cameras around. Still ... why the hell not? Some horny-ass vampires seduced our mothers and we were the ones being treated like shitbags? Like we owed them something? As more angry thoughts filled my mind, I realized my chest was heaving.

We were the vampire's children and they treated us like the help! My rage over the culling had been pushed down and locked away in a place I didn't go very often, mostly because I'm a big believer in not dwelling on shit you can't change – that does nothing but drive a person crazy. But I hadn't gotten over the culling. Not even a tiny little bit. Just barely hidden below the surface was my burning resentment that they had turned me into a murderer. That they used the killing of ash as a form of entertainment. Sure, I knew life was unfair for more than just ash, but things here needed a major shakedown.

Raising my arm and positioning my elbows correctly, I squeezed off six shots into the target dummy. Five of them went where I intended. Yes! Badass enforcer trainee with a gun. Shooting the dummy was quite therapeutic, enough that I could force the anger back into its box. The cage was a little shaky, but for now I was managing to keep it together.

I saw Markus squint. "Not bad," he said with a shrug.

I narrowed my eyes at him as he patted me on the back, his hands massive enough to cover my entire shoulder blade.

"It's just quite obvious that you were trained at a shooting range."

My expression morphed into something mulish. "What's that supposed to mean?"

Markus went over to the wall and pushed a large red button. Suddenly my mannequin target started zigzagging towards me, fast—like vampire fast. Crap, the enforcer was right, I did not have much experience with moving targets.

The heavy mechanical whirring of the machine filled the room. "Now try," Markus shouted.

Glancing down, I swapped out the first gun for a 9mm Glock; it would be more accurate for this type of shooting. Trying to focus on the zigzagging figure coming at me, I squeezed the trigger—missing. Damn, my concentration was not at its best with all the zipping around the figure was doing. Forcing my breathing to slow a little, I sighted along the gun again and shot until I heard an empty click. I lowered my weapon as I waited for Markus to halt the figure and bring the target toward us. It took a second for it to make its way across the long range. I counted the holes. Still my five from the first time.

"Well … shit," I groaned.

Markus' belly laughter caught me off guard. "You'll get there, rookie. We all did."

Rookie? Really? Was this shit going to stick too? I was kind of becoming partial to unicorn—it had a certain magical flare.

My walkie-talkie squawked. "Showtime, rookie." It was Kyle. "We've got a call."

My heart hammered in my chest as I quickly loaded my weapon and holstered it. Markus bolted from the room and I was hot on his heels. One of the first and most important lessons had already been drilled into my head. When we got a call, we needed to haul ass. A few seconds could mean life or death. Luckily, the elevator was open and waiting. Markus and I piled into it.

"You stay in the van. You do not enter the residence at any time," Markus said to me.

"Yes, Ryder," I replied, saluting him. Dude was channeling the head enforcer with his over-protective demands.

He gave me a serious gaze, uncharacteristic for the Scottish charmer. "You got off easy with the broken ankle last time. What's that you and Jayden call us?"

We were almost at our floor. "The sexy six..." I said cautiously, wondering where this was going.

He nodded. "Well, there used to be seven of us. So stay in the van."

The doors opened and he took off running. Holy shit, there used to be a sexy seven? That meant ... okay, maybe I would be staying in the van.

The rest of the guys were waiting in the garage for us, one of the Humvees already loaded, engine running. I was not at all surprised to see everyone decked out in all black. Even I had worn my blackest of army-style outfits for my first shift as an enforcer rookie. It was an unofficial uniform since there was no official uniform. That had just been their totally clever ruse so that I'd fall for their *really* funny trick with the chocolate.

The other enforcers in the Hive, who seemed to mostly undertake scouting missions and general peacekeeping, like making sure the ash in the community were following the rules, wore khaki fatigues. So I guessed the all-black thing was Ryder and his boys' preference.

It did give them a certain badass vibe. Which I was totally channeling in my own clothes. Ryder's gaze landed on me, his eyes trailing across my body as we jumped into the van. I'd love to think he was checking me out because he just couldn't help himself, but I'd seen that particular gaze before. He was making sure I had my gun and walkie-talkie. Mind you, there was no reason for his silvery eyes to stay on my butt for quite that amount of time, so maybe there was a little checking me out in there. Shit, now I was staring. And hot damn, I could totally perv on Ryder all day; he was a big ol' hunk of ash eye-candy, but right now it was time to focus on the current call-out situation.

We were all buckled in and powering out of the Hive compound when Kyle gave us the emergency run-down. This was the standard protocol. Not all of the enforcers were ever together when the call came through, and to save time and prevent miscommunications over the walkies, they waited for everyone to be in the vehicle before briefing.

"We have reports of six ash causing a bit of havoc on Alberta Street near the food trucks. Apparently there were more of the Deliverance group in the area, and they've riled them up. This should be mostly peacekeeping, but because there are six ash, we're all going along for the ride."

"Should be a good one for you, rookie," Jared said, wearing his relaxed, trademark grin.

Deliverance again. Seriously, didn't they have to go home and pray or practice how to stop being assholes? Ryder had told me this morning, when he dropped me at my door, that this extremist religious group believed they were here to deliver God's will, that their mission was to rid the world of any who were not God's children—namely, vampire abominations and their offspring.

"Tell me more about Deliverance," I said, leaning forward from where I was sandwiched between Markus and Oliver. "I did a bit of research today, and it seems that they are mostly kept under control by the humans. So between the humans and the Hive enforcers, I don't understand how they keep popping up as a problem."

Ryder flicked his head back and met my gaze. "Research, hey? Maybe this enforcer gig is rubbing off on you."

I fought the urge to reach across the seat and smack him in the back of the head. I might be a tad on the lazy side when it came to researching—it was always the job I hated the most when I was stuck in the call center—but when things interested me I was all over them. I was like a ninja private investigator with a degree in Google.

"Deliverance has risen and fallen over the years," Ryder said. "Under many names and banners. Originally they were known as God's Voice."

Shit, I had actually heard of that religious sect. When I was young there had been a lot of violent events linked to them, which had scared my mom. But then the news stopped reporting on them and everything had gone back to normal.

Ryder continued. "In those earlier days they had a strong voice, when there were many who feared that the Anima Mortem virus was the first stage of the apocalypse and that it was the end of days. They used this fear to create a small army of gatherers. But as the years have gone on, and the human governments have learned to work with the Hive Quorums, the voice of Deliverance has died off. Now they're mostly pains in our asses, creating a lot of paperwork and headaches for the leaders."

I swallowed hard. If they ever got a cure in their grip, I had no doubt their voice would rise strong again. There were still plenty of humans who feared the night. Right now they had no power and no legal rights to hunt the vamps, but imagine if they could cure them back to human. All of those families who had lost members to the virus, or who wanted to return humans to the top of the predator pyramid, would come out in force.

This could not end well for me. Not well at all.

Ryder must have been thinking the same thing. His voice deepened as he broke the silence again. "They will never touch you, Charlie. We look after our own, and you're one of us now."

A sense of resolve seemed to fill the car then; the men all wore identical expressions—very serious expressions. These guys needed a holiday or something. They hardly ever relaxed, and with everything happening now they were ten times worse than when I'd first met them.

I looked out the window to distract myself and saw a familiar landmark. Alberta Street was a mishmash of quirky shops and ethnic restaurants. Not to mention the scattered line of open-sided deli trucks with every kind of food imaginable—gluten free, non-GMO, vegan, Thai, you name it. My stomach rumbled just thinking about it. The food in the Hive was okay, but I missed my usual haunts. As the Humvee turned onto Alberta from 23rd avenue, I immediately saw the commotion.

"What the fuck?" It was Kyle who let the F-bomb fly, not me this time. Although the curse word had been on my tongue also.

In front of a Vietnamese food truck, an ash was strung up and nailed to a giant cross, humans—Deliverance I'd guess—standing around him chanting and spraying the tied-up ash with water. Of course that had to be holy water; there was no other insane reason to douse him. We weren't made of sugar. Water did not hurt us.

I strained forward in my seat and was able to see there were five other ash hogtied and face-down on the concrete, gun-toting Deliverance holding weapons to their heads.

Markus made the sign of the cross over his chest, then looked at me. "I'm a Roman Catholic and this shit is whack."

Whack was an understatement. How the hell was it even possible for humans to be able to overpower five ash? More of the Deliverance stepped into our line of sight then, standing near the back like guards, holding handguns. The one in the center had a really large, odd shaped gun. Its barrel looked wider and shorter than any firearm I'd seen before.

"They've got tranqs," Oliver shouted. His window was the side closest and he had as good a view as I did. "Bet they've finally managed to brew up some more of the AT20."

"AT20?" I asked.

His voice lowered slightly, but he was still pretty much angry-shouting as he explained: "The human government created a weapon to use against us, shit … years ago now, during the war. They decommissioned it once we reached peace agreements. Well, on paper anyways. Every now and then the zealots and Deliverance nutcases get their hands on some, or a version of it. Things get serious then."

Great, just what I needed, a freaking dart in my ass and lights out for a week. Well, there was one thing I knew for sure. If I woke up with nails in any part of my body, I was killing some humans.

CHAPTER 3

As soon as we closed in, Ryder gunned the gas and hopped the curb. No fucking around for the lead enforcer. The humans dowsing the ash with water turned as he slammed on the brakes, stopping the Humvee inches from the cross. I could see now that they had actually tied up the ash with razor wire and his arms were bleeding badly.

"Stay in the car and get ready to drive!" Ryder ordered me. Then all the doors flew open and the five enforcers leapt out, guns raised.

Holy fuck. Nothing like a front row seat. I was close enough to see the crazy anger across the humans' faces. It was this glint of insanity that had true fear cramping my gut. There was no way to predict what a group of unstable people would do and I was panicking, not just for my team, but for the hogtied ash with guns to their heads. This faceoff was raising the danger of them being killed.

The Deliverance humans straightened as they got a good look at the boys in black. The maniacs at the rear, the ones with the larger guns, turned toward them. Oh hell no. I slowly climbed in the front seat, put my foot on the brake and slipped the car into drive just in case. I would mow these bitches down if shit looked like it was going south.

Ryder and the boys had left the doors open, so I could hear every word. The lead enforcer's voice was calm as he pointed his gun at a greying woman, mid-fifties, who was short, stocky, and full of fire. She was standing center stage and Ryder had clearly surmised she was the one in charge. Not to mention she was the one clutching a Bible, her jaw set and her eyes angry. This bitch would kill for her beliefs. I could see it.

"Your actions are illegal. The human government has stated that unless provoked, ash must not be harmed. Walk away now!" Ryder's voice remained calm but the unspoken threat was clear. If the old bitch didn't walk away, shit was going to go down.

She smiled. "I follow one ruler! He is above all and *His* law states that you are an abomination that must be wiped from this Earth."

Shit. Markus, who was the closest to Ryder, took a small step forward. "As a Catholic of many years, I don't recall seeing vampires or ash in the Bible. We're all humans too, just different. It's nothing more than the results of a virus from infected bats. That's it. Nothing to do with the devil or evil. No apocalypse. Look…"

Markus pulled a necklace from his shirt and dangling there was a cross. The woman's nostrils flared, her mouth nearly foaming in anger.

"How dare you!" She reached into her jacket with her free hand and pulled out a gun. Now there was another human pointing their weapon at the enforcers.

"Stop right now or I'll shoot to kill. I'm well within my rights!" I recognized the register of Ryder's voice now. He was not messing around.

The woman wore a similar expression. I almost yelled out as I saw her finger flex on the trigger, and in that moment my movement must have caught her eye. Her face shuttered as recognition lit up her features.

"It's her," she whispered, but I could still hear her.

Shit. Out in the bright daylight, with silver eyes, I wouldn't be mistaken for anything else. Female ash. Unicorn. Antichrist most probably. I clenched my hands even tighter around the steering wheel as I tried to destroy her with an angry glare. A glint flickered across her eyes, followed by a wry grin, then she swung into action.

The next sixty seconds was the worst minute of my life. The time went by so slowly, and yet it was over by the time I sucked in my next deep breath. I still don't remember how everything went down—probably I had mentally blanked a lot of it out. The woman pivoted quickly and fired her gun like a drunken maniac, spraying bullets.

Through those first moments my eyes were locked on Ryder, who dived forward and away from the Humvee which would have protected him. Nope, instead it looked like he deliberately jumped in front of Markus, shielding the larger man. A scream froze on my lips as both men fell. Even with Ryder's heroic act, both him and the Scottish enforcer—not to mention the ash hung up on the cross—received the full brunt of her spray of bullets. Kyle, Oliver, and Jared managed to take refuge behind one of the car doors and were already returning fire. My foot bounced on the brake pedal, but since Ryder had dropped in front of the car I couldn't gas it.

I was just trying to figure out the best way to help the boys when the crazies holding the ash hogtied swung their weapons down and started firing—kill-shots to the ashes' heads, all of them dead in a moment.

"Nooo!" This time I couldn't hold back my panicked shouts. Shit. What the hell was going on here? How had this gotten so out of control!

Slamming my mouth closed, I breathed in short puffs. There wasn't enough air left in the world for me right now. I couldn't fill my lungs. Flashes of black and white crossed my vision and I knew I was on the verge of a panic attack. Ash were dead. Ryder and Markus had been shot. At least the other guys were okay, but I didn't know how bad Ryder was. Maybe the bullets had just skimmed him? I quickly talked myself down from the full-on-panic mode I'd been slipping into, knowing that I had to help, and calm was what I needed to properly assess the situation.

First thing: I needed to get to Ryder.

I flat out refused to believe he was dead. There was no way I could even think of that. It would literally drive me crazy.

No one was paying attention to me right then; they were all a little distracted by the massive gunfight going down, so I threw the car in park and slipped out the open driver side door, dropping to the ground and rolling underneath the Humvee. I had no problem army-crawling under the car. And thankfully, from what I could see, I had a direct path to the huge, not-moving body of Ryder.

Without hesitation, I started powering along, arms and elbows getting cut to shit but I didn't care. Ryder had slumped right beneath the front of the grill but Markus was nowhere in sight. Hopefully one of the other guys had pulled him to safety, since he'd been to the side and not dead center like Ryder.

When I reached the prone enforcer, I grabbed his belt and tipped him back toward me, laying him flat. I tried not to break down at the sight of Ryder's olive skin now as pale as snow, blood seeping from his stomach. He was completely unconscious.

Counting to ten in my head, a technique I'd learned to keep myself calm, I started to slide his body back under the car. As I backed up, I glimpsed the old lady and her psychos hidden behind a food truck. They continued shooting the shit out of our car, but only sporadically, as my boys were firing back. People were running and screaming down the street and

I heard sirens in the distance. This was followed by the empty click of a gun that had run out of bullets.

"Shit," Kyle said.

Acting on instinct, I pulled the gun from behind my back, and with the limited movement I had in the tight quarters under the car, slid it across the ground toward Kyle's feet.

Without missing a beat, he scooped up my weapon and continued firing.

Placing one hand under Ryder's belt and another under his armpit, I dragged him under the car. It was rough, slow going. I tried my best to be gentle, but time was a factor; he was losing too much blood. He groaned then, and I noticed he seemed to be semi-conscious now.

I huffed in and out, straining every muscle to move him.

"Shit! What the hell did you eat for breakfast, a small library?"

The mental counting slowed as my scattered mind started shooting questions at me. Was Markus dead? How long could we hold them off? How much blood could Ryder afford to lose? How the hell had all of this happened? This was supposed to be an in and out mission. Shit, I was missing Sam's crazy-ass presence right now. That dude would have Rambo'd his way through those Deliverance, smacking them down. Hard.

I dug deep into my stubbornness, dragging Ryder six inches at a time. I flinched and almost shrieked as bullets chipped at the ground and ricocheted up under the car. Effing shitheads, they'd finally noticed me. I heard the increase of bullets from the enforcers, and was glad to see the boys had put more than a few of them down. Bodies littered the path.

Finally, by sheer stubborn willpower, I got Ryder out to the safe side of the street. Hunching over him, I fluttered around trying to figure out how to haul his massive frame up into the car. Kyle appeared behind me and jumped up to stand on the edge of the back door, shooting over the roof.

He shouted down to me. "Charlie, I'm going to get Ryder in the back now. Jared and Oliver have Markus. We'll have to immediately try and stabilize them and control their bleeding, so we need you to get us all back to the Hive. We have to go now before the Deliverance call in backup. Do you think you can pull it together and drive?"

Okay, shit. Don't freeze up, Charlie.

"Yes." Because what other choice did we have?

Brave words. No idea if I could follow through. As I dragged myself back toward the door I caught sight of Jared's blond hair. He was shooting still, hiding behind the open back door. I couldn't see Oliver but knew he was somewhere close by. This car had to be bulletproof and reinforced, because it had taken a beating.

In one smooth movement I popped into the driver's side, keeping my head down best I could. I waited a few seconds and the suspension lurched as a thousand-plus pounds landed in the back seats. The enforcers shut the doors best they could, but the bullets had twisted them a little, and they didn't close properly. Oh well, it would have to be good enough for now.

Without thinking twice, I gunned the Hummer and lurched forward five feet, popping off the gutter. The Deliverance took the chance then to leave the safety of their hideout, running at us, guns blazing.

"Go, Charlie!" Jared shouted.

I slammed my foot down on the gas pedal, pulling the Humvee back onto the road. The right side of the car clipped one of the Deliverance on our way out, the tires squealing as I did zero to sixty in record time. My hands were slippery on the wheel, blood and sweat coating them. My heart was beating triple-time; I couldn't tell what was fear and what was adrenalin. Everything felt the same in my crazed mind.

A few bullets pinged off the back as we made our escape, but that noise faded away as I screeched around another corner. Once we were a safe distance away, I managed to slow the car down and get my breathing under control. A glance in the rear was enough to see that Ryder was in Kyle's lap. Blood and grime stained the enforcer's dirty-blond hair and he looked like he was seconds from losing his shit. Turning back around, I refused to think that crazed look in his eyes was because of Ryder. The lead enforcer was going to be fine—he was like Superman or some shit. Bullets could not kill him. Nothing could.

Dammit. A few minutes later I wanted to look again, to make sure that everyone was still breathing. "What's happening back there, guys?" I shouted. I couldn't turn at the moment, I was too busy white-knuckling the steering wheel while zooming through the downtown traffic.

"I'm fine, lass, just a few wee holes in me for luck." Hearing Markus' brogue was a welcome relief.

"Right, just a few holes," Oliver said drily. "He has eight bullets in him. He's just lucky most of them ended up in his right shoulder and leg."

"That's only because Ryder jumped in from the side and pushed me out of the way, which I will beat his damn ass for as soon as he's back on his feet." Markus sounded pissed, and worried. I knew he would have done the same for Ryder. They were a team, they had each other's backs, no matter what.

"And Ryder?" my voice shook just a little, but since I was almost totally focused on the driving I was doing, I managed to stop myself losing it too badly.

"I'm counting twelve bullets, six in the abdomen, five scattered about his extremities, and one grazed his temple, which is why he's out for the count right now."

I could sort of see in the rearview mirror that Kyle was applying a thick pad or pressure cloth to his best friend's stomach.

Our eyes met in the reflection. "Just keep driving, Charlie," he said. "I won't let him die. We just have to get back to the Hive."

I slammed my foot down even harder. Horns blasted at me as I sailed through a red light, but I seriously did not give a single fuck right now. I was a woman on a mission, and I was getting our asses back to the Hive in record time.

I still couldn't believe what had just happened? Massive shootout, dead humans. The six ash we had gone to save were dead. Not exactly the first day on the job that I imagined. Those Deliverance assholes … they were totally insane, and so much more ruthless and deadly than I expected. Ryder clearly had not been expecting it either; the boys might have had their weapons out, but there had been no real urgency, as if they never anticipated the others would retaliate with deadly force.

Fury washed through me again as I wrenched the wheel and pretty much drifted around the corner. The slickness of the roads would have been scarier if I hadn't been angry enough to set the car on fire. I'd been a bit on the angry side lately. Most of my ire was reserved for the selfish vampires who thought ash were their personal entertainment and slaves. But now there was some space in the Charlie-is-pissed vault for these religious extremist humans.

Everywhere I looked, ash were being shit on and killed by others who thought our lives were not important, that we didn't warrant the basic rights of survival. I knew that once upon a time I had been someone who cared very little for ash or the Hive. It was something I regretted. The ash were my friends and my family; the discrimination had to stop, and it had to stop right now, because as the Hives around the world filled further, there would be less and less room for ash, and even the few rights we had would disappear.

Guess there was now at least six spots freed up in our Hive, assuming those six had been from Portland. Gah, I was turning into a psycho. Seemed the moment my shock had faded out, I was less of the "human shaking and crying" and more of the ash "pissed and ready to kill".

As the Hive came into view, I was relieved to see the gates were open. One of the boys had called ahead. Which was good because I wasn't stopping. I screeched up the path and into the garage, my instincts urging me to go as fast as I could and slam on the brakes to stop. But knowing that might cause more injuries to the guys, I curbed those instincts and took my time to slow smoothly.

I threw it into park, and by the time I was out the door Kyle and Oliver were already moving. It took two of them to carry Ryder; they held him between them and were sprinting for the entrance. Jared and Markus were slower, but at least the Scottish enforcer was only limping. He didn't seem to be in mortal danger.

"Go, Charlie, I'll be fine. Ryder needs your support." Markus waved me off and I threw him a quick smile before I scrambled across the concrete garage.

The second the door to the Hive opened there were medical staff with a stretcher ready to care for Ryder. All vampires. WTF? Were ash not smart or something? Why were all of the medical staff and scientists full-on bloodsuckers? I'll bet it was because they didn't want us to be in control of any of the top-secret lab stuff. Wouldn't want us figuring out what bullshit was going on behind the scenes.

The vampires took charge, heaving Ryder onto the stretcher and hauling ass down the hallway and to the medical wing. Since I totally did not trust these vamp bitches, I followed close. There was no way I was leaving my man crush Monday with them. Oliver had dropped back to help Jared with Markus, but Kyle kept pace with me and the medical team.

Once we reached the door to the operating room, a tall blond woman put a hand out on my chest, stopping me.

"You'll have to wait outside." She was polite but glaring with her squinty-ass eyes.

I pushed her hand off smoothly. "Not a chance."

I stepped forward as she stood there with her mouth open. These people treated us like shit, put cameras up to spy on us, bugged our rooms. There was no way in hell I was leaving Ryder weakened and alone with them.

One of the male vampires that had begun cutting Ryder's shirt open narrowed his eyes at me as well. Still I refused to move, secure with the heat of Kyle at my back.

"Operating room is for the patient only," the male vampire growled.

Kyle and I moved further into the room, pushing the blonde out of the way. She didn't try to stop us.

Kyle was all casual as he leaned against the wall. Despite his stance, I could see the determined fierceness in his gaze; he would not be leaving his best friend either. "We're not leaving, and if he dies I'll kill you all, so I suggest you stop talking and start saving his life."

I heard the enforcer's teeth clank as he slammed them together. His eyes were wild, and the way his right hand was twitching over his gun should have been worrying the doctors. Even if it was a bit of a suicide run trying to take on three vampires, for Ryder, Kyle and I would not even hesitate. Striding to his side, I put on my best tough-unicorn face, leaning on the wall and crossing my arms.

The male vampire's nostrils flared as he prepared to retort, but the third scrub-attired vampire in the room, a female who looked kind of familiar, placed a hand on his arm. "You'd do the same. Besides, this one is the Quorum's favorite. We better do all we can to save him."

I remembered then where I'd seen her. She was one of Lucas' confidants. Often seen with the Quorum leader. That sort of had me feeling like we might have a slight ally in the room.

The male vamp looked like he was going to ignore her. He paused with a scalpel in hand and continued glaring at us. *You mother effer!* If he didn't start patching Ryder up in two seconds, I was going to go postal.

He sighed and shook his head. "Let's do this, he's bleeding out fast."

The breath I had been holding left me and I nearly burst into tears. As the first cut was made, I decided to find a spot in the room to stare at because there was no way in hell I could watch this. Even the knowledge they were slicing into Ryder had me on the verge of losing my shit and falling to the ground in tears.

I felt a strong warm hand take mine, a lifeline which pulled me back from the edge.

Kyle.

I wasn't alone. Holding on to him as tightly as I could, I decided on two things. One: life was too short to live half-assed. If you wanted something, you needed to go for it. And two: I was a hundred percent most definitely falling in love with Ryder. And who could blame me?

The next twelve hours were some of the most painful and scary of my life. The medical team kept asking for more blood to be hung. Not to mention all the cursing as Ryder's stomach continued closing over the surgeon's hands before he could patch up the damage inside. Even with the ash's advanced healing, the organs needed to be properly stitched together, bullets removed. Just like my broken leg had to have the bones set properly before healing or it would have fused together crookedly.

Kyle and I sat on the operating floor, against the wall. We were slumped together in a ball, my head on his shoulder. The surgery seriously felt like it had been going on for years, when the doctor finally stepped away from Ryder and rolled his neck to work out the kinks.

He met my eyes. "He'll be fine."

He turned then and made his way to a hand-scrubbing station. That was it, all the information I was getting, but it was all the information I needed.

I jumped up, my heart slamming against my chest as relief flooded me.

"Thank you!" I said, as gratefully as I could. Still hated the assholes, but they had saved Ryder's life.

I followed as the vampire female whisked Ryder down the hall and into a recovery wing. There were three other ash in there, all hooked up to blood and curtained off from each other. A wheelchair was set up next to Ryder's bed.

The nurse gave me some clear liquid in a syringe. "He can go home in an hour or so when he wakes. This will help with the pain. Stick it in his leg."

My eyes widened and Kyle nodded before thanking her.

Once we were alone with our boy, I exchanged a look with Ryder's oldest friend, a look that said *Holy shit we just survived something crazy and thank you for being there with me.* But we didn't say a word. Sometimes there are no real words that can describe what you've just gone through.

Kyle wrapped a warm hand around my shoulder; he looked exhausted and ready to drop. I, however, was so jacked up on adrenaline there was no way I was sleeping until Ryder was awake and talking.

"You want me to bring him to my apartment and take care of him?" Kyle asked.

My heart tightened at the thought of letting Ryder out of my sight. I shook my head. "No, I can do it."

Kyle nodded and pulled me in for a big hug. "You did good today, rookie."

I gave a lame attempt at a smile as he pulled away and met my eyes. "Get some sleep," I told him.

He nodded and yawned. "I'll check on Markus. I have to report to the Quorum before I can sleep."

Damn. No rest for the enforcers. I guess I should get used to it.

I sat in the wheelchair and held Ryder's limp hand. It took me about thirty minutes, but eventually that jacked-up feeling started to lessen. Some of the stress and exhaustion pressed in on me and I lowered my head to rest on the side of the bed. I knew Ryder could wake at any moment, and I really didn't want to drift off. Trying to stay awake, I started a slow, slurring murmur: *don't fall asleep, don't fall asleep...*

The sound of Ryder groaning jarred me awake. It took me a few seconds to orient myself, then the last twenty-four hours came slamming back. Ryder! Heart pounding, I fumbled for the clear syringe which had fallen into my lap. I was probably lucky I hadn't accidentally stabbed myself with it while I slept.

By the time I got my shit together, my gaze crashed into his wide silver and black eyes. They were filled with a tumult of emotions.

"Charlie…"

The rasp of his voice almost had me in tears. The way he'd just said my name, so much emotion in his tone—a tenderness rarely seen from the strong enforcer, except in vulnerable moments like these. His hand snaked out and touched my hair and I found myself sinking into his touch.

"Ryder…"

For once in my life I didn't know what to say. Was it too soon to blurt out *Don't ever do that again, I'm totally falling in love with you, and you scared the shit out of me*? Yeah, probably.

He looked down, noticing the gauze across his stomach, the blood dripping into his IV. His face scrunched in pain, and I was just about to freak out that something had gone wrong when his face shot back up to me. Clarity entered those eyes, along with some worry.

"Markus?" Ryder struggled to sit up.

I would guess he'd just remembered how he'd been a big hero and jumped in front of a bunch of bullets. We really needed to talk about that sometime.

"He's fine," I said, giving him my most reassuring face. Of course, I didn't know for sure he was fine, having not seen him since we got here, but surely if there had been an issue with his injuries, someone would have found Kyle and me and told us.

I palmed the clear syringe. "They gave me something for your pain, and it means I get to stab you in the leg."

A deep chuckle came from him before he winced. Laughter was not good for belly wounds; even the tough guy here was struggling. I waved the syringe a little closer and he gave me a glare.

"I don't like meds and I don't need any. Take me home. I hate hospitals."

Fair enough. Dropping the syringe on the side table, the first thing we had to do was remove the IV. The blood bag was almost empty now anyway. I might have closed my eyes just for a second as I gently pulled it out. It released easily, and apparently relatively pain free, as Ryder's expression did not shift.

Moving closer then, I put an arm under each of Ryder's armpits. Seemed like the safest place with all of his injuries.

"One, two, three," I said, and with a lot of help from him, we got him sitting with his legs dropped off the side of the bed.

I was both relieved and slightly disappointed to see he was in a low slung pair of sweats. One of the vamps must have slipped those on after the surgery. Of course, my female appreciation of his beautiful body was definitely diminished by the sight of his bandages, red seeping through some of the white.

As I swayed a little at the sight, I took a second to be grateful that his wounds were not on show. My mom might be a nurse, but I always knew medical stuff was not for me. I'd definitely have puked to see his body torn to shreds like that.

He noticed my inspection. "I'll heal in a few hours. As long as they stitched me up okay, it won't even leave a scar."

He was trying to reassure me, but we both knew the truth. He could have died today. Even ash can only lose so much blood and suffer so much damage before their genetics cannot save them. Forcing myself to focus on anything other than his almost death, I nodded at the wheelchair.

"Okay, let's do this."

It took some effort, but together we shifted him into the wheelchair. I was pretty sure I pulled my back doing it too. I'd thankfully healed all my injuries from dragging him under the car, so this was just a new one to deal with.

Ryder groaned, sinking into the chair. He looked as pale as a sheet and his eyes were on the syringe I had set down.

I smiled. "Want me to bring it just in case?"

After the briefest of hesitations, he nodded. Well, damn. If my big hardcore enforcer was needing pain meds, this was serious. I wheeled Ryder out of the medical ward, nodding to a nurse as we passed. After wheeling him into the elevator and down the hall, I stopped at my door and fumbled for my keycard.

Once we were inside, I noticed Jayden's door was closed. He was probably at his job. I wheeled Ryder around our couch and right into my bedroom. Careful not to bump the chair, I walked the long way around to face him. He wore a wan grin.

"What?" I asked.

"Not exactly how I imagined being invited to your bed."

Well hot damn. Ryder had thought about being invited into my bed. *Nice.*

"Want the pain meds yet?" I had the syringe safely stashed in the side of the wheelchair.

He shook his head. "Nah, I'm still doing okay."

Dude was a total liar; his normally bronzed skin was as pale as mine right now.

I sighed. Tough guys, they never asked for help. I reached out and plucked the painkiller free. I was betting whatever was in this thing was strong, especially if it would subdue an ash's pain. If Ryder didn't start looking better in a few minutes, I was totally using it on him.

Just as I had that thought, I noticed how much sweat had broken out on his forehead. Time to roll. I raised the syringe up high and he groaned.

"What's your obsession with wanting to hurt me?"

I shrugged, stepping even closer into his personal space. "Guess it's been harder than expected to get over the electrocution thing."

His attempted chuckle turned into another grunt.

"Ready?"

He nodded, and before I could think about what I was going to do, in a single smooth motion I drove the syringe into his leg, pushing down to disperse the clear fluid inside. He didn't even wince at the needle being jammed into his thigh. That pain probably paled in comparison to his stomach wound.

The mysterious clear liquid worked almost instantly. The tension which had racked his face lessened. His sigh of relief was music to my ears. Before he completely lost consciousness, I helped him out of the chair and tucked him into my bed. As his eyes fluttered, I went to step away, planning on running to the feeding station and grabbing some extra blood. But before I could he reached out and captured my hand, pulling me hard, using far more strength than an injured ash should have at their disposal. I fell onto the bed next to him.

"Lie with me," he whispered in a slur.

I kicked off my shoes and tucked myself into his side, careful not to lie against his injuries. I felt his head tilt down to rest against my hair, and as he nestled closer into me he breathed in and out deeply.

"This is all … all I want."

His last words were almost incoherent, but I heard them. Then he was fast asleep in a nice, drug induced state. As I was drifting off to sleep myself, I realized that this was what

I wanted too. Unlimited spooning with Ryder was totes on my more to do list.

Chapter 4

I awoke to the smell of bacon and immediately began to salivate. As I rolled over, I froze as I remembered the last twenty-four hours. I realized, with more than a little disappointment, that Ryder was already gone. My eyes alighted on a note propped up on the pillow. I reached across and snagged it.

Thanks for taking care of me. You snore in your sleep. Ryder

My mouth dropped open. I totally did not snore! Right? Shit.

"Hey, Jayden!" I was a lazy bitch. Shouting from bed was one of my favorite things to do.

Come to me peasants, come to me.

I knew my roomie wouldn't have left yet; the smell of bacon was the first giveaway. The second was that the clock on the wall said it was 6 a.m. Damn, that meant Ryder and I had been asleep for half the day and all night. I was starting to get a little too comfortable with that enforcer. There was a time a year ago when I could never have imagined trusting a dude enough to actually fall asleep with him. And look at me now.

Ryder was different. He made me feel safe, and that was a rare find.

"You hollered, bitch? You think I'm your dog now or something?" Jayden popped his fine ass in through my door, bounding across and slamming himself onto the end of my bed.

"Do I snore?"

His eyes widened, the silver ring barely visible—which was the way with most ash, except for Ryder and me.

"Of all the strange, freakish questions I hear from you, that's what you're spouting today? I expected: hey dude, did you know that Ryder shame-walked his ass out of my bed this morning. Or hey, dude, let's work out some sort of sock-on-the-door system so that I don't accidentally walk in on you and Ryder. Although…"

I punched him, right in the arm, which was way too muscled for knuckle comfort.

"Nothing happened. He was injured and we just slept together. As in *sleep*. As in no getting it on, no need for a sock on the door."

Jayden actually looked disappointed. "I was just messing with you, girl. Oliver told me everything, and after I almost cried—which I totally didn't because I'm badass—I waited up to make sure you were all okay. You must have missed me when you wheeled him in the room."

So he'd been behind that closed door. It was nice to know he was nearby if I'd needed any help. Leaning across the bed, I threw my arms around him, pulling him in for a hug. I might have lost a lot by becoming an ash: Tessa, my life with my mom, college—oh, and my humanity—no biggie. But I had gained so much also. I was trying more and more to count my blessings.

As we pulled back, Jayden's dark eyes twinkled. "Oh, and, Charlie, you totes snore, girlfriend. But it's cute little kitten snores compared to Oliver. Sometimes I literally have to stuff his mouth full to shut him up."

I cracked up then. Jayden was everything. Seriously, there was no way to feel all depressed with him around.

"I'm keeping you forever," I told him.

He grinned. "Yep, you're stuck with me, girlfriend."

After our BAFF moment, I decided to shower and get decent looking. I squealed like a pig as a few pieces of glass fell out of my ponytail and my shower water was tinged with blood. Probably Ryder's.

Not that long ago I used to wash glitter out of my hair after clubbing with Tessa. Damn, life had changed. I missed that chick.

After I was ready, I threw on my walkie and weapon and decided to find the other enforcers. I needed to talk about what the hell happened yesterday. Power-walking from my room, I slammed to a stop in the living room. Lucas was just casually sitting on my couch, wearing all white as usual, with a bottle of blood in his hand.

"Hey, Lucas," I said, recovering quickly. This was another obvious "how times have changed" moment. Vamp on my couch, no problem. Blood for breakfast? Sign me up. I was turning into a regular old champion at all of this effed-up shit in my life.

"Charlie…" He nodded to me. Something in his voice gave me pause. He seemed extra stiff… mad even.

I found myself stepping closer, eyebrows raising as I tried to figure out what was wrong. "What's up?" I finally asked, having no real clue.

Lucas took in a deep breath before letting it out slowly. "You haven't been honest with me, have you?"

It's amazing how quickly you can go from calm to full-on panic attack—heart racing, shallow breaths, weak legs. Shit. Did Lucas know I was the cure? Did I trust him? If he tried to take me, could I make it past him and to my boys?

"What do you mean?" I tried my best not to sound nervous, but dammit my voice shook.

Lucas tapped the couch and I reluctantly went to sit next to him. My gut said I could trust him. I always had this women's intuition thing; it had never let me down before.

Lucas's eyes pulsed silver for a moment as he inhaled my scent, but he had the grace to shake it off and continue: "Your father, the Original of the fourth house, is alive."

I released the breath I had been holding. Okay, that. Well, I wasn't keen on giving up the knowledge that he was still alive, but it was better than him knowing I was the cure. That shit needed to stay on lockdown.

"Oh really? I didn't know that for sure actually. My mom told me she got some money in her account every year and assumed it was from him." At least this was something which I could honestly answer him on.

Some of the stiffness left him then. "Yes, the Quorum acted against my wishes and tapped your mother's bank account. They have traced the sums of money she gets every Christmas to an account in Switzerland. It was registered under a fake name. Which was enough to raise suspicion further, suspicion which started with your very strong levitation abilities in the culling. They took the last image of Carter, and using facial recognition, cross referenced all CCTV footage they could get their hands on."

My heart was beating like crazy in my chest. What the fuck was the Quorum doing spying on my mother's bank account? And more importantly…

"Did they find him?"

This guy was my dad and my mom loved him, so if he was alive and walking around I wanted to know what the hell he was up to.

Lucas took a sip of his blood. "We have footage of Carter Atwater boarding a private plane in Canada."

"Holy shit!" I exclaimed. He was actually still alive.

Lucas' normally flawless and gorgeous face was strained and wore the lines of stress. He reached over and placed a hand on mine as he leaned in to whisper in my ear.

"Even though they have not tied him to the money transfers, they now know that Carter is alive. And, well, I think the Quorum has put two and two together about his relationship to you. Despite what I've managed to fake in your blood work, I'm not sure how much longer I can protect you in here, Charlie. The Quorum has been meeting in secret without me, and it may only be a matter of time before they decide you're too much of a risk to keep alive."

My blood chilled at his declaration. He pulled back, resting easily against the couch, and patted my hand.

"Let's take it one day at a time, okay?" he said, still whispering. "I just wanted to make sure you were aware, and if I know Ryder at all, he's already taken steps to ensure a timely exit if it's required."

Lucas's words reminded me that I needed to share this information with my enforcer team.

I nodded. "Okay, thanks for stopping by and letting me know."

I wasn't sure whether it was the events with Deliverance or this new threat to my existence, but something inside of me snapped. A fight-or-flight instinct was raging within me, demanding I either confront the vamp assholes or run so I never had to see them again.

I had no idea why the hell the Quorum feared the Originals so much. Why the fuck was I—one little ash female—even on their radar? It didn't make sense, unless they knew something about Originals and the cure or some shit. If my father was alive, maybe it was in our best interest to try and find him also, get some answers before someone decided to try and kill or kidnap me again.

One thing was for sure—these weak-ass Quorum vampires clearly had no issues with killing off someone they perceived to be a threat. And I hated to admit it, but they could wipe me out no problem if they wanted to.

I missed my old life then, and Tessa especially. I ached for her smartass comments about what I was wearing and the way she always seemed to look on the bright side of every situation.

As Lucas stood to leave, things felt a little awkward between us. He politely excused himself, leaving in a silent visage of white.

In a daze I made my way to the enforcer locker room, although I managed a chuckle when I saw someone had drawn a dress over the stick figure man on the sign stuck to the door.

Trust the enforcers to brighten my day. The last twenty-four hours had sucked the big one and I needed some happy. Where was my mutha-effing happy?

As I walked in, I was really hoping to find Ryder glistening with droplets of water and half naked in a towel. Come on, I did just ask for some happy, and that was a step up to ecstatic. Instead, I saw the sexy five—minus one silent enforcer—hovering around a whiteboard Ryder was drawing on. At the top, he had the words SANCTUM and DELIVERANCE in bold and circled, with small lines branching out. On a chair in front of him was a huge fishbowl of water with tiny black microphones floating in it. Okay, WTF? The boys had finally lost their damn minds.

Noticing me, Ryder tipped his head, giving me a tight smile.

Kyle winked at me. "Come on in, Charlie. Ryder was just about to detail operation 'Don't fuck with the ash or we will kill you,' aka: 'Revenge.'"

Operation Revenge? Awesome.

My eyes shot down to the bowl again and Oliver answered this time. "Kyle scanned the room and found twelve bugs."

Holy Shit. The enforcers' instincts had been right; there was definitely a spy in our midst, more than one if that number of listening devices was any indication. I took a seat as Ryder drew the word *mole* underneath SANCTUM, before turning back to face us.

"First order of business ... I've been trying for the past few weeks to politically deal with our response to the Sanctum attack. Finally, this morning, the Quorum ordered me not to retaliate against the group, and they denied my offer to sniff out who sent them to attack the Hive and steal Charlie. Not only does that make me a little angry, it makes me a lot suspicious."

I nodded. Why the hell would the Quorum order us not to find out who had attacked their home and tried to kill me? Unless...

"The Quorum wants me dead," I said in a resigned sort of manner. I really wasn't even surprised at this point.

Ryder's eyebrows furrowed and he and the rest of the enforcers turned to face me. I was startled to realize that it felt incomplete in here without Sam. These guys had quickly become friends and family to me, and now they were caught up in this bullshit because vamps were assholes.

The five were still staring at me, and I could see that they were waiting for me to expand on my previous statement. Without hesitation, I quickly caught them up on what Lucas had told me this morning. No one said anything during my story, but pissed-off-faces were being flashed all over the room. Once I finished with my speech, there was silence for like thirty seconds before the enforcers kind of exploded into action.

Ryder was the first to make himself heard: "We should just leave now. I don't want Charlie hurt. I have plans in place, safe houses and cash stashed around. I haven't figured out the blood thing yet, but I will." It shocked me at how casual he was about giving up his entire life here, his job— everything really—for my safety.

Kyle interjected: "Look, none of us want to see Charlie hurt, bro, but hear me out. We have an opportunity here to find out the bigger picture, to gather intel on the Quorum and to not only find out who sent the Sanctum but also what Deliverance is up to. I don't like not knowing what my enemies want, and I have a feeling this is bigger than just Charlie. If they knew one hundred percent what she is, she would be dead by now. I think we still have time."

Markus nodded. "Besides, we can't leave without Sam, and we need time to stash blood or figure out how we will survive. I say we stay friendly with the Quorum, and the second we catch wind of harm coming Charlie's way, we're out of here."

None of this was sitting right with me. So much sacrifice for one stupid chick. Okay, I wasn't a complete waste of space, but I always thought it was ridiculous in romance novels when all of these people just gave up their lives to save the damsel in distress. Now, in this situation, I see that this is what honorable males do to protect ones they care about. And while I would do the same for them, all of them, in a heartbeat, I still wanted to object.

"You guys, I feel bad about you having to leave because of me. Maybe we can just transfer to another hive. I've always loved Colorado."

Jared put an arm around my shoulders. "You're family now, we stick together. Plus, I reckon this fear of our beautiful unicorn goes deep and has spread to all Hives. That's the word on the street anyhow."

Even with his Australian accent prettying up that sentiment, it still wasn't nice to hear. I groaned. What was wrong with being different? Oh yeah, I was the cure to the one thing that gave them power and strength. I would fear me too. But we still had no indication this was about my cure, no way to know if they had this knowledge yet. Shit, *we* hadn't even known what I was when the Sanctum attacked.

Ryder touched his stomach then, those gorgeous silver eyes crinkling. I wondered if he was thinking about being shot up. "Okay, I think Kyle has a point. If we run, we would be completely in the dark, and knowledge is power. New plan is this: we lock down our intel, we have no more meetings unless we're out in the open or have scanned for listening devices. We stay on Charlie's ass—she's to have two escorts at all times—and I will tell all of you individually the escape plans if shit goes down." His eyes flashed to almost pure silver then. "And lastly, the Sanctum might be officially off our list to investigate, but the Quorum said nothing about Deliverance." The gleam in his eye gave me chills. "You don't try to kill me and my friends and get away with it. It's time for Deliverance to learn a thing or two about ash."

Kyle raised his hand. "Before you go Terminator on this one, I have a suggestion."

Ryder glared at his best friend. "I want them to hurt. Charlie was there with us. A lot of ash died. They had one of us wired to a fucking cross."

Uh oh, Ryder wasn't much for cursing. I was genuinely scared.

Kyle's relaxed features hardened right up, making him look less the fun-loving joker and more the scary-ass-sociopath. "Oh, don't you worry, they will hurt, but do you think it's a good idea to openly come at them? Last thing we need on top of our Quorum problems is the humans getting all pissy and freaking out on us."

Good point. More enemies was not what any of us needed. As Kyle continued, some of the fun-loving was back on his face. Actually, he kind of looked like a kid in a candy shop. "Remember when Sam and I built that computer virus that took a couple cents out of a few thousand bank accounts to get us through that rough patch?"

Wait, what? How long had these guys been together? Damn. How many laws did they break? I wanted to tie Ryder up and make him tell me sexy-six stories for hours. Well, I wanted to tie Ryder up period. The stories would just be an awesome added bonus.

Ryder nodded. "But if you suggest stealing a few cents from Deliverance, I'm going to punch you. They nearly killed Markus. They did kill our ash brothers."

Ummm, and they almost killed you! I wanted to shout, but I managed to hold it together.

Kyle's smile was crazy big now. "Deliverance is backed by the richest church organization in the world. They have billions to fund their ash-vampire smear campaigns. I say we wipe them clean, make them hurt where they care the most."

Ryder was smiling now too. "Bankrupt Deliverance? That's the best thing you've said all day. They'll go mental. So much of their power is in their money. It's what allows them to develop weapons against us and recruit all of these braindead humans who are looking for some sort of purpose."

Kyle shrugged. "It's not going to be easy. I'm sure they have security like you wouldn't believe, but we all know that there's not a computer program made which Sam cannot hack."

What, Sam was a genius hacker too? Geez, he was that kid I always hated in school, good at everything, hot as hell, and a complete enigma. Was I a little jealous? Hells yeah I was. I was the awkward girl who found most of my classes boring and had on occasion fallen asleep during math.

Markus shifted forward in his seat and I noticed he was moving gingerly, even though he looked completely healed. I guessed there was still some tenderness. "I like it. Where will we put the money?"

My hand shot up and I legit felt like I was in kindergarten. "We spread it out in even donations across the world's ten neediest charities."

Ryder's eyes met mine and there was a moment—a "maybe he's falling in love with me too" moment. I swallowed hard.

Kyle nudged me. "Aww, our little rookie unicorn is a Robin Hood."

I rolled my eyes, but everyone nodded their agreement.

"We steal from the psycho ash murderers and give to people in need," Ryder declared and we all did a fist bump.

"Maaaaate, Sam better get his arse back here, he's missing all the fun," Jared declared, drawling out the word mate, which sounded all kinds of hot in that accent. "Not to mention that we need him to double-check the virus before we send it out into the computer world."

Ryder nodded. "He contacted me this morning. Somehow he heard about the Deliverance attack. Said he was having trouble catching fish anyway, so he's coming back early."

How long had he even been in Alaska? Forty-eight hours? I don't know why, but this whole Sam thing was really on my mind. He was such a quiet guy and I felt like he was hiding something. Running off to fish in the winter … the things he said to me before he left—all of that stuff had every red flag going off in my mind. But he was part of the inner circle of the sexy six, which made me feel as if I had to give him the benefit of the doubt.

Only time would tell. For now I'd take Ryder's lead on this.

The next few days sped by quickly, and it totally took me by surprise when Jayden mentioned it was only three days until Thanksgiving. Holy crap, I'd been in the Hive for a couple of months. It was pretty amazing how quickly one can adjust to a completely new world.

I guess we had been busy focusing on all of the people who hated me, and the list seemed to be growing. Thankfully, there had been no additional drama since our last locker-room meeting. We were laying low, doing our thing. I spent most of my time training and researching. Call-outs were at a minimum, which gave the enforcers and me plenty of time to try and search out our dirty-little-rodent mole, trace the paper trails of the Sanctum hit—behind the Quorum's back—and also try and destroy the financial backing of Deliverance.

Sam had arrived back yesterday. Despite my constant barrage of questions, he was pretty much mute about his fishing trip. Yeah, I might have been trying to catch him out in a lie, but when a dude never says anything there's no need for lies. Plus, I couldn't badger him too much, he was being very helpful as he systematically catalogued the zillion and one bank accounts that Jermaine Winifred, the sneaky oil billionaire bastard leader of Deliverance, had funneled away everywhere. The guys wanted to make sure they hit all his accounts in one go. That way he had no time to stash any funds. No funds would make regrouping that much harder.

Nothing of investigative or revenge nature was done within Hive walls now. We'd taken to using encrypted computers up on the roof. Sunlight hated vamps, so it was our best weapon against the mole. For some reason we were all sure it was a vampire. Probably one on the Quorum, because they had the most money and power. More than enough to tempt Sanctum.

Today I was on the roof with Oliver and Kyle. I was never alone any longer after my "two guard assignment" started.

Ryder hadn't been back in my bed yet, but somehow he was always part of the Charlie night watch shift. Four nights in a row now we had sat on my couch and watched movies, the sexual tension between us pretty much killing me. I wasn't sure I could do it another night. Unfortunately, with two enforcers assigned to me at all times, having enough privacy for me to jump his bones was not readily available. I was also getting the gentleman vibe from him, like he was waiting for me to take the lead.

My dirty thoughts were cut off by a low voice.

"I think I've traced the entire network of his company and Deliverance." As always when Sam spoke, we all paid attention. "I'm preparing the virus. We have our own set of numerous offshore accounts ready for the funds. The cash will land there before my program divides again. Then it'll shoot between eighteen countries and multiple bank accounts, before wiring the cash to the charities we decided on. It would take them years and a supercomputer to follow the trail."

We all grinned. Hells to the yeah. You shoot up my boyfriend, I take your Mercedes, your private jet, your fluffy dog, and whatever else your money buys.

I wasn't sure what happened then, but all of a sudden Sam was staring at my eyes in an intense way. It was making me kind of nervous.

"What?" I asked, but he quickly shook his head.

My laptop screen beeped with an instant message from Jayden.

Tessa is here and she is hammered. I locked her in room 23, way in the back.

"Shit!" I popped to my feet and took off running. A quick glance back told me that Sam had remained seated, but Oliver and Kyle were already up and pounding across the track behind me.

"What's wrong?" Oliver asked, sounding worried.

I flew through the double doors and down the hallway. "Tessa," was all I said.

The sexy six knew enough about my current situation with her to know that she was a handful. What human wanted to be a bloodsucking, allergic-to-the-sun monster? Only my bestie.

I nearly slammed into a vamp exiting the feeding center while I was trying to enter. I managed to dodge the bloodsucker at the last minute, nodding at Jayden as I dashed past. He tossed me a key to the room. When we reached 23, I turned to my bodyguards.

"Give us a second, will ya? This chick needs some real talk and it's not going to be pretty."

They both nodded, and as I was about to turn the knob I heard her banging against the door.

"You can't keep me in here, you blood-loving assholes! I want to see my best friend." Her words were so slurred that I only understood them because of my years speaking drunk Tessa. I heard a crash, and with my heart in my throat I jerked open the door and she almost toppled onto me.

"Oh, Tess…" My hand flew to my mouth.

She swayed once, and then crumpled to the floor. Her normally pristine appearance was … that of a homeless lady—baggy sweatpants, a loose t-shirt, mismatched shoes, her hair in a ratted ball at the nape of her neck. She wasn't wearing make-up and was superbly drunk.

Her eyes locked on mine. "You!" She pointed and tried to stand.

Her shirt lifted and I saw a peek of her abdomen. "Is that a tattoo!" I shrieked. "You hate tattoos. You said they were trashy."

Tears rimmed Tessa's hazel eyes. "They are trashy! This is what happens when your best friend becomes a hot immortal ash and your only friend options are Valarie! I'm a mess."

She broke down.

Oh Tess. I knelt on the floor and tried not to wince at the reek of alcohol coming from my bestie. In moments like these, advanced ash senses were not good.

The second I opened my arms, she fell into them sobbing. No words needed to be said. I knew how abandoned by me she felt and I was feeling like the worst bitch of a friend. Not that it had been a party-time picnic for me, but I had met so many amazing people in here, and while I missed her like crazy, I should have known she would have a tougher time. Tessa's father was the only good thing in her life. After he died when she was young, her mom didn't pick up the slack. I was her family.

My chest tightened then. "I'm always here for you," I choked. "Fuck the Hive and their rules. If you need me, then I'm there."

I pulled her face from my chest and made her look at me. Her eyes burned a brilliant green, the brown tinge to her hazel almost completely faded away. Her lips quivered.

"Charlie, I don't know who I am anymore," she moaned. "You and Blake are the only things real to me."

My body shook. Seeing someone I loved making such a desperate plea for help ripped open my insides. I pulled myself together, holding her firmly.

"You're Tessa Grace McNair, my annoying best friend who generally wouldn't be caught dead out in public like this." I touched her hair and she laughed.

"I drank a bottle of tequila. Now the room is spinning." She lay her head on my lap and I stroked her hair.

"How dare you get hammered without me." I joked, and she laughed before promptly rolling over and vomiting. A blond curl bounced out of her ratty bun and I snagged it, pulling it back as she puked. Because what are friends for if not for times like these.

"Oh good," I said, trying not to gag as I laughed. "The one thing your homeless look was missing was the smell of vomit."

Despite the dry heaving, she laughed with me then. It warmed my heart to know that in a few days I would be stuck with my mom and this crazy chick for Thanksgiving. I wouldn't have it any other way.

I sat with her for longer than was usually allowed in feeding times, but eventually she had to leave the Hive. Jayden called my mom to pick her up and Oliver and Kyle helped me get her into the car.

My heart felt both overfilled and fractured at the sight of my beautiful mom. I used to see her at least once a week, and now we could go a month with nothing more than a few emails. It's not as if I couldn't arrange to meet up with her on rare, secret, occasions—like the upcoming Thanksgiving trip. Ryder would definitely figure out how to get around those rules. It's just that it felt wrong to drag her into this dark world—people chasing me, trying to kill or kidnap my ass, knowing I was the cure and it was only going to get worse. How could I keep her close when she could easily become a possible victim or target in all of this?

I couldn't. So distance was the key. But that didn't make my heart ache any less.

Just before she left, my mom gave me a tight hug. "I can't wait to see you for Thanksgiving. Remember to be there early so we can cook together."

I nodded. We would have this day together, me, Mom, and Tessa. Just like old times, one last perfect holiday memory. It was so hard to release her; she smelled like home, like everything good and familiar, and I relished the close contact.

"Take care of Tessa, she's just having a hard time adjusting to this."

My mom nodded, and for the first time I noticed the strain in her face. "We all are, dear. I wish the rules were different. I wish the ash were allowed to come home. It's not like you're contagious."

She kissed my cheek and got in her car, but what she said replayed in my head long after she drove off.

"Oliver, why don't the humans let the ash live among them? Only the vampires risk spreading the virus, and surely many of the ash families would prefer they stayed with them rather than being killed off in the culling."

Oliver gave me a side glance. "It wasn't the humans that made that rule. I think the vampires like having us around to do all their dirty work. They declared that once the ash transformation took place, they were no longer classified as human and had to follow the rules of the vampire world. The humans were powerless to fight against it."

My stomach threatened to bring up my lunch. WTAF! I thought there were no choices, that the humans wanted nothing to do with ash and that the culling was the best chance at survival. Were they seriously telling me it was the vampires keeping all ash from being with their families?

From me possibly having my mom and Tessa permanently in my daily life, all so I could work for them, fight and kill for them? Oh *hell* no.

There's only one word for the feelings that were rising up inside of me. *Anarchy*. Fuck the vampires and fuck the Hive. How many years had this been going on? Killing their offspring, using us as their foot soldiers? They kept us weak and scared, killing off most of us in the cullings and then making the survivors think they were lucky to be part of the Hive world. Mind-screwing bastards.

If the humans never rejected the ash, or relegated them to the Hives, then we should be joining forces with them, rising up to demand that the vampires stopped their barbaric practices. My head was aching with all of these thoughts and questions, the anger smashing inside until I felt like I was going to go crazy.

My two bodyguards remained with me while I watched my family drive off, back to the human part of Portland, back to normal, leaving me here in blood-soaked crazy town.

Chapter 5

The next day was on the depressing side. Seeing Tessa like that and thinking about the sucktastic life for us ash ... well, it had shaken me.

Seeking some sort of comfort, I found myself ditching my guards—they thought I was just ducking to the feeding room—so I could take a minute to myself outside in the garden. My new badge was all kinds of awesome, allowing me access to areas I had never been allowed to go alone before. I began wandering aimlessly, bypassing—avoiding—the many groups of ash scattered around. I couldn't be bothered dealing with the males of the Hive today. I was still the unicorn ash, and the only thing which kept me from being harassed a lot was the fact that my wolf pack was a bunch of killer enforcers.

Knew those guys would come in handy for more than brooding and chiseled abs.

I traveled further than ever from the imposing Hive building. The grounds were quite extensive, and I knew from the "welcome" package, which was as dreary as the ones you probably got in prison, that there was about ten acres of land here. A large chunk was taken up by the enormous building, but still plenty of nature remained. The government had forbidden the vamps from building more housing or extending the Hive. They were trying to keep the numbers contained.

I found myself in a section of the forest which I'd never been before, the canopy thick and dense, and it was dark and cold on the ground level. Winter was so damn close I could feel the chill in the air, smell the fresh scent which usually meant ice or snow was around the corner. As I strolled further through the tightly-packed forest, I fought for a sense of ... something. I was lost. On the other hand, things were actually okay in the Hive. I had Ryder and the guys, I was going to be an enforcer— which was a hell of a lot better than "hello, can I take your call"—but still, this feeling of unease remained.

As the trees thinned, I emerged out into a large open space. I could see the high, wired fences in the distance, and hear cars, so I was probably close to the front entrance. It took me about five seconds to recognize where I had ended up. Since arriving here I'd tried to avoid this particular spot, consciously and subconsciously. I really hadn't wanted to deal with it. But of course, like all suppressed things, something eventually forces them to the surface.

Sucking in a deep breath, I squared my shoulders, got all brave and stomped across to the very spot where I had been dragged and almost raped. Everything looked a little different now. The ground was rough, the grass browning off and starting to die. The last time it had been dark, the shadows casting the entire world into something that seemed sinister and petrifying.

Crouching down, I dropped both of my hands into the grass, scraping across the hard dirt below. I had fought my attackers, but there were two of them and they were so much stronger than me. I knew at the time there was no way for me to escape, and that if I just lay there and accepted my fate, they might let me live.

But of course, I would have preferred death over letting those two animals think they had broken me. I was a fighter.

I had to squeeze my eyes tightly as images and emotions flashed through me. It was disorienting and overwhelming, mostly because I had refused to let myself dwell on it too much. After it happened I wouldn't speak on it, only giving my mom and Tessa the very barest of information. I had gotten very good at suppressing that night, and instead had focused on becoming physically stronger. Emotional strength, as always, was a lot harder.

It took me a while, sitting there on that cold, hard ground, eyes closed, emotions a mess, tears leaking from my eyes. Eventually the ache in my chest and stomach started to abate, until I could finally open my eyes and see the world around me again.

On the rare occasions I allowed myself to remember that night, it was only to wonder who the male was who had saved me. At the time I'd been out of it, overcome with fear, and the entire thing came back in flashes. But the Viking male, with his broad, strong and kind face, was permanently imprinted on my mind. A vampire who was actually caring enough to stop a human female from being raped. Seemed as if Lucas wasn't the only one I could trust, but Viking vamp had completely disappeared.

It kind of made me sad that I would never know his name.

My legs protested as I straightened. I wondered how long I'd been crouched there for. Probably long enough that someone in the Hive was looking for me. No doubt the enforcers had realized I was not with Jayden and were probably storming the place searching for me.

Shit! I hadn't meant to stay out this long. It was a real asshole move to make them worry about me. Stupid memories.

I spun around, preparing to sprint my butt back through the trees, knowing I was going to get majorly ass-kicked by Ryder, which I totally deserved. But before I could even take a step, the figure standing about three yards from me had me grinding to a halt. The enforcer looked kind of pissed off, and yet at the same time he didn't.

I cautiously approached Ryder, wondering if he was going to throw me over his shoulder and spank me or something. More importantly, did I want him to and was that even a punishment?

"I'm sorry," I said, as I stepped closer. "I really just wanted a minute by myself. Some fresh air. I got a bit ... distracted."

Ryder's eyes flicked across to where I'd been crouched, before coming back to rest on my face. "It's okay, you're not a prisoner. I just don't want to see you hurt."

Those were surprisingly calm and reasonable words from my hotheaded boyfriend. Yeah, I totally used the B-word. Couldn't think of what else to call him, and I liked having the claim on him. I paused inches from him, my body doing that thing where it gravitated toward him, like he was the magnet pulling my metal form straight into his grasp.

"What happened here, Charlie?"

Both of our gazes shifted back to the spot behind me. He must have been standing there for some time. He had seen my little breakdown. His hand brushed across my cheek, and I felt a slide of wetness.

"You were crying." His voice went a little low and growly, and I knew that the calm, collected dude was about to disappear.

I pressed my cheek tighter to his palm, allowing his warmth to eliminate some of the cold which had seeped into my skin. I lifted my eyes to meet his blaze of swirling silver. The black was almost gone at the moment.

"I should have told you this a while ago, but there never seemed to be a good time to bring it up." I shrugged a little, trying to make it seem less intense than it was. "The day that I woke up in the hospital wing was not the first time I was in the Hive. The first time was about a year before my ash genetics kicked in."

If I hadn't been watching so closely, I would have missed the tightening of his features. He was working very hard to remain calm, but I was starting to get a good read on him, and I knew he was upset.

I didn't want to be there any longer, I didn't want the negative energy seeping into me and Ryder. I laced our fingers together and led him away, back through the forest and out into a small patch of sunlight which had some flat rocks scattered around for us to sit on. The entire walk I felt Ryder growing grimmer and tenser, and I realized that starting my speech and not finishing it was the worst thing I could have done. He was probably imagining a bunch of terrible things.

With that in mind, I didn't waste any time once we were seated close enough that I could feel his hard thigh pressed against mine. "So, like I said, I have been here before under pretty horrible circumstances. That's partly why I was so negative about ash and vamps when I first arrived."

Taking a deep breath, I told him everything. Ryder didn't say a word during my story. I tried to keep my voice clinical, just listing the facts. I had been out at a club. Coming home, two ash had attacked me and dragged me into the compound. They knocked me around a bit before tearing my shirt off and half of my skirt. I was about ten seconds from being raped when some sort of guardian angel Viking saved me.

Ryder's hand tightened around mine, falling just short of being painful. He was not dealing so well with this story. Shocker. Finally, when I was finished, and the silence was getting a little uncomfortable, he leaned forward and wrapped me in his arms. "I'm so damn sorry, Charlie. *Shit!* I recognized the spot you were sitting at—I'll be honest, I'm feeling the need right now to go off and punch some things."

I pulled back a little, sitting straighter. I wanted to see his eyes. "You recognized the spot?"

Ryder cupped a hand around the back of my neck, pulling us closer again, resting his forehead against mine. "Yes, last year we found two dead ash there. They had been ripped apart. I investigated, but since these particular ash were both arrogant and dishonorable, my search was half-hearted at best. Not to mention I saw the torn skirt, and could smell blood that was unusual enough that I knew it wasn't from them. I closed the case without finding their killers. The vamps didn't care. Ash are nothing more than cattle." He pulled back and our gazes clashed. "Then ... to see you kneeling there, tears running down your face, in the very same spot ... let's just say more than a few scenarios were running through my mind."

I let my eyes drop down, trying to compose myself. "I fought them—all the way—but it took another male to save me—which I hated. So, from that day forward I trained. I got stronger. I needed to know that I could be strong enough on my own."

Ryder leaned in and pressed a kiss to my forehead, letting his lips linger there for a tantalizingly long time. As he pulled back, his voice was low and serious: "You've proven more than once that you're strong enough, Charlie. But for the sake of my sanity, tell me that if anything dangerous ever happens you'll always come to us, to me and the guys. We don't think of ourselves as your babysitters. We're your friends. We're your team. We have your back the same way I expect you would have ours."

I nodded at him. "Yes, I know. And I think all of you are amazing."

The sexy six were the toughest of males, but they never made me feel weak or indulged. They treated me like one of them, and I loved each of them so much for it.

Ryder tilted his head back a little, letting the sunlight bathe his face. His tawny skin looked extra bronzed in this light, and I got the sense that he loved the outdoors. His eyes twinkled when he noticed me ogling him.

"I used to come out here a lot. Like you, I sought comfort from nature. Away from the vampires who are the reason I'm an ash … the reason I turned into a monster and killed Molly."

He never spoke about his fiancée, like ever. It sort of bothered me, because it seemed like even after all of these years he wasn't over it at all. On the other hand I understood.

I strained forward as he continued. I wanted to hear every single word, even if some of it was going to be painful.

"It was easier to blame them than myself, you know. That's part of the reason I went rogue and into Sanctum. I was so angry when I first turned into an ash, the pain was killing me. Funnily enough, I always knew I was going to be an ash. Molly knew also. Kyle and my mother went out of their way to become pregnant to a vampire. It was all the rage at the time."

Kyle had told me bits and pieces of this, Ryder a little more in the restaurant, but I was greedy for every single detail.

I cautiously chose my next words: "I thought all the males who knew they were going to turn ash, well, the government kept a close eye on you? Especially when you were in your early twenties."

Ryder laughed then, a low derisive sound. "I turned about a year before they expected. For some reason, the closer your sire is to the original line, the less they seem to know about you and the fewer rules you follow. I was young and stupid. In love. Molly and I were barely out of high school. The funny thing is that I've been holding on to the damn guilt and pain for so long that I didn't even realize how bitter I'd become."

A blaze of silver wrapped around me. His look was intense and potent. "When I met you, everything changed for me. You broke down my walls with your persistence. You never let me get away with anything. You called me out on every single shitty thing I did and said. I realized that your fire was exactly what I needed to warm the coldness which had seeped into my soul."

Whoa. Maybe Ryder had missed his calling as a poet. That was pretty deep and so romantic. I couldn't stop from throwing myself at him, and as his arms wrapped around me I felt comforted.

"Molly and I would have been happy. I know that." His muffled words were as painful as I expected them to be. "But happy is not the same as what I know I could have with you, Charlie. You're more. You're everything. This is not young, first love. Not for me. It's the real deal and I'm ready to let go of the guilt and bitterness now. I'm ready to let go of Molly."

Holy shit. Could one, like, die of happiness? Because I was pretty sure I was having a heart attack. My chest actually ached, and my head was a tizzy of emotions. I knew Ryder had pulled out something emotional to try and even out all of the baggage I'd spilled on him. He was trying to share some of himself with me, and in doing so had given me the best gift I could have hoped for. I tilted my head back and gave him a quick soft kiss. Something had settled inside of me, the thing that girls have when they grow up without dads, that unsettled feeling around love interests. Mine was gone, replaced with something amazing.

Before the mood could get any more serious, he gave me that crooked half grin, and standing, pulled me to my feet. "Come on, Charlie, it's time for our shift now. I know Markus is waiting to whip your butt in the weights room."

The serious mood was broken but the euphoria remained inside. I was genuinely happy, more than I ever remembered being. I just wondered how long before something came along to destroy it.

As we started to walk back toward the Hive, I yanked gently on his hand, pulling him to a stop. "I have hated being an ash from the second I started to turn. But right now, for the first time in my life, I think it's the greatest blessing I could have received."

Standing on tiptoes, I brushed my lips against his, and before I could pull away, Ryder tightened his hold and deepened our kiss. My eyes closed at the pure orgasmic joy I was feeling as his tongue brushed against mine. The feel of his soft lips was addictive.

I wondered then what the world record for kissing was. I was totally up for trying to break that one.

An hour later I was in gym clothes, face-down on the stinky-ass workout mats.

"Markus, you are an asshole. You know that, right?" My words were muffled, exhaustion too much for me to even lift my head. "You are now number six on my list of favorite enforcers. Maybe seven."

Markus' deep laughter filled the gym and bounced around, giving the illusion that there was more than one big, mean enforcer trying to kill me in here. "I'm trying to show you the best way to take down an attacker who has both size and weight on you. Those self-defense classes gave you a good basic idea, but you're dealing with ash and vamps now. We're mean bastards, and we do not play nice or fair."

I rolled over. Seriously, it had to be every muscle, joint, bone, nerve, artery, and vein that was currently hurting. There was no other explanation for this much pain.

"I swear to God you were a torturer before turning ash," I grumbled as I pulled myself up, my body screaming at me to stay down—*just stay the hell down.*

Markus laughed again. I was so glad I amused him so much. Ass. Hole.

"I was actually an earl from a well-respected family back in Scotland. I was born in Edinburg, early 1950s. My life growing up was incredible, but apparently no one knew that my mother was hiding a big secret—one fun night away from her husband. Imagine everyone's surprise when I went through the ash transition twenty-three years later." Some of his laughter sobered up. "Guess you can say the family name was ruined. My father cast my ass straight out into the world. No title. No inheritance. No freaking clue how to survive."

I found myself crossing to his side to place a comforting hand on his arm. Did anyone have happy stories in this damned place?

His eyes were dark as he stared down at me from his mammoth height. "I learned quickly. It was fight or die, and I am determined you don't find yourself in the same position. If we aren't here one day to protect your back, I need to know you can do it on your own."

I gave an exaggerated sigh, before patting his muscled forearm one last time and striding back to take my position again.

I waved my hand at him. "Okay, guilty McGuilt-trip, bring it on."

Bring it he did. I was lucky I walked out of there on my own.

Later that afternoon, after an ice bath, hot tub, and another ice bath, I managed to regain use of my limbs and made it back to my apartment, bodyguards attached again. Jayden, who must have just finished his shift, catwalked through the door just after me. He was acting strange as hell, giving me all these serious looks. Eventually, we ended up alone in the kitchen; the boys were on the couch chatting. I confronted him by the fridge.

"What's up? You're being weirder than usual."

Jayden picked at his nails—eyes so dark no silver was visible. Made him look like one of those demons off *Supernatural*. A hot, buff one.

"We need to talk alone," was all he said. Well, shit. That wasn't good.

Giving him one last flinty stare, I strode out into the living room and begged Kyle and Oliver to give me some alone time with my BAFF.

Oliver shook his head. "Ryder said two guards, and we already let you escape once today."

Jayden, who had followed me from the kitchen, put one hand on his hip and gave his boyfriend the staredown. "Are you saying I'm not capable of protecting Charlie?"

Uh oh, that was a question Oliver was going to want to think long and hard about before answering. The enforcer clearly knew that; he was looking quite trapped, like he didn't know what to say. Finally Kyle, attempting to save his friend, spoke gently: "Jayden, you're not a trained—"

Jayden cut him off with a raised palm. Oliver groaned at the same time. He knew his man well enough now to know this was turning into a code red.

"Excuse me?" Jayden was all narrowed eyes, one hand in the air and the other on his hip. "Did you watch the culling? I'm a killing machine, bitch. I can take care of my best friend for an hour."

I grinned. Oliver was trying to hide a smile as Kyle narrowed his eyes but I could see he respected Jayden. I decided it was time for me to step in again, reassert my own authority.

"Look, guys, I love ya, but I need time alone with my BAFF. I have a gun, Jayden has a nail file. We'll be fine."

Jayden gave a nod when I said nail file. "That's right," he said. "We get attacked, I will file a bitch."

I grinned. With a shake of his head, Oliver took off his walkie-talkie and tucked it into Jayden's belt. Bit of overkill considering I had my own. Sure, I on occasion left it places that weren't on my person, but still … overkill.

"One hour," Oliver commanded in a stern tone.

Jayden put his hand up in an army salute and Oliver rolled his eyes. Jayden and I left the apartment and made our way to the ground floor so we could go outside. It was the only place

I didn't feel like a member of the Hive. Plus, I knew for sure Jayden did not want to be overheard by any spying vamp asshats.

When we got to the creek, we both sat on a log. His expression was hard to read, but he was definitely having deep thoughts.

"Sooo ... are you pregnant?" I said in a dead-serious voice.

Jayden lifted his perfectly-shaped eyebrows and gave me a devilish smile. "Girl, I wish."

I laughed. "Seriously, what's up?"

His face darkened. "If bad shit is happening but there's nothing you can do about it, are you one of those people that wants to go about life not knowing and thinking everything is sunshine and rainbows or—"

I interrupted him—no thought required on that question at all. "Or. I'm the or. Tell me."

He swallowed hard. "The feeding center has become a hub of gossip. I hear it all. Most of it probably isn't even true."

Okay, he was definitely priming this for a bad news drop.

"But...?"

"But..." He picked at his nails again, one of his few nervous tics. "So there are always these rumors flying around this place that the vampires give out high interest loans to humans in exchange for stuff. Until today I'd never known for sure, but there were these two vampires talking in the feeding room—"

I raised an eyebrow, which was admittedly much less groomed than my BAFF's, and interrupted him: "So, I gather that mostly what you do for your job is spying."

He pursed his lips. "No! Maybe. Whatever. Anyway, I overheard the vampires saying they finally got something on Senator McGreelie. Pictures his wife wouldn't want to see."

"Who is Senator McGreelie?"

Jayden rolled his eyes. "That's not what's important. Charlie, it's all true. The vampires have blackmail files on all of the major politicians. Despite the fact that their numbers are greater, the human world is secretly ruled by the vampires."

Holy shit. Unbridled rage swept through me. Enough was enough. This was not okay. I pulled out my all-access keycard. Jayden had more than piqued my interest, and now I had to know for sure. Because if this was true, it had cemented something inside of me which had been brewing since I found out I was the cure.

"Want to have some fun?" I asked.

He gave me his grin, the one which told me he was down for anything.

Chapter 6

Ten minutes later we were in a room full of filing cabinets. Jayden had told me plenty of times about this secret little room. Since he had to constantly log in blood donations and keep records of blood types and schedules of feeders, he knew the administrative side of the Hive. My fancy badge got us into the room and hopefully no one would pay attention to the security log, because while Jayden had a legitimate reason to come in here on occasion, I had none.

We were alone. The ten-foot-high rows of filing cabinets were menacing, casting shadows on the cement floors, making me paranoid. The room was small, maybe fifteen feet long and ten feet wide.

As we crept along one row Jayden whispered: "I overheard one of the ash saying that a few years ago the vampires were hacked and lost a lot of precious info. Since then they have printed everything and kept it in hard copy form."

Everything? Holy shit. Could it be that easy? Their paranoia was going to make our snooping on the vamps that much easier. Not to mention, so many of the vamps were older than dirt, and found it hard to assimilate into the twenty-first century. Here's hoping that we would just open one of these cabinets and find the dark secrets of the Hive. Why hadn't Ryder and his boys done this before? Probably something to do with pit-style punishment if they were caught.

Eek, we'd better not get caught.

Knowing time was short, I began scanning the cabinet labels: *Blood Types, Feeder Data, Hive Construction Permits…*

"Boring," I murmured, before moving on to the next one. It was equally as useless. As I rounded the first row I noticed that Jayden had stopped dead in front of a cabinet that looked different from the others. It was sturdier and had a key lock on the front, while the others had a simple push-button to open. Moving in behind him I read the label. *Classified.* And there we had the perfect example of the arrogance of vampires. Jayden jiggled the locking mechanism, and it was solid. Thick.

Dammit! Of course it wouldn't be that easy. One of the Quorum members probably had the key. Oh well, we would just have to find another way to get the Hive's dirty little secrets. Turning to leave, I did a double take as my bestie reached into his pocket and pulled out two bobby pins. He then started tinkering with them, straightening one and twisting the other.

He flipped up his head and gave me a sheepish look. "Don't judge me for what you are about to see."

I just stared at him, mystified, until he inserted both pins into the lock and began to twist them around. No way! My sassy BAFF knew how to break and enter with the skill of a master thief.

"Dude! Where did you learn to pick locks?" He'd told me he was a Portland native, and lock-picking was not a big skill around these parts.

"Girl, you don't want to know. Growing up ... the struggle was real." He quipped and I laughed, stepping forward to give him a hug from behind.

Suddenly I heard a click and Jayden opened the drawer in one smooth move. Holy crap, we were going to be in serious shit if we got caught. Looking left and right to make sure we were still alone, I began to riffle through the folders. Names, dates, and businesses were labeled at the top. I picked one at random.

Jeff Burns, CEO of Global Oil, the label read. Popping the folder open, I scanned the contents. Holy hell on steroids. There were multiple payments issued from Global Oil to Portland Hive. In the back of the folder was a series of photographs showing who I assumed was Jeff Burns wearing a gag ball and leather bondage outfit, posing half naked on a bed. Okay, that shit was going to be burned into my brain for a really long time. Jayden, who was pressed close to my back, was reading over my shoulder. I had the uncomfortable feeling he was taking mental notes. Ugh. Just no. I had to draw the line at ball gags. Putting the folder back, I grabbed another.

Union Blood Bank, it read. Scanning the folder, I began to seethe. My mom worked for the local hospital. I recognized Union Blood Bank as one of the main donation centers for humans to give blood to save other humans. But no, according to this file, Union Blood Bank only gave twenty percent of their blood from humans to the hospitals. The rest was funneled to the Hive, against the humans' knowledge or wishes.

These files were like crack. I needed more. Looking at Jayden, who was now on his own set of files, I saw he was open-mouthed staring hard.

"What? Another bondage scene?" My laughter died as I leaned over and saw a photo of an absolute bloodbath, a massacre I didn't even want to describe or ever see again—

pooling of blood, decapitated heads, entrails, organs. The victims had been torn to pieces.

Jayden spoke with a hollow voice: "Operation Freedom …when they killed all of the Originals."

I gasped, opening and closing my mouth, trying to make sense of that carnage.

The sound of a slamming door jarred me out of it. *Shit!* Footsteps and voices could be heard coming towards us. Frickity frak! Jayden and I both shoved our files in the cabinet, uncaring where they ended up, before slamming the door shut. There was no sneaking out of this room. Every sound echoed off of the walls and there was only one exit. Trying to alleviate suspicion, we crept away from the classified cabinet, moving toward the more boring stuff.

"Who's there?" a deep male voice called out.

We froze, and Jayden looked at me as if waiting for me to do something. Time to improvise. I quickly yanked off my shirt, exposing my bra. Jayden gave me a solid WTF look, before raising his brows like I was a crazy person who had just escaped from a padded room.

"Kiss me!" I whispered. His *you're insane* look quickly morphed in one of disgust.

I smooshed my body against his and pressed my lips to the corner of his mouth. The footsteps stomped closer and with a faked gasp I pulled back from Jayden, feigning a caught expression and covering my chest.

It was a bit of a relief to see that it wasn't a vampire, but Jose, the ash who had given me my first Hive tour. Another ash was close behind him. Jose looked at me, shocked. His eyes went from my shirt on the ground, to Jayden and then back to me.

"I … what…?" Jose started. The other ash looked just as confused. "I thought you were…"

Jayden smirked. "Sometimes I like to bat for both teams. Plus, it's Charlie. Everyone wants a piece of unicorn ass once in their life."

Luckily no one mentioned the fact that we were roommates, and could have just made out in our living area if we wanted to. I think the shock had fried their brains. I grabbed my shirt, throwing it on, already making plans to beat on Jayden later for calling me a piece of ass.

Jose recovered first, and started flapping his hands in an agitated manner. "Get out of here, you're not supposed to be in here," he said. Jayden grabbed my hand and we booked it out of there. The second we were far enough away, we broke into laughter.

Jayden shook his head back and forth. "I'm totally telling Oliver I kissed a girl. He will get a kick out of that."

I chuckled, but then my face darkened at the memory of what we found. How deep did the Hive's control go? We had spent five minutes looking through those files. What would we have found if we had more time? Was there a file on me in there? Shit, I should have looked for that first.

Each new piece of knowledge only cemented my feelings that I needed to do something to change the Hive world, to shake up the evil little vampire leaders. Not yet, but very soon. For now I would bide my time and suppress all that shit I'd just read.

Jayden and I wordlessly went back to my apartment. I decided that next time we were up on the roof together I would tell the boys what we'd discovered. I wondered if it would surprise them how deep the corruption ran. Probably not. They were already suspicious by nature.

The next day passed slowly, and by the afternoon I still hadn't seen Ryder and was feeling bummed. We hadn't really hung out since our kind of intense and emotional conversation and I was feeling insecure.

After visiting Jayden at the feeding center, I made it back to my apartment with Oliver and Kyle at my side. As my door came into view I couldn't help the broad smile which broke across my face. Ryder was leaning against my door, one hand in his pocket, looking all kinds of sexy.

Ryder nodded to the boys. "I'll take over watch now."

The pair exchanged a glance, all smirks and raised eyebrows. Kyle gave me a wink as they walked away. I swallowed hard, and my belly heated at the thought of alone time with Ryder.

Dear God, please let this very hot ash badass finally take advantage of me. Love, Charlie.

After letting us inside, I realized there was no one else waiting for us. No other enforcers. Jayden wouldn't be back for hours. He was working the late shift at the feeding center. I wondered why Ryder had relaxed the two guards at all times rule. It was the first time in days we'd been alone in my apartment.

"Wanna watch a movie?" I set the keys on the counter and turned around to find Ryder a few inches from my face, silver-black eyes scanning my body.

"Not really," he said, his eyes falling to my lips.

Oh my gawd.

Ryder reached out and brushed my cheek. "Since becoming an ash I've barely slept more than a few hours straight. Until that night I slept next to you." He paused, his expression turning playful. "Could have been the drugs, but I know in my gut that it was you. You have bewitched me, and now I can't stay away from you."

I grinned. "I thought I snored."

He palmed the back of my neck. "You do, like a little kitten."

I laughed and met his gaze as something intense built between us. We stayed locked in that stare for what seemed like forever.

"Charlie…" He stepped closer, and my hands found their way to his hips and the tight muscles there.

"Yes?" I panted in anticipation.

His lips brushed close to me. "You drive me crazy. I've never wanted anyone as much as I want you."

He pulled back just in time for my lips to crash into his. He didn't hesitate, gripping under my butt and lifting me up so I could straddle him. Our kiss deepened as he walked us back to my bedroom. I wrenched myself from him long enough to peel off my shirt, exposing my red lace bra. His hooded stare, as his gaze devoured my body, nearly sent me over the edge. Thank God Jayden had picked out my clothes today. Yep, even my underwear.

Ryder carefully laid me down on the bed, before kneeling between my legs. Pulling his shirt over his head, the entire time I was mentally chanting *slower, slower, slower.* Okay, I actually couldn't wait to see him naked, but the show was so freaking good that I also wanted to draw it out. When he was finally naked from the waist up, I reached out a hand and dragged it across his hard abdomen. It was perfect again now, no marks or scarring from his surgery.

And holy lord of all things sexy, Ryder was a piece of work. Tan tight skin wrapped around rock hard muscle, swirling silvery eyes and twenty-four hours of stubble—he was so fine that my insides were constricting in pure need. Ryder seemed to be enjoying my perusal, but eventually our gravity grew too strong to ignore. Our lips met again, and the taste of him was like a shot of orgasm right to my girly parts. Somehow we got naked, magically, because I don't even remember that part happening, but I sure as hell was glad that it did.

Ryder's lips left mine as he started to kiss down my cheek and along the ridge of my jaw. My eyes rolled back in my head as he made his way along my neck. "You are insanely beautiful," he murmured between kisses.

Perfect. Of all the shitty relationships I'd had, and there were more than a few on that list, Ryder and I had started off the rockiest and ended up the most perfect. I never in a million years would have imagined that this scary, military, badass ash enforcer who had electrocuted me my first day at the Hive, would end up loving me like this, with just the right amount of tenderness and passion. You know what they say? Don't judge a book by its cover? Well, I had Ryder all figured out now; all bark and the hottest bite ever. He was mine and I was keeping him.

There was no stopping us now. I had been dreaming about touching him like this for so long. As he kissed his way to my stomach he lifted his head and our eyes met.

"You okay, Charlie?" There was lust in those eyes, but also concern.

I reached out and linked my hand through his. "You treat me right, Ryder, so don't worry. I'll let you know if I need more time."

A low, rumbly growl rocked his chest, and he shifted up so our faces were even again. His strong arms framed either side of my body as he lowered himself down to me. "I will never hurt you. My every need is to protect you from whatever storm is coming. Just know you are always safe with me."

I never realized love was strong enough to actually cripple an organ, but right then it felt as if my heart was going to explode. I laced my hands behind his neck and yanked hard enough to pull his weight onto me. Our kisses were frantic as we moved past any doubts or fears. Now was time for loving. Tomorrow we would worry about the storm.

The next morning, I rolled over to see Ryder asleep on his back, one arm behind his head, sheet pulled down to his waist. I took the second to stare, because he was yum. Holy yum. Last night had brought the relief we both needed, uh twice, and hopefully moved our relationship out of the hot and cold weird zone and into the solid steady zone. Something told me I was going to be using the B-word more frequently now.

I found myself grinning like a loved-up idiot, and despite that I wanted nothing more than to go for round three, I slipped out of the bed to brush my teeth and get ready.

When I came out of the bathroom, Ryder was standing next to my bed, wearing just his unbuttoned enforcer cargo pants, looking sleepy and sexy as hell.

Uh, round three please.

"If you're not in the bed, then I'm going to need coffee," he grumbled.

I laughed. "Aww, are you not a morning person?"

Some of the tired faded from his eyes, and I almost blushed as he took a slow leisurely inspection of my body. "I can be if you want me to be."

Well, hello man of my dreams. I grinned. "Go shower. I'll make coffee with a shot of blood."

He smiled, before prowling across to me. "Perfect," he said as he captured my mouth in a devastatingly sexy kiss on his way into the bathroom.

I needed a few moments after that to pull myself together. And to walk without my legs collapsing. Finally able to move, I strode out into the kitchen and saw Jayden was already at the table. He was wearing a big-ass grin, coffee mug in his hands. When I got near him, he squealed before dropping his cup and flapping his overly-excited hands.

"Shh, Ryder is in the shower," I said, snorting out my laughter at his manic expression.

Jayden leaned forward, eyes wide. "Oh my God, tell me everything."

I rolled my eyes. "I don't kiss and tell."

Jayden's face quickly turned deadly. His pointer finger came up in my face. "Bitch, I have been waiting months for this to happen. Like a soap opera, I've hung on every drama. You need to give me something."

I chuckled again. He grabbed my hand and pulled me close, whispering, "Did you, ya know?"

I humored him. "Yes."

Jayden's mouth dropped open. "And? Is he like a dominatrix in the sack? I picture him tying you up and giving orders."

"Oh my God, no. He's a weirdly perfect mix of strong and sweet."

Jayden looked disgusted. He let go of me. "Sweet? How boring."

I shook my head. "Remind me never to ask about you and Oliver. I don't even want to know what goes on behind those closed doors."

Jayden batted his long eyelashes at me. "It's anything but sweet, I'll tell you that."

Before I could retort, Ryder flung open my bedroom door looking pissed. The swirls of silver in his eyes were practically glowing. Unfortunately he was already dressed, wearing his clothes from last night. They looked slightly wet, like he had thrown them on without drying.

Shit.

I was on my feet, coffee forgotten. "What's wrong?" My heart was racing. My hand went to my hip where I should have been wearing my walkie-talkie. I'd left it in the bedroom. Double shit!

"We got a call." His voice was clipped as he ran through my kitchen, "A vampire infected a little girl ... on purpose."

"Oh *hell* no," I breathed, and took off after him.

The more shit I heard about the vampires, the more I was sure I hated them.

Kyle and the boys were waiting for us at the Humvee. Thankfully one of them had the foresight to bring coffee and a few bottles of blood. Oliver looked as smug as Jayden when he scanned Ryder's outfit and saw it was the one from the night before. He gave me the same knowing smartass smile as his boyfriend. Nosy ash.

The second we jumped into the car, Kyle gunned it.

"Give me a report," Ryder ordered while chugging the coffee in one go.

Kyle's face looked thunderous, his eyes black as night, and I was pretty sure he was flashing fang. "A fucking vampire infected a twelve year old girl. He attacked her."

"God damn vampires!" Sam was the surprising owner of the angry voice. "They should all be eliminated." There was that darkness which simmered under the surface of our normally silent enforcer.

"Where is the girl?" My heart was hammering. This was so not okay.

Kyle gritted his teeth. "That's the really messed up part. She's in the medical wing, recovering with the permission of the Quorum. They're acting like this isn't a big deal."

Ryder's face took on a stone cold deadly look. "What? Then where are we going?"

Kyle pointed to the road. "The humans found out and there's a riot outside the gates. Our orders are to disperse the crowd."

As we neared the gate to exit the Hive, I saw a bunch of picketers wearing masks. They had signs with *Don't touch our children!* and *Monsters!* written on them.

"Stop the car!" Ryder ordered, and Kyle screeched the Humvee to a halt.

Ryder turned to all of us, staring each in the eyes. "We no longer take orders from the Quorum. I'm not doing this kind of dirty work any longer. If the vampires want this crowd gone, they can do it themselves."

"That's the sexiest thing you've ever said," I told him, and he graced me with a rare grin.

"I reckon we head back in and mess up every vamp we find. What do you think, mates?" Jared called out.

The Aussie was growing on me. He was hot, he was lethal, and he was not taking shit from the Quorum any longer.

Ryder turned to Kyle. "I want you guys to go back to the locker room and wait for me. I'm going to see the Quorum. Alone."

"I'm going with you," I stated as Kyle turned the car around.

Ryder glared at me. "No way. The Quorum already has it out for you."

I crossed my arms. "Yes way. Lucas won't let them hurt me."

I knew the second it came out of my mouth that it was the wrong thing to say.

Ryder's features hardened, but there was a wounded look in his eyes. "I won't let anyone hurt you either, Charlie."

My face fell as the guys all started to stare with great focus out the window.

"I know," I squeaked. I hadn't meant to imply that Ryder couldn't protect me. I just did my usual speak before thinking thing.

Thankfully a distraction arrived in the form of Kyle parking the Humvee back in the garage. None of us wasted time exiting the vehicle and dashing through the Hive. I stayed right by Ryder, even after we left the other five guys at the locker room. I could tell he still wasn't happy about me coming along, but he was learning not to argue with my stubborn butt. Of course, I had no doubt that if he'd felt that strongly about me staying behind, I'd probably be tied up next to Kyle right about now.

We made our way to the medical wing. Before using his key card to open the door, Ryder turned to look at me. "Don't do anything stupid." His tone was serious, but there was a spark of humor across his eyes.

I feigned an innocent look. "Who, me?"

He pressed a quick kiss on my lips. "I didn't get a chance to say good morning."

Grinning further, I nodded. "It was a good morning … could have been even better."

Hello, round three...

Damn the vampires for ruining our morning afterglow. Another reason to hate the child-turning evil fuckers.

Upon entering the medical wing it was immediately obvious something major was happening. The staff was running around with bags of blood in their hands, all wearing flustered looks.

Out of nowhere, a big tall male vampire zoomed into Ryder's space and placed a hand on his chest. Ryder looked down at the hand and I saw his jaw clench.

"I want to see the girl." Ryder's voice was clipped and deadly. I knew him well enough to know he was three seconds from ripping this asshole's hand off.

"No. Your orders are to disperse the mob outside the gates," the man said in an equally deadly voice.

Ryder flicked the man's hand out of his way and pushed forward. "I don't take orders until I speak with the Quorum." His voice was so cold I was pretty sure I now had frostbite on my cheeks.

We kept moving, and the vampire seemed unsure about stopping the deadly enforcer again. *Smart move, asshole.* The next hall we crossed into was one I hadn't been before. Each door was frosted glass. Ugh, this place gave me the creeps. I heard a strangled noise from behind and turned to find the bodyguard vampire bolting after Ryder. Dude must have found a pair of balls after all. He barely even glanced at me, so it was easy to stick my foot out and trip him. He stumbled forward but caught himself, turning to give me a deadly look.

"Oops!" I put my hand over my mouth and batted my eyelashes. *Dick.*

Before this shit could escalate and I no doubt got my ass kicked, Lucas and a few other Quorum members trickled out into the hallway. From the room they exited I could hear a young girl's voice: "I want to go home! I want more blood!"

The Quorum member known as fugly, the hideous dude with slicked-back hair and a bent nose, was my least favorite of any living creature. He was the leader of the fourth house, and a total pain in my ass.

When fugly saw us, his eyes went all silver swirl and he charged straight into a faceoff with Ryder. I was about to interfere when Lucas gave me a stern look.

"Since when do you defy our orders?" Fugly sneered at us. "We keep you fed and employed, don't forget that."

With clenched fists, Ryder stepped closer to him. "I work for you willingly, to help save ash from making the same mistake I did. I do not help you animals infect children and cover the evidence up. Or PR goodwill to the humans. I'm thinking about joining their picket line actually."

Holy shit. He wasn't holding back at all. For the first time I feared for Ryder. If they wanted him dead, we were vastly outnumbered.

Fugly sneered again, which made his nose look even more crooked. "It was an accident, enforcer, calm down! The *animal* is in the pit."

Ryder didn't seem pleased with that answer. "Not good enough. I want him dead."

Fugly barked out a laugh, which died off as his arm snaked out and he wrapped his hand around Ryder's neck. "Who do you think you are? Demanding such things? How about I kill you and make the other robots do as I say."

Oh hell no.

I stepped forward. "If you kill him, the other enforcers will revolt. They won't work for you. They take orders only from him. Look outside. Do you see any enforcers breaking up that mob? No. Because Ryder told them to stand down."

All eyes were on me now, and Ryder chose that moment to use himself as a distraction. He knocked the vamp's hand, and despite the fact that the evil suckers were so much stronger than us, it took him barely any effort to free himself. There was anger brewing in the enforcer's eyes, but the way they flicked between me and the Quorum, I could tell he was afraid to start anything while I was down here too.

Ryder and I remained side by side, neither of us backing down, the child's cry in the background. The Quorum members exchanged looks then, looks I didn't particularly like, because they were very much on the evil and calculating side. Something more than this little girl was up with them.

Finally, when the tension was almost unbearable, fugly turned to us and said, "You ash are so sensitive. Fine, we will kill the vampire. Now get back to work."

That was much too easy, which only increased the bad feeling in my gut. They were planning something. No way would they let Ryder get away with this shit otherwise. He might be important in the ash and enforcer world, he might have a token seat on the Quorum, but their arrogance ensured they did not allow others, especially ash, to question their orders.

Ryder was a statue beside me. Something told me he was as suspicious as I was. He was a better actor though. His next words were friendly, offhand even: "I appreciate your support in this matter. I'm going to go now—not feeling so well—think I'm coming down with something. I'm going to take a few days off."

Before they had a chance to retort, he captured my hand and we both hauled ass out of the creepy medical wing. As soon as we were back in the elevator, I leaned forward, and speaking as low as I could asked: "What's the few days off for?"

The tumult of emotions was strong in his eyes. "Remember that storm I mentioned last night, well, I'm pretty sure it's on its way. The Quorum is up to something, and I have no idea when the hurricane will hit. You deserve to have the holiday with your family, but there's no way you can go without me and a few of the boys. I was on duty, but now I'll be able to keep you safe."

I grinned. "So what you're saying is that you're coming to my house for Thanksgiving?"

Ryder gave me a sexy side glance. "If that's okay?"

"It's perfect."

We both leaned back against the elevator, silent again. There was no safe place to speak in the Hive. That didn't stop the multitude of questions, worries and fears which were as much a part of me now as my heart and lungs.

The next day Jayden, the sexy six, and I sat clustered around the laptop on the roof, our unofficial hide out place.

Leaning forward, Ryder motioned to Jayden and Oliver: "Can you two go run some laps? We should probably make our meetings a little less obvious."

Jayden nodded, springing to his feet. "If he can keep up with me."

Oliver gave him a look which was a combination of exasperation and adoration. These two dudes were seriously the cutest couple ever. They both took off.

Markus chuckled. "Jayden is a good match for Oliver. He loves a challenge, and I can tell our unicorn's BAFF is definitely keeping him challenged."

One of my favorite things about this group was that there was never one ounce of awkward about the boys' love, and I for one thought that said everything about how absolutely secure and awesome they were.

Sam's fingers suddenly went into super-fast mode. "Our Deliverance window is open! Kyle, tether with me."

Kyle hunched over his laptop and began to type rapidly. We were all frozen with anticipation. This was it. We were bankrupting Deliverance.

"We're completely untraceable now, and I've got all of the bank accounts online," Kyle said.

Sam nodded. "Sending virus." His finger punched a key before he sat back, relaxed—well, relaxed for him anyway.

Ryder opened his hands. "That's it?"

Sam nodded, his eyes half-closed. Kyle was still monitoring his screen closely and I could see his pupils rapidly darting across the computer. Finally he broke into a huge grin. "Our selected charities are now a couple hundred million dollars richer."

Markus gave an excited shout, followed by a groan. "Don't get me wrong, I love that the needy will benefit from a corrupt bunch of assholes, but I'd have liked it if we'd taken just a wee bit of that money and bought a little something for ourselves. I've had my eye on this Audi R8 for a while now."

Ryder clapped his shoulder in sympathy. Most of these boys were car enthusiasts. Poor babies were stuck with vampire-issued, probably bugged Hummers.

Sam slammed his laptop shut and handed it to Kyle. "Incinerate them."

Kyle nodded, and jumping to his feet dashed away with the two slim-line computers. Movement caught my eye and I was laughing again as Jayden playfully fell behind Oliver, just so he could smack him on the butt. My friend, seriously, you just could not take him anywhere.

Ryder leaned forward. "Okay, now what are we doing about the little girl?"

My attention instantly focused. I had not stopped worrying about her for a moment and I needed to hear what the plan was. I was worried everyone would forget as all the drama died down.

The riots were slowing down outside the Hive, and the vampires were doing what they did best, covering their tracks and creating positive publicity. Publically, the Quorum had paid the girl's family a large, undisclosed, sum of money, and the human media was having a field day with this information. In the end, the girl's family accepted that vampires were the only ones who could now properly care for their daughter and did not press charges, so the humans couldn't do much legally.

The men kind of fell silent. Clearly there was no plan forthcoming, so I blurted out what I had been thinking all along. "I want to cure her." I managed to keep my voice low and still convey every ounce of my determination.

Kyle was back now from the incinerator and he froze mid-stride. Ryder shook his head. "Absolutely not."

Aww, poor thing. Ryder thought that because he was sleeping with me, he could tell me what to do.

I crossed my arms. "Let me put this a simpler way so you all can understand it. I *am* going to cure her and you can either help me or get out of my way."

I gave Ryder my serious big girl face and was rewarded with the slightest twitch of his lips before he exhaled. "Do you have a death wish?"

"If it means giving an innocent twelve-year-old her life back, then yeah I do."

I could see the vein in his neck throbbing and I had to push down the memory of the time I drank from him to confuse the Quorum's blood results.

Sam stood, distracting our standoff. "There will be a time for that, Charlie, but it isn't now. Be patient."

Then he walked away.

What the hell? "What's with Yoda? He's been acting weird since he came back from 'fishing.'" I did air quotes.

I could see the concern on the enforcers' faces as they watched Sam leave. No one said anything. I knew they had all long ago decided to let Sam keep his secrets.

Ryder held a hand out to me. "Just put a pause on your aspirations to heal the world until after Thanksgiving, okay?"

I shrugged. "Fair enough. But I'll bet this little girl is going to cry her eyes out knowing she can't spend the holiday eating turkey with her family." Never hurts to remind them what our delay was costing her.

The gravity of the situation hit us all then. The boys' faces were somber. Life in the Hive wasn't just affecting us, it affected all of society. When an ash was brought in or a new vampire infected, that was a family member taken away, a gaping hole left in the hearts of those people. Maybe there was a greater reason for why I was the cure. Maybe I shouldn't be hiding it. Maybe it was time to do something.

Chapter 7

The next morning as we made our way to the garage, I realized how damn quiet the Hive was in the early hours. Vampires were probably asleep in their coffins. Okay, I was pretty sure they slept in beds, but there was no denying that they were creepy enough for coffins. At least the enclosed building, locked down with heavy shutters, felt less oppressive without the bloodsuckers around.

There were two Humvees waiting for us. Ryder suggested this in case some of the boys were called back to the Hive. At this stage, all of the sexy six, plus Jayden, were coming to Thanksgiving. Ryder cleared it with Lucas and Lucas chose not to tell the rest of the Quorum. If anyone asked, we were out on a call.

Jayden was extra hyped today. Apparently Thanksgiving was his second favorite holiday. Easter was first. My BAFF loved fluffy bunnies. I ended up in SUV #1 with Ryder, Kyle, Silent Sam, and Jared. The Australian enforcer had never celebrated Thanksgiving. Apparently it wasn't a holiday in his home country. He'd been in America for years now. His Hive in Sydney transferred him out to the Portland Hive after the incident which will not be named, but vamps didn't celebrate human holidays, despite the fact that once upon a time they were human, unlike ash, who were never anything other than a hybrid. Funny which one of us had kept the most humanity intact.

The sun was bright as we exited. Spending so much time indoors made the sight of the rising sun extra beautiful. You don't realize how much you take some of these things for granted until they're gone. This was what I was trying to tell Tessa, but my stubborn, stinky-drunk friend refused to understand what I was saying.

Thoughts of evil vampires had my mind flittering back to the little girl. I hadn't been able to stop thinking about her last night, even with Ryder and Kyle sprawled out on my couch eating all my snacks and keeping me entertained. The only way I could shut my mind off was when pure exhaustion knocked me out. I ended up crashing out between the boys, Ryder's warm arm holding me against him. We were back to no alone time or privacy, especially with the Quorum on the radar again.

"Is this the first child to ever be turned vamp?"

The small talk which had been going on died off, and all eyes were suddenly on me. Ryder's hand snaked out and covered my mouth before I could speak again, before I could demand information.

His voice was all casual-like: "Yeah, as far as we know. The Quorum are really strict about that law. This girl was a random accident."

I wasn't confused at all by his sudden defense of the Quorum. He was reminding me that despite their repeated searches of the Hummers, there was a chance they missed a listening devices and we should be cautious about what we said.

Dammit!

Our speed picked up and we pretty much screeched around the corner and onto my old street. The large trees which lined the sidewalks were looking a little barren. Winter was coming, and the chill in the air told me it was going to be brutal this year. Pulling up in front of the familiar little house, pangs of homesickness shot through me hard. It was easy sometimes to compartmentalize my life, push away the losses, but seeing it again ... there was no way to forget.

The five of us piled out. Ryder was at my side in seconds. We moved from the car to the opposite side of the road, away from my house.

"I'm not sure what they're using to bug us, but there's every chance your mother's place is compromised also. They can be very thorough, and they'll be looking for your father, with the Original blood so strong in your system."

The boys closed in tighter. "Every year there are a few cases of children being turned, far less than there used to be, say a hundred years ago. Vamps are policed pretty closely now. Still, there is always one screwed-up vampire who likes little kids and decides he wants one around forever."

Okay, that was just freaking sick.

"So what happens to the kids who are turned?" The second Hummer was parking behind ours now. We'd draw attention if we stayed out here any longer.

"I don't know of any vamp children in the Hives around us. They're all transferred out to European Hives. Apparently they have the facilities to deal with them. The virus messes with children. They never age, and their brains don't develop properly after the change. They're too young to deal with the virus."

Jared snorted, and I turned to him. "They're transferred on the books, but I've visited hundreds of Hives over the years, plenty through Europe, and I've never seen a single child. So who knows what happens to them."

Sam didn't speak, but the way his muscles were trembling, rage was consuming the silent enforcer.

"Is that girl in danger?" My voice rose slightly, even though I was trying to keep it locked down. "You better not have stopped me from curing her, thereby giving the Quorum time to kill her."

Because I was starting to see that was what the vampires did with the children. If they were difficult to control, if the virus messed with their minds, they would either have them locked away in some dungeon somewhere or they'd kill them. They wouldn't risk the bad publicity and possible war with the humans.

"We have a few days," Ryder said. "They never do anything until all of the media attention dies down. It's all secret, hush-hush stuff, and right now there's too much attention on our Hive. It gives us time to plan things out properly. If we're going to cure her, we have to make sure there's no chance of getting you or the rest of us killed."

I calmed slightly, even though I was fuming inside at the extra few horrible points I could add to my "vampires are assholes" list. Could they actually stoop so low as to murder children who had done nothing wrong except be preyed on by evil itself?

Hell yeah they would.

I was beyond words as we made our way back across the street and up to the front porch of my mother's house. The others were already waiting for us, Jayden pretty much bouncing on the spot as he tried to guess what we'd eat.

"Will there be green bean casserole? Mashed potatoes … oh man, I love mashed potatoes."

Just the sound of his inane babble, and Oliver's encouraging yet disinterested responses, was enough to lighten my mood. I closed my eyes and took a deep breath, calming myself and sucking down as much of the negative energy as I could. Today was about family and enjoying stolen moments together. The vampires would not ruin it for me. Dealing with them could wait until tomorrow.

I rang the doorbell, which felt odd, but now that I carried around a bunch of large ash enforcers with me, I didn't want to just barge in and give Mom and Tessa a heart attack.

Standing there, I let my senses free, and found that if I really concentrated I could feel the warmth of humans inside my house. I never spent much time outside of the Hive, so it was odd to realize that the warmth, heartbeat, scent … everything really, was different to the ash. We had heartbeats—it wasn't like we were dead—but it was different; ash heartbeats were slower. Humans were so much more … full of life. I was glad we had all chugged down blood before leaving this morning, enough to keep our hunger controlled for most of the day. We could act like humans again.

The lilac and spearmint scent hit me first, so familiar, so many memories associated with it. Then the door swung open and the still-youthful and beautiful Joanna Bennett stepped into view. My mom's blonde hair was piled up on top of her head and her cheeks were flushed, which was how she looked when she was cooking. Yep, the frilly white apron topped off the outfit perfectly.

"Charlie Anne," she practically shrieked as she pulled me into a hug. "I've missed you so much, baby. A few emails and one drunk Tessa pick-up is just not enough time."

I sank into her, laughing, careful of my strength. It was easy to forget how breakable humans were. I could easily hurt her without realizing it. "I've missed you too, Mom. It's so great to be back here."

The scent of food was already wafting out of the open door. A mixture of everything good in the world was currently in my mother's kitchen. I was so sure about it.

"Mom, I was supposed to be helping you cook," I said, as we finally pulled back from our hug and moved into the front hall. Jayden was practically skipping as he followed along behind us. Which, honestly, he pulled off, despite his massively muscled frame.

"I just got a head start since there were so many of you coming today. It's wonderful to have a full house."

Another blonde popped up in front of me, and thankfully this time she wasn't covered in her own vomit.

"Tessa!" I threw my arms around her and pulled her close. Our hug lasted almost as long as with my mother. The boys sidled around us, following my mom into the kitchen area. Tessa and I remained locked together.

"I'm sorry I showed up like a hot mess at the Hive," she mumbled against my shoulder. "I just get really depressed some days. I can't cope with you being gone, with the loneliness. Even Blake ... like today, he can't be here because of the sun. I'm always on the outside of your lives."

I gave her an extra squeeze. "You know the saying, babe: the grass is always greener on the other side. You have serious FOMO, but there's nothing you need to fear you're missing out on. The Hive is dark and deadly."

The look on her face told me she was tuning me out again. I forced myself not to bitch-slap her. Despite the fact that I was so happy to see her, she was also pissing me off a lot lately with this moronic stubbornness of wanting to become a stupid vampire.

Pretending the tension between us wasn't there, she flashed me a smile and linked her arm through mine. Her face was only lightly made up today and she looked pretty, fresh-faced, and healthy. "So Blake is meeting with the Quorum again tonight. Apparently they have conferred with other Quorums, and the international vampire council. They're the ones who keep track of the world numbers or something. We should have a decision in the next week."

My mouth dropped open. "Tessa!"

She elbowed me sharply. "Shh, don't ruin this day. Your mom and I have been planning it for a week."

I gave an exasperated sigh. The pissed-off was growing, but I didn't bother to argue with her again. There was almost a hundred percent certainty they would deny the request. It was next to impossible to change humans any longer. The human-vampire truce was on shaky grounds, and we didn't need more bad publicity, especially with the newly-turned child. Actually, if anything good could come out of that horrible happening, it was that Blake's odds of being granted permission to turn Tessa were probably now at minus one.

I relaxed as we crossed through the sunny living room and into the open-plan dining area which bordered the kitchen. The extension on the dark wooden table was open, and extra chairs had been brought in. There were already settings out, ten of them by my count, delicate white china which we had inherited from my grandparents. They had passed on ten years ago, but it was almost as if they were here with us when we used their stuff. It wasn't just the china. Everything in this room held a memory for me. It was home.

My mom wasn't wealthy like Tessa's, but we'd always done okay. I loved our furniture, mostly dark wood and antique, rich with age and history. Crossing into the white and turquoise country-style kitchen, topped off by dark timber bench tops, I ground to a halt, before peals of laughter ripped from me.

Holy shit. The sexy six were cooking.

The enforcers were stationed around the kitchen, their hulking forms making the room look positively tiny. Each of them was wearing a frilly and feminine lace apron and my mom had them hard at work with food prep.

I couldn't stop staring. Ryder and Sam especially had me in hysterics. Both of them looked absolutely lost for words, as if they couldn't even understand how my petite mother managed to get them into this position. Still, I was happy to see that each of them were making the best of it, Ryder kneading bread, Sam snapping the ends off of green beans. Markus had even started to sing, his Scottish brogue deepening as he basted the turkey. I wonder if he'd been informed that that amazing liquid was a secret concoction passed down from Grandma May. Knowing my mom, he definitely had been.

Jared flashed me a white-toothed smile; he was on cranberry sauce duties, which we made from scratch in this household. Oliver was slicing cheeses, and Jayden stood at his side, sampling the fare and giving orders, sticking to what he was good at.

And my mom, who was totally in her element, was dashing between all of them, giving instructions.

"Is this really happening?" Tessa's voice was a bubble of amusement. "Or did we just wander into an alternate universe?"

"Let's hope it's an alternate universe and we can expect this room filled with sexy man cooks in frilly aprons to stick around," I murmured. I turned to her and waggled my eyebrows up and down.

We both burst out laughing then, and I was so distracted that I never even noticed Ryder duck around the kitchen island, until he was right in front of me. He looked hot as hell, even with the streak of flour on his cheek and the pink and lavender frilly apron around his waist.

"You're not laughing at me are you, Charlene?"

Ugh. No doubt he was taking great pleasure in using my full name. He knew how much it grated on my nerves.

Of course I'd give him no satisfaction by reacting. I smiled. "Lace really suits you. I think you should think about incorporating it into the enforcer unif—"

Quick as a flash he lightly palmed my face with flour. My mouth dropped open—damn, no doubt he'd been waiting for the perfect moment to do that. Before he could coat me any further, I quickly tackled him, laughing as he still somehow managed to rub more on my face.

Suddenly Mom was standing over us with a huge grin. "So he's the one? I was trying to figure out which one of these good looking fellas had caught my daughter's attention."

Ryder scrambled to pull me upright, and wiped his palms on his apron.

"It's nice to officially meet you, ma'am. I'm Ryder Angelson."

Whoa! Ryder had a last name? Ash and vamps tended to just stick with first names, most of them shedding that last formality of their human persona. I'd never even thought to ask him for a full name.

My mother gave me an approving look. "A boy with manners, I like it. You can call me Jo." She shook his hand. I could tell immediately that she wasn't just saying the words, she really did like Ryder. My mom was a great judge of character; she'd already looked past the lead enforcer's outer persona of tall, dark, and deadly to see the man beneath. Glancing between my mom, Ryder, and around the rest of the kitchen, my heart filled with enough joy to last a lifetime.

Thanksgiving was beyond perfect; I didn't want it to end. We ate until we were stuffed to the brim. Everything tasted so good. On top of the food, it was the atmosphere which made it so special—relaxed and peaceful. It felt like the last few months of blood, murder, and drama in the Hive had never happened.

The enforcers made a few halfhearted efforts to duck back and forth to the Hive, but most of them spent their time snacking and napping lazily on the couch. A few of us played board games with my mom. Can I just say that Jayden is a competitive bastard—and he cheats.

Eventually, though, as the day faded out to night, and with the blood thirst gnawing at the back of my throat, we said our goodbyes. Ryder pretty much had to pry me from Tessa and my mom's arms. It was only the knowledge that I couldn't drag them into my shitty life that forced me to leave.

As we piled into the Humvees and drove out of my neighborhood, I looked back at my house, my heart and throat aching as I fought my tears. That life was gone. I guess I just needed to come to terms with it. A strong hand squeezed my thigh.

"It was a good day," Ryder told me, and I could tell he was trying to ease some of my heartache. "Keep those memories safe, and I promise I'll do everything in my power to make sure that's not the last holiday you spend with them."

I managed to smile, before turning away to lock my burning eye on the world outside. I didn't want to cry. I'd probably never stop if I started. Ryder pulled us onto the freeway and almost instantly the car sped up—like in a pedal to the metal way. I swung my head back around to see what was happening. Ryder's face was hard now, furrows along his brow as his eyes flicked to the rearview mirror.

"Black van. Three cars back," Kyle said from the back seat.

Ryder nodded. "I see it. Radio the boys."

Oh shit. What now? Not on Thanksgiving. Did these people have no patriotic pride?

Sam leaned forward, close to my ear. "Buckle up, Charlie."

My heart began to pump harder, fear burning through my body.

"Who is it?" I asked as I clicked my seat belt on.

Ryder was still moving fast, far too quickly to be safe on the roads, especially as we swerved in and out of traffic.

Kyle's voice came from the back seat. "Sam's running plates but nothing is coming up. Looks like humans though. My guess is that it's a little bit of payback for our recent financial do-gooding."

Deliverance. Those bastards had almost killed my boyfriend and now they were ruining Thanksgiving. I popped open the glove box and grabbed the gun Markus had been training me with.

Ryder gave me a side look and grinned. I think the boy liked me when I got all pissed and weaponed up.

"Hold on," he said as he jerked the car to the right, crossing over three lanes and exiting on Murray street.

Screeching tires behind us indicated the Deliverance truck had managed to stay right on our ass. Our other Humvee, with Jayden, Oliver, and Jared inside, slotted themselves in behind the van.

"Can we call the human police? Wouldn't they want to know these maniacs are doing this?" I was having flashbacks of a bleeding Markus and nearly dead Ryder. I didn't ever want to relive that.

Kyle actually chuckled, before sobering a bit. "Maybe before our evil bosses stole and infected a twelve-year-old girl."

Shit. Good point.

I was watching the rearview mirror and my stomach dropped when the van's sunroof opened and a guy holding a large machine gun popped up.

"Ryder!"

"I see it! Hold on!"

Static sounded from behind me and I heard Kyle radio across to the other car. "Van sandwich," he said.

Sam was at my ear again. "Brace yourself, Charlie."

I had a split second to reach for the "oh shit" bar before Ryder slammed on the brakes. The Deliverance van's brakes squealed and I saw the entire vehicle wobble as they tried to avoid us, but they'd been way too close. The crash was loud and hard, and I was thrown forward against my belt. At the same time, I heard a final gunning of an engine and another crash and jolt as the second Hummer smashed into the van, pinning it between the two of our vehicles.

Without skipping a beat, Ryder slammed his foot down again, our tires spinning for a second before there was a wrenching of metal on metal and we were free. A quick glance back told me that Jayden's car had also managed to reverse out of the crash, and was now following us. I could see the slight crumple to the front of their Hummer but nothing too crazy. Okay, clearly these vehicles were army-spec reinforced, because that had been a hard hit.

Wanting to see the Deliverance van better, I tried to turn my head all the way around, wincing at the twinge in my neck. I twisted around far enough to see that the van was completely crushed and clearly undrivable. Humans were stumbling out of it.

My attention was back in the car then as Ryder reached out and gently touched my lip. "Trust me, that hurt worse for them. You okay?" As he pulled back I looked down at his thumb to see a little blood. I must have bitten my lip by accident, something which tends to happen when you go from eighty miles an hour to a dead stop.

As the metallic and sort of sweet scent of my blood filled the car, Ryder's eyes began to slightly pulse—silver to black—the way the vampires' did when they couldn't resist my blood. It had been a while since anyone vamped out on me. The enforcers especially were used to my unicorn blood now. I was pretty sure there was more than blood on Ryder's mind right then, though.

"Happy Thanksgiving…" Kyle's sarcasm distracted us from the surge of adrenalin, bloodlust, and attraction rocketing between Ryder and me.

Before I could come up with a sarcastic reply, Ryder was slamming on the brakes again. For fuc—what now?

A roadblock, about ten yards away from our vehicle. *Shit.* Two blacked-out Chevy Tahoe's were parked sideways, with about seven people crouched and standing around them. That first glance was enough to tell me that these people were very different from the douchebags following us, but still human.

Their clothing reminded me of some sort of defense force or military uniform, but of the hardcore variety. Their attention was locked on us, and even as we gave them hard stares back, they didn't flinch at the full convoy of ash enforcers. They remained serious-faced, weapons in hand.

Yep, the badass vibe was totally making sense; they were definitely some sort of special forces. Based on my many hours of television watching, they looked a hell of a lot like SWAT, with face shields and all.

As Jayden's car screeched up to halt beside us, I pulled my gaze from the GI Joe humans across from us, and turned to Ryder. I was opening my mouth to suggest we U-turn and head back past Deliverance, when the enforcer's eyes flicked up to the rearview mirror. It was rare to see anything but confidence and lethalness cross his face, but in the moment I swear there was a flash of fear and uncertainty.

It was only there for a second, that minor creasing of his brows, shadowing in his eyes, but it had been there for a reason. Swallowing hard, I turned in my seat.

Frickity frack, we were toast. Barreling down the road were six black vans, exact replicas of the Deliverance van we'd just trashed. One held some crazy-ass firepower on top, looking like a freaking war machine ready to kill thousands.

I spun to the guys, ready to start beating a plan out of someone. We might be in a bulletproof Humvee, but something told me the Bible freaks had learned a lot from our last attack. Hence the big guns, which were no doubt armor piercing.

Jittering in my seat, I managed to halt my tirade of spewing panic as I noticed Ryder was already busy. He was leaned forward in his seat, and there was no fear on his face now, just a calculating expression. I followed the line of sight and found myself staring at one of the SWAT men. The massive dude stood way out in front and wore authority like no one's business. Definitely some sort of leader. He was tall, built like a truck, and had piercing blue eyes.

Ryder and Blue Eyes remained engaged in their epic staredown silent conversation. WTF, guys? We so did not have time for any sort of male pissing contest. If we didn't move in the next few minutes, we were dead.

I was just about to start kung-fu fighting someone's ass, when finally Blue Eyes nodded and waved Ryder over with his head. The enforcer let out a very low exhalation of air, and I realized how tense he was.

Kyle, who had been following the silent conversation too, picked up the radio. "Take position behind the blockade."

No one hesitated, the tires on both cars screeched as engines roared to life and the boys maneuvered our vehicles to the side of the blockade, out of the way. Doors flew open as we all popped out of the Hummers, and crouching low, weapons held close to our bodies, we ran across to get behind the blockade of the human SWAT team.

As we passed him, Blue Eyes glared at Ryder. "My beef is with the Deliverance today. I have no orders to take your kind in. But don't get in my way."

Your kind. *Ouch.* Something told me Ryder and Blue eyes knew each other, but there was definitely no friendship there.

Kyle looked them up and down. "You military now, bro?" Okay, they definitely knew these guys.

Blue eyes shrugged. "That's classified."

More of the SWAT guys turned their hard stares at the enforcers. Both of the groups were doing the whole dominance staredown thing. Except for me, because I was born with a brain instead of a penis. Although I did take a second to turn flinty eyes on one of the SWAT boys who was checking me out a little too thoroughly. Yes, I was the mythical female ash, but there was no way he was going to learn anything about me by staring at my ass. Before I could tell him to put his eyes back in his head, a bullet sailed past my ear and tires screeched behind me.

"Down!" Blue Eyes yelled and I dropped to the ground, rolling underneath the Tahoe. I heard scuffing feet, and from my spot on the ground saw the SWAT team situating themselves around the vehicles.

Wanting to get further from the bullets, I rolled myself fully under the Tahoe, keeping the momentum going until I emerged out the back. Ryder was right behind me, Kyle to my right. Popping up to my feet, I was much more secure at the back of the two huge cars, facing toward the oncoming attack.

Blue eyes was speaking into a bullhorn, his deep voice echoing around the entire area. "Deliverance, you have officially been categorized as a terrorist organization. Get out of your vehicles and place your weapons down or we will shoot to kill."

Around me, my enforcer team stepped up into firing positions, spread across the back of the vehicles. No way would these boys sit out in a firefight like this. Sam almost looked gleeful as he loaded his gun. I flicked off the safety on mine, grateful for all the hours I'd been clocking in the firing range. I could almost always hit the moving targets now. Which was important. Very important.

Markus tossed an open duffle bag at Ryder's feet. The enforcer dropped down and rifled through it to pull free bulletproof vests. Sweet. Maybe I would walk away with my life today.

"Armageddon is upon us!" A high pitched female voice whined out of another speaker. Did all of these humans carry around loudspeakers or something?

I knew that whiny voice. It was the crazy bitch who'd killed those ash and nearly killed Ryder.

Ryder grabbed a vest and helped me slip it on, securing the last strap as the gunfire began. Oliver did the same for Jayden, who was the only one here unarmed.

Ryder leaned in close and whispered in my ear. "We could run, but we may need a favor from these boys in the future, and they're outnumbered. They could use our help."

I nodded. It was the right thing to do.

As the noise of bullets increased, one of the SWAT guys tumbled off one of the cars and slid backward into Kyle's outstretched arms.

"Man down!" Blue Eyes roared.

"I got you, bro." Kyle ripped open a med kit—seemed the boys had emptied the Humvees of the important stuff when we'd ran here—and began to treat the fallen guy.

Blue Eyes was still barking orders, and at the same time seemed to be ducking between the two vehicles constantly. His shots were scarily accurate. I saw him take out at least five Deliverance in under a minute.

Actually all of these guys were highly trained and absolutely brutal. They definitely shot to kill, and a small, sick part of me enjoyed that. Deliverance should not exist. They were murderers, killing innocents for their sick sense of right and wrong.

Deciding I wanted to be a little closer to the action, I snaked my way around the side of the closest Tahoe. The back door was open, offering me some protection, and I propped myself up on the step so I could shoot over the top of the window. A quick headcount had at least twenty Deliverance assholes, and they all seemed to be armed. *Shit!* Was that a freakin' AK-47? Steadying my hand over the doorframe, I breathed deeply, allowing my mind to release the fear and panic and step into the zone.

The weapon bucked in my hands as I shot once, twice, a third time. I heard two shouts, and knew I'd nailed them hard. The third bullet had clipped the crazy old bitch, whom I particularly wanted to kill, because she'd shot at my guys. No one touched my boys.

Blue Eyes swung around to me then. "I don't want an untrained female on the front line. Stand down."

Oh hell no. I flipped him off before lifting my gun up again. I heard a bark of laughter from behind and knew it was Jared. He would find that amusing; he had a particular distaste for authority.

With a shake of his head Blue Eyes resumed his previous position and went back to taking down crazies. After a few more rounds from us, the Deliverance had lost at least half their members, which must have been their signal to start gearing up to use the big machine gun on the roof. I saw two of the guys crawling their way up, others flanking around them to provide backup. I squinted again, taking aim, and fired. A female spun off the side of their car then, but another stepped in to take her place. Dammit. Were they multiplying?

"Take cover!" one of the SWAT bellowed, and on instinct all of us hit the ground. Under the Tahoe I could see Ryder and Sam, who had been exchanging fire with a small group of Deliverance to the left side.

I flinched as the first bullets from the heavy machine gun started raining across the ground and cars. Bullets pierced right through the door above my head; nothing was stopping those shots. *Shit.* I army-crawled my way backwards, sticking close to the car until I could scoot back around to the rear. I expected to find Kyle and company back there, but it was only Jayden. His eyes were wide, the silver swirling into the black as we both pressed ourselves to the rear panel.

"That is one hardcore gun," my BAFF whispered. "How the hell are they going to take it out?"

Oliver popped up beside him then, scaring the absolute heck out of both of us. "Ryder and Lincoln are going to come in from either side. One of them will be able to take the rest of the Deliverance down, no worries."

What the actual ... seriously? "Who is Lincoln and where can I find Ryder so I can kick his ass? Dude just got out of hospital for being a hero."

I was so angry I was literally shaking. Well, angry and scared. No matter how lethal Ryder was, he was not bulletproof.

"Lincoln is the head of this special forces division. We've had a few run-ins with them. Generally we live in an uneasy truce, but they do seem to just be waiting for the day we fuck up and they can nail our asses."

Ah, Blue Eyes.

I'd already tuned out of the conversation, trying to figure out how the hell to chase down Ryder and haul him back to safety. I was crouched again, attempting to see along the ground to find where all the men were. But I kept getting blocked by a bunch of debris which had been smashed off the cars.

The bullets died off then and the ringing in my ears intensified. Hadn't even realized how loud that machine gun was until it stopped. Using this moment, I popped myself up and launched onto the back step of the car to see above the roofline. I wasn't stupid enough to go any higher; there were plenty of Deliverance there still, but I needed to see Ryder. Before I managed to fully take in the scene, which was pure carnage—that gun had shredded the cars and debris was absolutely everywhere—Oliver yanked me back down. Just in time too, as the heavy bullets started up again.

"Heard them reloading," Oliver said. "Figured you'd like to keep your brains on the inside."

I gave him a quick hug, my breathing a rapid. "Yep, totally. That's where I like my brains."

Oliver gave me a nod, before turning back to Jayden. The two of them were trying to creep around the back, I think to help out Kyle, who was stuck in an awkward and not so safe position. Everyone had something to do except me, and I was not okay with that.

I caught a glint of metal then, a few yards away, against one of the abandoned looking buildings which had us boxed in here, a ladder leading up to a platform or rooftop terrace. The building was only two stories high, but that would be more than enough to give me a decent vantage point. If I made it to the ladder I'd be okay; it was on the backside of the building, and the only people who would see me were ones in the same position I was in right now.

Flicking the safety back on, I tucked my gun into my holster, and taking a deep breath forced down my fears and lifted myself off the ground, keeping my head as low as possible I ran, using whatever cover I could find.

"Charlie!" Jayden whisper-screamed after me.

I ignored him because there was no time left to do anything but sprint as fast as I could. The entire time I was waiting for bullets to rain into me. If the losers manning that massive machine gun caught sight of me, I was dead.

The building closed in and I found myself encased in the shadows, protected and safe.

CHAPTER 8

I pressed myself against the building, breathing rapid and hard. Keeping my head firmly against the rough brick, I faced the firefight to make sure no one had followed me. I remained like that for a few extended moments, my heart pattering away from fear and adrenalin.

Crappity crap. Had I seriously just gotten away with that? Hells yeah.

Another surge of adrenalin coursed through me and I felt both jacked up and tired as hell. If we managed to survive today, I was totally taking a nap. Naked. No clothes and no worries. That's what my tired soul needed.

Checking my gun was still secure, I started to climb rapidly, scaling those rungs in seconds. They were a little rickety and rusted through in places, but nothing broke away as I ascended, which was a definite bonus.

Beams of the dying afternoon light hit me as I passed above the shadow of the building next to this one, and I knew I was almost at the rooftop. Up here I would be more exposed, but since I was way above the others, and hopefully no one knew I was coming up here, they wouldn't be prepared.

Reaching the edge, I slowly pulled myself over, keeping my head down. The space up here was not huge, only about fifty feet across. I could see the remnants of garden beds, and an old sun lounger. Once upon a time this had been someone's terrace, and now it was just a muck-load of dirt and desiccated bird crap.

I basically glued myself to the disgusting ground—bullets were the greater evil in this case—as I army crawled across to the edge which bordered the zone above the gunfight. Part of me was cursing the amount of time it had taken me to put my plan into action, and the other, much larger part, was praying and hoping that Ryder and the boys were okay, and that no one had been gravely hurt. Upon reaching the edge, I pressed closer to the small bricked-up wall, which provided a decent amount of coverage, and lifted my head to peer across and down. *Shit!* I was a little far south of where everyone was. Ducking back down, I scurried further along the wall before popping up again in a new spot.

Perfect.

This time I ended up right above the wreckage of humans and ash, my senses firing almost as rapidly as bullets as I tried to take in the entire scene. It took me no more than a few seconds to find Ryder; it was as if I just knew his energy. My heart actually stuttered as my eyes locked in on him and Blue Eyes ... Lincoln, whatever his name was. They were trapped on the edge of the Deliverance's area. Those freaks were keeping them at bay with the massive machine gun.

It looked like in the time I'd taken to get up here almost everyone on the evil side was dead. All that was left was the crazy old bitch, and three around the large gun.

The rapid fire of bullets cut off again, and this time I had the perfect view of them reloading another lot of ammo into the machine. I was distracted then by the two heroes slash dumbasses of the hour, Ryder and Lincoln, as they left their safe little area. The Deliverance hadn't noticed yet, they were too busy trying to maneuver what looked like fifty tons of bullets into the gun.

Ryder was keeping low to the ground, and I heard pops—Sam and Kyle were now covering the boys from behind, which was good and bad. The bullets drew the attention of old bitch lady, and she noticed Ryder and Lincoln.

With a bark to one of her minions, they both pulled out smaller weapons and began spraying bullets at my man. *Muthaeffer.* Ryder may have been wearing a bulletproof vest, but nothing was protecting his head. Forgetting about staying unnoticed, I jumped up and took aim straight at her, standing firm like Markus had taught me.

I knew from my training that a bullet from this gun could shoot over forty yards, well within the range I was at now. It might not be as accurate from this far away but I didn't care. All I needed was to add my protection and distract her until the boys could reach the machine gun.

Ryder and Lincoln were also popping off shots, trying to take out those Deliverance shielded behind the monster weapon. The old lady sneered as she took a huge step toward the guys, firing a random spray of bullets.

Nope. Not happening.

Holding my breath for absolute accuracy, I fired off three quick shots, aiming for her head. Two of the bullets landed and the old lady flew back with the force, her shoulder dripping bright crimson. Not quite her head, but that would do for now.

All eyes turned in my direction then, and not only eyes but guns. I hit the ground in time to cover my head as the area around me got absolutely smashed with firepower. After an agonizing minute of flying plaster, brick, and other debris—my heart pounding so hard I thought it might explode—the shooting stopped. I expected a deafening silence, but instead there was a strange whirring sound. A helicopter was circling the area. And I could hear police sirens in the distance. Yeah, now they come to help...

Taking a few moments, I lay there catching my breath and debating what to do. I didn't want to peek my head up and have it blown off. Just when I was about to decide, Jared poked his head up across the other end of the rooftop.

"It's over. The SWAT called in backup and their helicopter is keeping things under control. Let's get out of here before the media arrives." His thick Australian accent was the best damn thing I had heard all day. I sighed in relief and popped up, walking over to the enforcer, who helped me down the ladder.

When we reached the bottom, he turned to me: "Oh and that was damn good shooting, for a rookie." He winked.

I scowled briefly before it turned into a grin. "Good ladder climbing, for an enforcer," I said, and he nudged me playfully.

Suddenly Ryder was there, eyes blazing, looking every inch the deadly enforcer. Jared took the hint and left me alone with him.

"Don't ever do that again." The silver swirl of his eyes was almost mesmerizing.

Focusing the best I could, I dragged a small slice of attitude up from my tired depths, and putting my hands on my hips, channeled my inner Jayden. "Same to you, bud. You nearly got yourself killed, which is the second time this month in case we were keeping track!"

He took a deep breath and I could sense he was trying to calm himself. A few more deep breaths and he seriously looked as tense. At the fifth breath he stepped into me so fast it was a blur and then our bodies were pressed tightly together, the wall of the building behind me.

Ryder's forehead pressed against mine, his words tumbling out. "Sorry, Charlie but that was the last day you will be allowed out of the Hive until we deal with both the humans and the Quorum. Something has to give soon, and I won't let that something be you."

It took a minute for his words to register. I was a little distracted by the press of his body and the fire in his eyes and the scent of spice and cedarwood. Then he was kissing me gently before striding off to bark orders at the team. Pushing myself off the wall, my legs were a little too shaky for my liking as I followed his path across to where our Humvees waited. Our vehicles had been spared the bullets which had ripped apart the SWAT cars and it looked like we were bailing now.

Oliver and Jayden were already inside when I climbed into the middle seat. The door next to me opened and Ryder slid in too. We didn't want to wait around another moment.

As we drove through the scene, all I could see was the mess of bodies and parts scattered around. *Holy shit.* I was grateful it had been none of my guys. Beside a few war wounds, we were all leaving here alive. Then an awful thought struck me: "What if Deliverance retaliates on my mom? Did they see me leaving her house?"

Oh God, that would be the icing on the cake.

Ryder answered straight away. "I'll have the other boys go check on them and warn your mom and Tessa. At least we know there are not many of them around here left to retaliate. Not after today."

That was true. They'd lost a lot of their people this afternoon.

Ryder was all business as he relayed the information to the boys over the walkies. Listening in and worrying about my mom gave me a pain in my stomach, which I was pretty sure was an ulcer. Could ash even get ulcers? Seemed like this unicorn ash could.

Oliver was foot-to-the-floor smashing his way through Portland. The sun was set now, and the cold was seeping into my body.

"I never wanted to drag my family into this mess," I said, my voice monotonous as I stared out the window, seeing nothing of the dark streets as they flashed by. "They already lost me, and now they might be under attack from some crazy-ass human Bible bashers."

Ryder reached across to me and I met him halfway. A slight ease entered my being as he laced our fingers together. I wasn't alone in all of this; there were others to watch out for me and my family, and that in itself was a huge gift.

"It will be okay, Charlie," Oliver said. "Deliverance tend not to target their own kind. They focus the hatred straight at the Hive."

I nodded, and as he turned back to give me a confident, perfect-teeth smile, I managed to return the gesture. His words did make me feel a little better, and if I stayed away from them and my family hid out for a few days, hopefully Deliverance would never think to use them against me.

CHAPTER 9

The next few days passed by agonizingly slow. I wasn't allowed out on calls, and no matter how hard I snooped I couldn't find out where they were keeping the little girl. For the most part I was back on "who is the mole?" duties, trying to figure out who in the Hive was a backstabbing, lying piece of shit. I had about eight thousand suspects, and no reason to wipe even one of them off the list. Every single vampire was there on principle now, except for Lucas. I would give him the benefit of the doubt until he did something which revoked that trust.

After dinner I was sprawled across my couch, about to die of boredom. Jayden, Oliver and Markus were in the kitchen, talking about something dude-like—cars, I think. Jayden was probably trying to figure out how to drag his man into his bedroom for some private time. As much as my BAFF loved my new bodyguard detail because Oliver was often in the apartment, it also sucked because the enforcers were always on duty. No time for fun.

At the knock on the door I sprang up and dashed across the room, flinging open the door to find Ryder standing there dressed in his gym clothes.

Boredom fled. Along with saliva in mouth and clever words in brain.

"Want to go for a rooftop run?" he asked.

Hells yeah I did. Wasting no time, I dragged on some sweats, laced up my shoes, and waved goodbye to the boys. Jayden was flashing me his eyebrow and hip waggle, so he was very happy about this change in circumstances.

It took five minutes, but then we were out of the building and on the roof. The second the cool night air hit me, clearing away some of the funk I'd been in, I knew this was a good idea.

Ryder took off down the track and I followed, focused on the large swollen moon. I'd always found something so mesmerizing about the moon, especially when it was full. Its light seemed to highlight the beauty around me, remind me to stop and take a second to appreciate everything.

After a few laps, I heard the doors open and nearly stumbled over my feet when I saw the little vampire girl walk out. Following her was a stern-looking redheaded vampire.

Ryder caught my arm and we slowed as the pair walked out on to the track. The girl had headphones on, but when she saw us she took them off.

The redheaded vamp found the closest wall and got to the really important business of relaxing against it. "You have ten minutes," she told the girl with a thick Russian accent.

The young girl gave a single head nod and then began to jog. I sped up next her.

"No," Ryder whispered.

I shot him a death glare that hopefully conveyed how closed my legs would be if he kept trying to order me around. He lifted both hands up in a placating manner, before backing off me a tad.

"You like running?" I asked, turning back to the girl.

I couldn't halt the sadness and anger which welled inside of me. She looked depressed. Her alabaster skin was shining in the bright moon, but her eyes were downcast, stress lines fracturing her perfect features. No child should have stress lines.

Of course she was beautiful, with short brown hair naturally curled into tight ringlets, smooth skin, and a thin athletic build. The vampire virus was working in full effect. But it was still wrong somehow, like looking at a weird doll.

She wet her lips before answering me: "I used to run and like it but now I don't know what I like." Even her voice was low and sad. "You don't smell like a vampire, but you're a girl?" For the first time a sign of actual interest crossed her solemn face.

I nodded. "I'm an ash, a special one-of-a-kind girl ash ... and I can help you." From the corner of my eye I could see Ryder was reaching for me again. Clearly I was overstepping the safe boundaries he was trying to keep me in.

With a burst of speed, I moved out of his reach again. The girl kept pace, and as she stared longer at me, her eyes started the silver pulsing thing. "Your blood smells really good," she whispered, blinking a few times, her face falling. "Which is totally gross."

Dammit. I was curing this girl or I would die trying.

"What room number are you staying in?" I pressed her, knowing my time was short.

Her lashes fluttered at my question, as if she was trying to understand what I'd just said. There was something wrong with her cognitive functions; she was slower to think and was void of personality, almost as if she was stuck in some sort of robotic and depressed state.

"Katelynn, time's up!" the redheaded Russian screamed at her. The lazy bitch had not moved from the wall, and it looked like she'd been on her phone the entire time. Great babysitting there.

Katelynn ground to a halt, all obedient-like.

Time to break out the big guns. The very thing I would have used on a daily basis if I had ever been a mom. Bribery. "Tell me your room number and I will bring you a present. A stuffed toy." My heart started to hammer as footsteps sounded behind me. There was more movement, and I heard Ryder's deep tones as he moved to intercept the redhead.

"They have me on the forty-ninth floor. Room sixteen. I like unicorns." Her innocent voice shredded my heart.

Room 4916. Gotcha.

"Then I'll bring a unicorn. Just don't tell anyone or I can't see you again."

A small smile graced her mouth. "Okay."

She turned and went to her Russian nanny, who was both conversing with my enforcer and glaring at me. I didn't care. My eyes were glued to Katelynn as devastation at letting her go rocked through me. I just wanted to grab her up, hug her tight and keep her safe. Dammit!

Okay, I needed to focus on what I could do. She said she liked unicorns and she was going to get one. Or at least the blood of one. I might not be able to save her today, but it would not be long before I could.

After they went through the double doors, Ryder took a few long strides to stand before me. He took my face in his hands. "Sometimes I wonder if falling in love with you will be the death of me."

My breath hitched at his use of the L word. That was a definite declaration, or a roundabout one anyway. Before I could reply, his lips fell on mine and we were locked in a kiss.

This wasn't the first time we had kissed since our night together, but it was the first where heightened emotions and our fiery attraction merged into one cataclysmic event. I lost all sense of time, worry, fear, and regret. I lived in that moment with Ryder, and if I could have prolonged it forever I'd be signing on the dotted line. Unfortunately, as was the norm of late, all good things had to come to an end.

We mutually pulled apart, both of us a little out of breath, and a lot silver-eyed, I was sure.

I leaned in closer to him, which somehow was still not close enough. "Geeze, I'm so sweaty from that run. I really need a shower but I'm afraid of getting attacked." My words were light, like I was just making idle conversation, but I was eye-screwing the hell out of him and he knew it.

Ryder's laughter was so rare that it made it that much more enjoyable to hear; that low rumble warmed my belly. "Why, Charlie Anne, there's no way I could leave a lady to shower alone in these sort of dangerous times. In fact I'm going to have to insist on this protective shower duty becoming a daily occurrence."

I grinned, losing all sense of chill as our lips met again, but only briefly this time. It was not a good idea right now, our need out of control, to be kissing in any sort of hardcore fashion. Our bodies were too impatient to be together, so we'd hold back the lust until we got to that shower. It was moments like these that I wished ash had magic powers too. Instant transportation would be very useful right about now.

The next day I was in my living room playing cards with Ryder as Sam sat quietly on the couch, flipping through a magazine. We'd just come back from the rooftop, arguing about when was the right time for me to cure the girl. Ryder wanted to wait until we were ready to run, but I was afraid they would "transfer" her, or whatever bullshit they pretended to do to get rid of the children.

"Boom! Full house!" I slammed my cards down, showing off the three aces and two kings.

Ryder's face was carved from stone, no smile, no hint of defeat.

"Shit," I groaned, knowing he must have a better hand than me to be keeping that mask of calm.

Ryder placed his cards down and smiled. "Straight flush."

I fake pouted. "Cheater."

Before he could retort, a loud bang-bang-bang came at my door. Sam was up and across the room with his gun drawn in seconds.

"Who is it?" Ryder demanded from behind Sam, his own gun-held in a strong grip.

"Oh God, Charlie, I'm so sorry." The male voice came through clearly, familiar and sounding desperate.

"Blake?" I pushed past my guards and wrenched opened the door.

The vampire's eyes were red-rimmed, blood crusted around his mouth. His hands were shaking almost uncontrollably.

"I'm sorry," he said again.

My voice could have cut glass then. "What did you do?" This motherfucker better not mention my best friend.

"I changed Tessa and now she's dying. It's not working. Her body is rejecting the virus." He dropped his head down, those shaking hands clutching at his Cabbage Patch Doll-like curls.

Using his distraction, I leaned forward and ran at him in a football tackle, slamming him against the far hallway wall and cracking the plaster. "I'm going to kill you!" I screamed in his face.

He didn't flinch, didn't fight. He looked desperate. "I love her."

"Where is she?" The words sounded inhuman as they left my throat.

"Medical wing, room five." Blake was crying, as I pushed him to the ground and took off.

The sound of the two enforcers' footsteps close behind gave me strength. If the vampires thought they could take my best friend's life, they were about to learn just how deadly I could be. I would burn this entire Hive to the ground before I let one undead asshole touch Tessa.

I kicked open the medical wing doors, hitting a nurse, who shrieked. Ignoring her, I bolted for room five. The frosted glass door was half open, and the second I saw the pale, emaciated form of my best friend limp in the bed, an animalistic wail ripped from my throat.

The vampire doctor tending to her turned to me, startled. "No ash allowed!" Same old story as the last time we'd been here. I felt a sick sense of satisfaction as Sam whipped out his gun, holding it to the vamp's head. Asshole backed right off then.

"What's happening to her?" I shouted at him as a few other medical staff crowded in behind us. Ryder was doing his best to use his bulk to hold them off. I couldn't focus on anything but my best friend though—or, well, what was left of her. At that moment Tessa wasn't Tessa. She was a shell of a human, a sack of pale skin with dead, white hair. Oh my God.

The doctor seemed annoyed with my question. "She was changed with permission. I have all of the proper signed forms. Her body is fighting the virus too aggressively and it's killing her." He shrugged. "It happens."

Tears spilled onto my cheeks. "No! No! We have to save her. That's my best friend."

A flash of something crossed the doctor's features. Surprisingly enough, it seemed like sympathy. "I have never understood why anyone would willingly want the virus. It's dangerous. Many more humans die than become vampire."

Sam moved to the side as I stumbled towards the doctor. "Does she need more blood? Antibiotics? What can we do?"

Because if he didn't give me an answer in five seconds I was saving her with my blood and outing myself to this entire Hive. I could see now that over a dozen medical officials had crowded the doorway, watching, one of whom I recognized as a Quorum member—too many here to hide what I was, but for Tessa I would do it in a heartbeat.

The doctor shrugged again, and if the POS did it one more time, I was going to punch him in the throat. "There is an experimental vampire plasma that works in twenty percent of cases like these."

Twenty percent wasn't good enough. Tessa's life was worth more than mine. I extended my arm. "Use my blood, it's the—" Before I could say "cure," Sam's gun came out of nowhere and cracked me on the back of my head and blackness took me.

The moment consciousness returned, a sense of panic surged in strong waves through my body. I could feel the rapid beat of my heart, the pulsing of blood in my veins, but I didn't remember why that was—for the first few moments anyway. Then all of reality came flooding back, and despite a raging headache and an incessant thirst, I forced my heavy eyelids open and wrenched my body up.

"Tessa!" My words were supposed to be strong, angry. The panicked rage inside of me needed a place to go. But my dry throat produced nothing more than a rasp of my best friend's name.

I looked around, finding two enforcers up against the wall of my room in the hospital wing. No Ryder though. Kyle and Oliver were the stooges today.

I swung my legs off the side of the bed, relieved to see I was still fully dressed and didn't appear to be hooked up to any machines.

"Where the fuck is my best friend?" My voice gained strength as I stalked forward, ignoring my blood hunger. Although, if someone didn't start talking soon, I was going to let the red haze consume my mind.

Kyle straightened, taking a step toward me. As he stopped inches away, I flashed back to the hours we had sat and prayed here together when Ryder was injured. It reminded me there was a bond between us, and I did not want to hurt him.

"She's okay, Charlie. They gave her the vampire plasma and it counteracted some of the virus long enough for her cells to start the transformation. Ryder and Jared stayed behind to make sure no one screwed anything up."

My relief allowed some of the hot rage to die down. Of course that made way for the true sorrow. I turned to the boys. "How was this permitted? The Quorum rarely allows for new vampires, and with the young girl being turned…"

I rubbed at my temples, trying to relieve the pounding ache. I understood why Sam had hit me. I'd almost outed myself to every vamp in that room, but that didn't mean it wasn't still painful.

Kyle's golden features hardened. "Sam and Markus are investigating now, but we think that maybe this was allowed because of you. Somehow the vamps know how important Tessa is to you, and now they have her exactly where they want."

Shit! I had never even thought about that, always just assuming and hoping that the normal rejections would happen with Blake's request.

Blake! "I'm ripping that bastard's throat out. What the hell was Blake thinking? He almost killed her."

The rage was back. I didn't even care that he said he loved her, you don't do things like that to people you love. Blake was a vampire. He should know that it's not all perfect nighttime strolls and blood milkshakes. His emotions had blinded him and he put his own needs before Tessa's. Not good enough for me, and not good enough for my BFF.

No one tried to stop me as I stormed from the room. In the hallway I glanced around, trying to orient myself. I'd been spending enough time here lately that this place was becoming way too familiar. I was pretty sure I was at the far end from where Tessa had been. Ryder probably stashed me there in the chaos and told the boys to keep an eye on me. By the time I made it to room five again, Kyle and Oliver were right on my heels. Both of them had their hands resting close to their guns.

"Is there something else I need to know?" My words were hard. I was at the limit of my niceness today.

Kyle's eyes flicked to Oliver for a second, and I was just about to scream some more when they both met my flinty gaze.

"The vampires want to test your blood again. They want to know why you think your blood would help Tessa when the doctor clearly said they needed vampire plasma, not ash." Kyle sounded sympathetic and a little pissed on my behalf as he explained.

Shit. Damn. Shit.

Okay, I totally didn't regret trying to save my best friend. I would have cut my arm off if that was what it took. Though now that she was going to survive all on her own, all I had done was raise suspicions about my blood and cast attention back on me and the enforcers.

"Is it safe for me to walk into this room?" The hallway was empty. If we had to run, I could do it, but we'd be grabbing Tessa and bringing her too.

Oliver nodded, lowering his voice. "So far there were just some comments, but Ryder shut them down pretty fast. Hopefully once the excitement dies off, they'll forget about your little slip."

Sure, because that sort of luck just happened for me. Sucking in a deep breath, I clicked the door open and stepped inside. The room was a lot emptier now, just a few nurses scattered around. Ryder and Jared were standing vigil either side of Tessa's bed, and it kind of warmed my heart to see how much they cared, how much diligence they were putting into her safety. That was for me. I knew without any doubt the boys thought of me as one of their team now, and since I loved Tessa, they protected her for me.

I jerked as I realized Lucas was also in the room. He was sans his usual white trench coat, wearing just a dark shirt and slacks. I almost hadn't recognized him. He rose from his chair and crossed to my side.

"Charlie, I'm so sorry about your friend. I tried to dissuade Blake, but he ... he couldn't see the situation clearly. I voted against it on our council, but was in the minority."

His silver eyes were swirling at me and I felt he was trying to tell me so much more than what those few words were saying. Was this entire freaking Hive bugged?

"I thought it was very rare for the council to approve something like this. I was sort of wondering why they jumped on board?" My voice was low and casual. There were way too many witnesses around for me to lose my shit like I wanted to. We were laying low now apparently. I knew what that actually meant: more days of being locked in the damn Hive.

"I don't know for sure. There must be something in the files."

Again, Lucas was telling me shit with just his eyes, and again I was having trouble speaking silver swirl. He dropped his head and gave me a kiss on the cheek. "I'll leave you in the capable hands of your enforcers." As he pulled back, I heard the barest of whispers: "Be prepared to run."

I blinked a few times as he left in a swirl of vampire energy. Pulling myself together as best I could, I crossed to where the four guys were waiting. As far as I could tell, Lucas was telling me the Quorum was acting very out of character, and that he was worried for my safety, which meant time was running out for us to decide what to do. My eyes fell on Tessa, who thankfully was back to looking like my beautiful bestie ... more beautiful actually, if that was even possible. The virus was working through her body, making her strong and immortal—not to mention evil and bloodsucking. Shit. Forget first world problems, we now had Hive world problems.

Her timing really couldn't have been worse. These Quorum problems were going to be tenfold once she woke up. Tessa was about to find herself right in the midst of vamp politics. And possibly a war.

When I reached Ryder, I found myself snuggling into his side. "Thank you."

He didn't say anything, but as his warm hand ran across my lower back in a comforting gesture, I realized how much he meant to me, how far he'd wiggled into my life and my heart. He was the first man I'd been comfortable with since my attack, and I was the first woman he'd cared for since his fiancée. Were we perfect? Nope, but together I was hoping we would find something perfect to hold on to in all this chaos.

"How long will she be unconscious for?" I asked, not having a clue how long it had even been since I was knocked out by Sam.

"It generally takes a full day for the transformation once it has started." Jared's accent was strong at the moment, which usually meant he was upset. "Since the plasma, which was four hours ago, she's already well into the change. She'll be screaming for blood in another four or so hours."

Okay, so that meant we had time to get to the roof for a team meeting. Ryder must have seen the determination in my eyes, and somehow knew what I wanted. "Jared, you okay to stay here and keep an eye on Tessa while the rest of us check in with the enforcers?"

The Australian nodded once, before settling into the chair which Lucas had just vacated. I leaned down and kissed the smooth, porcelain cheek of the unconscious girl in the bed. "I'll be back for you soon, Tess," I whispered, turning to exit with the boys.

No one spoke as we made our way to the elevators, and the silence remained even after we reached the rooftop. It was daylight again, which was a relief; it felt as if the sun was my friend now, the big baddie that kept the vampires away.

Ryder led the way, his stride strong, face locked in the pissed-off range of emotions. He must have had this already planned, because as we rounded the corner, out of the doorway line-of-sight, Markus and Sam came into view. They were camped out, laptops in front of them, a cooler at their side.

My dry mouth increased then, and I sensed eyes on me as I pretty much drooled. Markus had the lid up and bottle in his hand before I even made it to his side.

"Thought you might be thirsty. Grabbed you some O-negative." The Scottish enforcer was as serious as I'd ever seen him, and his accent was strong. Emotions deepened their accents, and right now we were at our emotional peak.

"Sorry about … your head." Sam's low words sounded quite emotional too, for him anyway.

I waved. "All good. I know why you did it. But if Tessa hadn't made it, you and I would be having a completely different conversation."

Sam just gave me a single nod, as if to say he'd have been okay with that too. I knew that even at the time, in the heat of that highly emotional moment, he'd weighed up the risks and had decided my life was worth more than hers—which was sweet, but not his call to make.

I wasted no more time as the burn in my gums signaled my fangs descending, and as they pierced the top of the bottle I chugged down the blood; relief to my parched throat and mouth was instant. It annoyed me that we were so reliant on this now. Sure, even as a human I'd needed water and food, but for the most part I could get that from anywhere. We would never easily find enough blood for us all to leave. The Hive had us trapped.

Wiping my mouth, I discarded the empty bottle, reaching for another. "How much blood will we need if we run? It would have to be what … a pint a day, each?" I expressed my concerns to the enforcers, shifting the icy bottle. "Lucas pretty much just told me that the Quorum is acting strange and we need to be ready to run, but how the hell can we?" My brows pinched together as the pure enormity of the situation crashed into me. I couldn't drag the boys into this.

"Charlie, get that damn look off your face." Ryder towered over me; his eyes were almost pure silver. "We will have no sacrifices, no martyrs, and no heroes running off on their own."

I jabbed my finger at him. "Get out of my head. I'll do whatever it takes to keep everyone safe, and being around me is not safe."

Sam stood then, and because he was such a presence—he had badass down almost as well as Ryder—we all turned and stared at him.

"I have a plan. You need to trust me."

He sat back down then, and I gave Ryder the side-eye. What the eff?

"You have twenty humans willing to travel with us to a safe place and go on a rotation of donating blood?" I asked.

The silent enforcer was up to something and "trust me" was alien to my controlling take-charge personality.

Sam didn't answer me. He just looked at Ryder. Something passed between them, something without words. What was with all these people speaking with no more than a few exchanged looks. Words, use them. They existed for a reason.

Ryder eventually gave a nod. "We are going to trust Sam on this one. I have no doubt his plan is solid. When are you ready for us to move out?"

"I'm going to need at least a week to get everything sorted. Especially if Charlie plans on curing the little girl."

Oh, I planned on doing that.

"I want to bring Tess and Jayden," I said. "I promised my BAFF that I'd never leave him behind, and he'd be the first victim of the Quorum if I did."

"I second that," Oliver said. "I won't leave without Jayden."

"Already counted him," was all Sam said.

"And Tessa?"

The enforcers exchanged a single look. It was fast, almost unnoticeable, but I freaking noticed. My anger was at boiling point again, and I was wondering if my hair might be smoking from all of the heat in my head.

Kyle was the first to try to reason with me. "Charlie, you have to understand that a vampire is a massive liability for us to carry around. She can't travel in the sunlight, she needs a ton more blood than we do, and she's going to be pretty hard to control for the first few months. If we take Tessa, we are pretty much signing our own death warrants."

No. Just ... no. I couldn't leave her here to the mercy of vampires.

Still, he made some really valid points.

Ryder had a look of sympathy on his face, which immediately told me I was going to be pissed by what he was about to say.

"How do you even know she'll want to run with you, Charlie? She's been going full-throttle for the last couple of months to get into the vamp world, and according to you, she was obsessed with them for most of your lives. She also loves Blake, so I think she'll resist you. There's nothing you can do but let her learn the hard way that this is not the world for her."

Fuck! Dammit, why did he have to be attractive *and* intelligent? Really, was it just too much to ask that he blindly agreed with everything I said?

"Well, I'm at least going to give her the option to leave with me. She always said her main reason for being in here was so that we would be together."

Markus snorted. "Vampires and ash are rarely encouraged to be together. She'll be part of the elite, and all too soon will start thinking of herself in the same way that all vampires do. As the superior race."

My bestie was not shallow like that, but there was a part of her that had always wanted to belong somewhere. She had that with me and my mom, but once I was gone that had all fallen apart for her. Maybe what the vamps would offer her, a large and secure family, would trump me. This reminded me of something else I hadn't had a chance to tell the boys yet. It was time they knew what we were up against, if they didn't already.

"I have a confession," I squeaked, and suddenly every enforcer stopped what they were doing and all eyes were on me. Shit, I hadn't meant to make it sound that serious. Taking a deep breath, I rambled:

"Jayden overheard some rumors about the vampires being big assholes, so I used my keycard to get into the file room. Jayden picked a lock with a bobby pin because he's like MacGyver or something, and then we read some crazy shit then got caught and pretended to make out as a cover for being in the room and then we ran."

Whew. Got it all out in two sentences and I felt better already. I'd been meaning to tell them for ages. There should be no lies between us all.

Ryder and Oliver shared a look, no doubt reflecting on the fact that I said Jayden and I made out. To my surprise it was Sam who spoke. I could see the thoughts churning through him.

"What did you find?"

I explained in detail the blackmail files, the oil industry payments, the blood bank, the photos of the Original bloodbath. As I went into detail about each, Sam's face darkened, until he exploded:

"I've been searching for this information for a long time, but never guessed it would be in paper form, in plain sight in the damn middle of the Hive."

Yep, that was why simple minds worked best. Like Jayden's and mine. With a grimace, Sam dropped his gaze and began typing away on his computer. I started to tell the enforcers a few more things about that day, before Sam growled, interrupting me.

Stepping over, I dropped down next to him. "What? What happened?"

The others also crowded closer. "Your discovery gave me an idea about where I've been going wrong in my search for information. I was going too deep, and needed to step back to the simple and old ways. There used to be this site which was almost like a notice board for the underworld. Jobs of an unscrupulous nature would be posted there, and people would apply for them. I never would have thought that this would be how Sanctum was hired. But looks like I was wrong. They tried to cover it up. They seem to have use of a technology expert with a skill-set almost as good as mine. Almost as good." He did not sound boastful, just factual. "I've found encoded messages for the hit on Portland Hive, and Charlie. Tracing those back leads me to…"

He paused, his fingers flying across the keys again, and I was about to punch him in the arm when he finally continued: "Shit, traced it twice now, and both times leads back to our Hive. The hit was ordered by someone in here, someone with a high level clearance. They're punching about twenty levels above Ryder's security pass. And they have a lot of cash."

Well, damn, we all knew who had the most money and clearance in this place. The Quorum. Those sneaky bastards had been behind it the entire time. But what was their end game?

CHAPTER 10

The silence was too much for me. I had to start talking. I needed answers. "Why would the Quorum order me to be kidnapped? Why didn't they just take me out when I first got into the Hive? Or in the culling? It would have been easy to end me in those battles. Instead they made my run through quite smooth."

Lucas ... *shit.* Was he in on this too? Why warn me that they were after me then?

Ryder stepped closer to me. "I have had my suspicions for some time that the orders for Sanctum were from someone on the Quorum. I went over the log of events on that night, and the council was ferreted away very quickly, almost as if one or more of them knew in advance."

Kyle nodded. "When you mentioned you were looking into Allistair, I figured you had suspicions on the Quorum."

"Who is Allistair?" I asked.

"The creepy looking head of the fourth house," Kyle said without missing a beat.

Right, fugly. I stood then because I needed to move. Of course, maybe I just needed to be closer to Ryder. The moment I stepped into him, and that familiar scent of spices and cedarwood wrapped around me, I felt better, calmer even, able to organize my jumbled thoughts. Speaking them out loud helped even more.

"So we're saying it's probably not all of the Quorum, which is why I'm still living in the Hive and not dead or locked away in their laboratory. Still, one of those bastards hired someone who almost killed Jayden, and tried to coerce Ryder to their side so he'd help to kidnap me. They've been behind the scenes this entire time, manipulating everything ... playing with our lives."

Tension filtered through our group, built on fear and pissed-off-ness.

Kyle snarled: "The thing with Tessa is starting to make much more sense. I know we were only guessing at it before, but I have no doubt now that they allowed her change because of you."

I lurched forward as worries for her came back full throttle. I'd been trying to suppress the fact that my bestie was now part of the "nightmare club."

"Do you think they'll hurt her?"

If that was the case, even if she refused, I was knocking out her undead ass and dragging her out of here by her hair.

"No, they won't," Markus said. "She's much more use to them alive. They're going to try and manipulate her, use her to ferret out your secrets. You have to assume anything Tessa knows, the Quorum will now be able to access."

Which was pretty much everything. She was my best-friend-sister, I told her everything.

"She doesn't know about your blood, right?" Markus finished, locking me in his stare.

Everything except that.

I shook my head. "No, I never had a chance to tell her."

In hindsight, maybe I'd held that back for a reason. I sort of knew that with her close proximity to Blake it wasn't knowledge to just hand across.

Ryder shook his head a few times, as if trying to sort his thoughts. "This complicates things. Even if Tessa doesn't know of her blood, I still don't want Charlie in here one more second than necessary. If a Quorum member is after her, then she's not safe anywhere, even with us on full-time guard duty." He turned to Sam. "I know you need a week, but I won't give a second more than that."

Sam gave a decisive nod, but his eyes looked lost. Again I was struck by how much I hated that we were blindly trusting him. Don't get me wrong, Sam was family, but this was a life or death situation and my gut said he was hiding something. As if he'd read my mind, Sam's dark gaze shot up and our eyes clashed. His look suddenly changed to something more biting. Was that … fear? Before I could say anything, the moment was gone.

In a smooth movement, Sam stood, closing his laptop. "Don't worry, a week is enough time. I'll get everything rolling. Be ready to go at a moment's notice."

After running out some of my aggression on the roof, I showered and went to find Tessa. A few feet from the medical ward, I heard her voice, demanding and shrill.

"More blood!" she screamed.

My hand froze on the door handle. Tessa, you stupid, stupid bitch. How could you want this life? Breathing to center myself, I entered the room and saw Tessa chugging a bottle of blood. My eyes were immediately drawn to the shine of her hair. It had been beautiful before, but looked absolutely stunning now. The pale blond ringlets were tight and glossy.

But unnatural. I preferred when she looked more real.

Now she was like a perfectly crafted doll, skin flawless and smooth. Not a single mark of her previous life remained, not the tiny scar that had been on her chin from when she got hit with a softball in gym, or those couple of persistent freckles which she did her best to cover with concealer. Nope. Nothing.

I flinched as her swirling-silver eyes swept over me. She squealed, dropping her bottle and pushing a nurse aside to reach out and grab my arm. She yanked me into a rib-crushing hug.

"Charlie! My bestie." Her voice was full of happiness and I didn't want to bring the world crashing down around her, but the roil of emotions inside guaranteed there was no way I could fake anything in regards to this.

My voice wavered, tears so close to falling. "You have no idea what you've done," I choked out, my senses filled with her odd new smell, all vanilla and coppery blood. "I can't believe you did this to yourself ... to me."

She released me from my hug. "I figured you would be pissed for a few days. But once you realize how amazing it is having me around you'll see this was the best idea ever. Where's Jayden? Have you seen how incredible my hair is?" She was actually grinning and it had my stomach churning. No real surprise that she was bouncing like a five-year-old on a chocolate high. I had always been the responsible part of our duo. She was the naïve, carefree one.

My voice was clipped: "Jayden is working in the blood feeding center. Ash are given ten hour a day jobs and made to live separately from the vampires. We live in cramped dorms and you will get your own fancy suite. I'm only permitted five minutes to visit you today and then you'll be taken away to your new life and we'll barely see each other."

She scoffed, rolling her eyes. "Charlie, don't be such a mom. I'll go meet with whomever to sort out my new apartment and stuff and then I'll come over tomorrow for movies and pizza." She bounced again.

Then her face dropped as soon as she caught her mistake. "Blood and movies, whatever. Pizza is overrated."

Now my arms were crossed because my BFF just talked shit on my favorite food. Pizza would never be overrated.

Knowing my time with her was almost up, I had to move forward and deal with the most important reason for my visit. There were eyes on us, so I did the only thing I could and pulled her in for another hug.

"Meet me on the roof tomorrow night, at midnight," I whispered, and as I released her, turning to walk away, her perfect face was prettily creased in frowns.

I had to bite the inside of my cheek to keep from crying, because something told me Tessa would not be running away with us. Tessa seemed to like her new life just fine.

Craptastic.

The next day we were on the rooftop getting some sun. Two of the enforcers remained on rotational Charlie guard duty, and all of us had started to notice a pattern of random vampires outside the hallway of my apartment. It was a floor completely dedicated to ash housing, so they had no reason to be there. Bloodsuckers were keeping tabs on me.

We continued to keep all of our conversation inside the Hive general and light. We had confirmation that the bastards had bugged my apartment. The boys swept for them and found a few. We didn't bother to destroy them; they would only replace them again, and we didn't want them to know we were on to them. The ones they'd killed in the locker room were different. They expected the enforcers to be suspicious and to keep up security in there, but bugs in the apartment of the Hive, well, they knew we'd only sweep in there if we were suspicious of something.

For now, Jayden was laying low and staying out of our little rooftop planning session, but was ready to go with us at any moment.

Shit was most definitely going to hit the fan soon.

That morning, as we all sat in a little huddle, I decided it was time to inform the rest of them of my plans. I met Ryder's gaze, knowing it would make him rage.

"I'm going to sneak into the girl's room tomorrow in the daytime, when she's sleeping, and feed her my blood. Then we can bust ass out of here." Finding the bugs in my room, and vamps in my hall, had really shaken me. I felt like they were closing in on us, and I did not want anyone caught in the Hive's deadly clutches. I didn't care about Sam's timing, I wanted out of here.

Ryder gave me a look—you know the one men get when they're torn between exasperation and annoyance. It was a look Ryder had down to a fine art. "Charlie, I admire your spirit ... but that's a stupid plan."

My mouth popped open. Did he just say ... did he call me stupid? Anger fired my blood and I opened my mouth to rip him a new one, but before I could speak his hand came up to stop me.

"What will you do about the guards at her door?"

Great. Twenty questions time. I crossed my arms. "Knock them over the head!"

He chuckled. The man actually chuckled at me.

"What about her nanny that most likely sleeps in the apartment with her?" Markus added.

I didn't have a reply.

"How exactly will you force her to take your blood?" asked Kyle. "What if she goes crazy, as new vampires are known to, and drinks too much and you pass out?"

My face was beginning to redden as they teamed up on me. Dammit, it wasn't just Ryder. All of these sexy bastards had beauty and brains.

I suppose I had jumped in with little to no thought, but I seriously needed her safe. It was keeping me up at night. "Fine, assholes, you design the rescue mission, but this is happening, and soon, because I can't sleep knowing this girl could be killed."

All of their faces softened then and it surprised me when Sam spoke: "You're good for us, Charlie. We've been doing this so long, watched too many cullings, seen too much death. We've become desensitized to the evil of the vampires."

A silence settled over our small rooftop group. What Sam just said had struck a chord and rang true. Something within me shifted. It had been slowly chipping away for the last few months, but finally the last iota of my long-held belief that the ash were evil by association with the vampires was gone.

I could see now that the vampires had created a perfect little society with ash as their slaves, brainwashed them into killing, made them feel less powerful and more dependent on the Hive for survival. Rage boiled up inside of me. This was not okay!

I met Sam's eyes, which were blazing with almost equal parts silver to black. "I will bring down this Hive if it's the last thing I do. I'll bring down all of them."

Kyle nodded. "Now we're talking."

But when I turned to Ryder, something in his face made me falter—a shade of vulnerability. He didn't like that we were going to take on the powerful vamps. I had no doubt he would back me and his boys all the way, but I guess the responsibility of our lives weighed heavily on him. I reached out and took his hand.

"We're all adults here." My gaze flicked across to Jared, who was laid back with his mouth open, asleep and lightly snoring. "Okay, most of us are adults here, and we make these decisions knowing full well what the consequences could be. You don't carry this alone. You don't have to shoulder the burden of our choices."

He was all fierce now. "You guys are my family, and I will tear down anyone who tries to mess with that. It is my responsibility. I know we have no options left. The vampires are going to act soon. My clearance level is practically gone. The information I had available to me is no longer there. The Quorum is gunning for Charlie, and even though I only have theories on what their end plan is, we can never let them get their hands on her. She will be gone, and they have the money and resources to keep her gone forever."

I actually shivered at that thought. Definitely couldn't let that happen. I would not want to find myself at the mercy of creatures who demonstrated daily that they had no mercy.

Speaking of…

"Have we heard anything about Deliverance?"

The news on them had been pretty much non-existent since we'd commandeered all their money and had a major street fight that was somehow covered up and didn't even make the local news program. Which was probably to do with SWAT and their interest in the religious group. At least it was nice to see reports of the charities who received the money. They'd been overjoyed by their windfalls and it made my heart happy to see some of the work which was already in place through the generosity of those Bible bashers.

"Gone underground," Markus said. "They have to regroup, and I heard there was a mass call put out for donations, but the human population is getting a little tired of their hate mongering."

Which hopefully meant it would take them many years to rebuild. Still, they would always find someone with too much money and hate in their soul. I had no doubts they would eventually be back.

Sam shifted then, his fingers flying over the keyboard. He'd been practically buried in his laptop the last few days. It was one of the few we had left which was completely safe. "I think I've found a place to stash the little girl when Charlie cures her," he said, his voice very quiet. "There are pockets of humans who are sympathetic to ash. They have reserves scattered around the world, offering short-term safe passage to ash if they decide to run from the Hives. Human law enforcement check in on them, so there is no way ash can stay long term, but that won't be an issue once the little girl is human."

"Yep, as long as she is hidden from the Hive's prying eyes, so they don't come looking for whomever cured her," Ryder agreed.

Whoa! I had not known about those reserves and ash sympathizers. I mean, I knew ash were not hated on the same scale as vampires. Just the fact that we needed to eat and could be in the sun, they didn't see us as quite so alien.

I leaned forward. "Why can't we use those reserves when we escape? We could go between them, stay for a short time…"

Sam nixed my idea immediately. "No, we're a well-known and large group of ash. The vamps would hear about us very quickly."

Markus nodded. "The Hive will make a token effort to search for the girl, but if there's no trail of carnage they'll just think she's dead. They won't expend much of their resources looking for her. Children are liabilities they do not want to deal with. Us on the other hand … they're going to be beyond pissed. They will hunt for us. Charlie especially."

Okay, all good points. I liked that the enforcers had not dismissed my need to cure the little girl. They knew it was important to me, and it was starting to look like it was important to them too. I had to do it; I could feel it in my very cellular makeup. Before I arrived with my magical unicorn Nutella-flavored blood, there had been no cure for the virus, despite millions of dollars spent every year by the humans. But somehow nature found a way. I was that way.

Jared cleared his throat, leaning forward to join the conversation. He was awake now and apparently following along no worries. Something told me the Australian enforcer had only been dozing. None of these guys let their guard down for very long.

"We better get our arses into gear. If we plan on busting out of here next Friday, that only gives us five days to sort our shit here."

The others all nodded, so it looked like Friday was the day.

Five days ... could I convince Tessa to leave with us in that time? I freakin' hoped so.

We dispersed after about an hour on the roof. With the increase in surveillance on us, spending too much time in a group was a bad idea. No doubt it hadn't escaped the vampires' notice that we were using the sunlit rooftop a lot, even if we did leave random enforcers—Oliver today—in the control room with some of the other non-sexy-six enforcers. You know, keeping up appearances. Still, it was unfortunately true that while the vamps were evil, they weren't stupid.

I was restless for the rest of the afternoon, pacing my apartment to the amusement of Markus and Kyle, who were on Charlie duty. Eventually, after dinner, I had reached the end of my patience. It was almost time to leave to meet Tessa.

"Is it midnight yet?" I asked for the zillionth time in the past hour.

"It's a quarter to midnight." Markus was generally patient and kind, but at the moment he sort of looked like he wanted to strangle me.

"Where's Ryder?" I was about to haul ass and leave without him. I couldn't miss this meeting with Tessa.

"He'll be here, Charlie, and he's not going to be happy if we let you meet a newly-turned vampire on the roof without him."

Well, I gave zero fucks right about now. Ryder had two more minutes or he was going to have to hear the story from us later. The door flew open then and I jumped to my feet, but it was only Jayden strolling in with Oliver.

As my face fell, my BAFF gave a shout of laughter. "Bitch, you better be happy to see me. I've been slaving away at the feeding center—you know, doing stuff." He raised his eyebrows up and down, and I knew he was talking about all the crates of blood he'd been ferreting away for us. We were going to need a decent supply when we ran, and Jayden was in the perfect position to facilitate that.

I managed a smile for him. It was not his fault I was a stressed out hot mess. In fact, if it hadn't been for his never-ending smartass humor, I'd be rocking in the corner right now.

Pushing down my impatience, I bounced over and threw myself at him. He hauled me up into his strong arms. "There's my BAFF. Come on, girl, it's going to be okay."

"I leave for two minutes and you're already stepping in on my woman." Ryder's amused voice washed over us, and I realized he'd walked through the doorway which had been left open by Oliver and Jayden.

I wrinkled my nose at him as I stepped out of Jayden's arms. All of the enforcers had taken to giving us crap about our make out session in the filing room. They all thought it was hilarious. "You've actually been gone for four hours," I said. "But hey, who's counting." I tried to be pissed, but the way he called me his woman was totally hot.

He strode across and dropped a kiss on my lips, and like magic all of my pissed-off-ness just floated away. Sneaky ash bastards, using their good looks and animal charisma to cloud a lady's senses.

He pulled back, silver eyes pulsing at me. His emotions were as heightened as mine. "Sorry I'm late, Charlie. We ended up with a call out. I had to detain and bring in a new ash. He'll be in the next round of culling."

My mouth popped open. "There's another culling? I thought we were full?"

Ryder's face hardened. "The ash that Deliverance killed opened up some spots."

WTF! "So why doesn't the Quorum just give the next five spots away? Why build up the numbers of ash and then make them fight for it?" My fists were balled. This was total bullshit. The more I stopped to look around, the more I felt this entire ash/vampire system was royally fucked and needed a complete overhaul.

Ryder leaned in to me. "The Quorum gives nothing away," he whispered.

The vampires were the stronger race, and yet they sat in their penthouse apartments drinking blood wine and doing God knows what while we were fighting for our lives. But they had weaknesses we didn't, weaknesses which could be utilized if there was ever a chance to take those bastards down.

"It's two minutes to midnight, better move your asses," Markus said, and I was on point again. I couldn't dwell on this culling shit anyway. I wouldn't be here to see it this time. But just like everything else on my bring-down-the-vampires list, I would give my all to end that barbaric practice.

As I left, Ryder and Kyle stuck close to me, the three of us silent as we took the lift up to the roof. We had to be careful at this time of night; there were vampires everywhere, and they often used the jogging track for their nighttime outdoor activities.

As soon as we were on the right level, I strode quickly, an enforcer on either side of me. I liked to think I could handle myself now. I had my weapon and the constant training—aka beat down on Charlie—was starting to pay off. But still there was something inside of me which felt safe being sandwiched between these two ash.

The fresh air was a relief, and besides a few groups of creepy suckers scattered around, the top level was fairly deserted. I swiveled my head, looking for Tessa, but there was no flash of her signature blond curls. We strode further across, and I was getting the creepy feeling that someone was watching us.

My breathing started to increase, the fear in my body catching up before the fear in my brain. Ryder and Kyle reacted in an instant. Both of them drew their weapons and fell in back to back on either side of me. The three of us were silent as we observed the area around us. We weren't out in the open, we'd stuck close to the walls as we searched for Tessa, but something was stalking our footsteps.

Lucas popped out of the shadows then and Ryder nearly took him down. At the last second, he pulled back.

Lucas' face was pinched in anxiety. "Charlie," he whispered, his voice husky. "I've been voted off the Quorum. They no longer trust me, but I overheard them. Your mom, they're going to take her."

I sagged against Ryder's side, the air knocked out of me.

Kyle had to speak for me because I was at a loss for words. "Who is going for her mom and when?"

Chattering reached me and I noticed a group of vampires coming over to us. In the center was Tessa. She was beaming smiles and entertaining, being a social butterfly as usual.

"Vampires. Working for the Quorum. It's all going down right now. At her work … at the hospital," Lucas murmured before turning away from us and crossing to the advancing group of vampires. He intercepted them before they could reach us. "Enjoying our little Tessa?" I heard him say. "She's a doll, isn't she?" He was using his best weapon to distract that group from us. His charm.

My friend finally noticed me then. She'd been a little busy laughing and sucking face with Blake. Asshole. My heart pulled in two directions as Tessa waved me over.

I shook my head at her, before turning away. "Let's go," I told my boys, and a quick glance back had Tessa staring after me, a frown marring her pretty face.

Not up to dealing with her pain, I turned away and practically raced off the rooftop.

"Charlie!" Tessa called, and it tore my insides to leave her. But some motherfuckers were after my mom and that was the final piece of information I needed to snap. It was like I was back in the culling again, seeing red, hell bent on murder.

We didn't have time to get the other boys or try to communicate with them. We had to assume every move we made was being watched and listened to. We moved as fast as possible without arousing suspicion. Ryder led the way, right into the locker room. Inside, Sam was on one of the weight machines, but he dropped it and jumped up when he saw our faces.

Ryder reached out and grasped his friend by the shoulder, leaning in closer and talking to Sam in another language, which I was pretty sure was French. My jaw was on the floor right about then. How could I not know he spoke French? My boyfriend's hotness had just skyrocketed. Dear God. That body and he speaks foreign languages.

As Ryder finished Sam nodded swiftly, and strode across the gym, flipped open his laptop, and within seconds was typing like a crazy person.

Suddenly the siren over the locker room, which told us that there was a call coming in, started wailing. I met Sam's eyes and grinned as he winked.

Jason, one of the call room ash, came running in. "We've got another suspected ash. On Alberta Street, may have attacked a human." He was out of breath.

Thanks to Sam, the world's best hacker, we'd just been handed the perfect excuse to get out of the Hive.

Ryder nodded at the panicky ash. "Thank you. Don't bother to call out anyone else. We're on it."

We suited up quickly, tossing on bulletproof vests, and guns, before jogging out the door.

In the Humvee, Ryder sat shotgun and Kyle drove, while Sam slid in beside me. We peeled out in a rush of screeching tires and engine acceleration. I noticed when we were halfway across the grounds that the gate wasn't opening like it normally did.

"What's happening?" Ryder leaned forward, his eyes locked in. I knew what was worrying him—dispatch always radioed the gate to open it for us. If they hadn't, that must mean...

Mother-effers. "They're stopping us!" I pounded the back of the seat.

Sam was hammering away on his laptop as Kyle slammed on the brakes. We had been barreling along and had to slow or we'd have smashed into the fence.

"They're not blocking me," Sam said, and I breathed out a huge sigh of relief when the gate opened. "But they didn't dispatch through like normal."

Thank God he'd thought to bring his computer with him. Maybe he had anticipated this happening. Why hadn't they dispatched it through? Was the Quorum not even trying to pretend they weren't targeting us now? The thought was partly liberating but mostly frightening.

Kyle gunned it. A guard had stepped out of his tower to stop us, but when it was clear we were not slowing this vehicle, he did the smart thing and jumped out of our way.

"Where did they say the ash was? Legacy hospital?" I asked, playing my part for the listening vampires. It was also the easiest way to let them know that was where my mom worked.

Sam played along. "Yeah, just near that on Alberta."

After the longest eight minutes of my life, Kyle hopped the Humvee onto the curb outside of the emergency room where my mom worked. I had the door open and was halfway out before the car had even stopped. I was powering toward the entrance when a familiar scream rang out into the night and had me changing direction toward the smoker's alley. That shriek had sounded an awful lot like my mom.

The boys were close behind me, and as I turned the corner the scene was definitely not what I had expected. There, standing in the alley was the guy, the blond Viking-looking vampire who had saved me from my attack over a year ago. He had my mother in his arms, cradling her gently, and there were three mangled bodies at his feet.

"Mom!" I screamed, shaking off my stupor, stumbling toward her.

She looked stunned to see me, but that didn't stop her from tearing herself from Viking dude's grasp and running at me. In the dull light I noticed her scrubs were torn, and I could smell fresh blood on her. Looked like there were some gashes on her arm.

No surprise that she looked like she had put up a fight. There was nothing more badass than a single working mom.

"Charlie, thank God you're okay!" Pulling me in for a hug, my eyes wandered back over to the blond vampire who was standing there, barely moving. Why had she been hugging him?

"Who's that?" I gestured to the Norse god before us.

My mom sighed and met his gaze before turning to me. "Charlie, this is Carter, your father."

What the…?

The one who saved me from my attack was my father?

I was happy to see I wasn't the only one standing there dumbfounded.

Ryder, Kyle, Sam, and I were all frozen, mouths open, staring at Carter. An Original vampire. In real life. Alive.

Eventually Carter cleared his throat and walked closer to us. "Hello, Charlie, I've been keeping an eye out for you and your mother for a long time, but it's nice to officially meet you."

Okay, this was not exactly how I'd envisioned meeting my father. Not only had I just stumbled onto a scene where he'd killed a bunch of vamp douchewads, but then his first words were an admittance of stalking.

I guess no families were perfect.

With barely a hesitation, I reached out and shook his hand, before blurting out the first thing that came into my head: "You have blond hair?" I'd always thought I got my dark hair from my father. My mother raised me believing that her boyfriend who died in the war was my father. He had been a human with hair as dark as mine. But when we found out I was an ash and fathered by Carter … well, I had just assumed that he was the one I had inherited the hair color from.

Carter's lips raised in an easy smile. I could see he was amused. Ryder stepped forward then; his hand slipped into mine and he gave a gentle squeeze, which felt both supportive and encouraging.

"Can you fly?" Kyle asked him, and Carter's smile turned into a laugh. My mom's eyes lit up at the sight of him laughing. Oh my God, she still loved him. Who wouldn't? He was gorgeous, ya know, in a good looking dad kinda way.

"Something like that," Carter told Kyle, and winked. Whoa, so the rumors about the Originals were true. They were totally scary and powerful.

"Oh shit. Cool," Kyle replied.

Carter was suddenly all business, turning back to the bodies in the alley. "Hive will come looking for their boys soon. We need to move."

Crap! There was no way the Quorum wouldn't trace this back to us. We had left the Hive at the perfect time for this attack, and now all of the vamps were dead. Hopefully it would still be a few days before they came for us. Our plan was hinging on it.

An hour later, I was sitting in a remote wooded park with my mom, Carter and the enforcers. Carter and I were spending a lot of time staring at each other. I was fascinated with the Original vampire. He seemed different from the other bloodsuckers, a strange combination of lethal Viking and refined gentleman. I could definitely see why my mom fell for him. He was enigmatic. I sat beside Joanna, and Carter stood before us. My enforcer bodyguards were lurking around, making sure we remained alone.

"I need you to get my mom out of Portland, it's not safe for her here anymore." I turned to face the unflappable Bennett mama at my side. She'd just been attacked in an alley and was as calm as anything. "I'm going to have to run soon, and there's no way I can do that if I know you're here and they could come after you at any time." I told her.

Finally, some worry pulled down the corner of her lips and eyes. It wasn't worry for herself though, it was all for me. "Charlie, baby, come with us. Carter already told me he has a safe house set up."

I shook my head, Jayden and the rest of the gang were waiting for us back at the Hive and I didn't want to lead trouble to my mom. She was better off nowhere near me. I turned back to my father, forcing myself to not lose focus again. He was just so mesmerizing. I opened my mouth to ask him where he planned to take her, but other questions emerged instead. "Why did you leave her ... us? How could you do this and leave both of us vulnerable to the Hive?" Anger tightened my voice. Ever since I had found out I was an ash, all I'd wondered about was him, my vampire father, and how he could abandon his family.

Emotions flickered across his face; sparks of gold were really strong in his silver eyes. They were not like regular vamps' color, nope. His were flecked through with golden stars or some shit.

"I'm hunted for my blood, Charlie, for the purity of the original virus. I wanted to stay. I tried to make it work, but in the end I had to do what I thought was best to keep you both safe, which was to keep myself alive to look after you. Your mother and I thought you were human because you were female, and me being around was only going to get both of you killed."

"So you ran?"

He nodded, those blond braids scattered through his thick tresses of hair flying around. "I ran. But I always came back, checking in, making sure you were cared for. I deposited small amounts of money, never enough that anyone would check into you. If either of you ever needed me, I would have been there."

Like the night I was attacked. I stood then, unable to remain sitting, and took a step into his personal space. He didn't move back; his eyes tracked across my face, as if memorizing me.

"Thank you for saving me from those ash," I said, needing him to know that I remembered. "I have no idea what would have happened if you weren't there."

I could see sprinkles of tears in my mom's eyes, and the sight hurt my heart. I cleared my throat, blinking a few times to get myself under control.

Carter nodded, placing a hand on my arm. In that moment no words were needed.

"One more question," I managed to mumble out. "How the hell am I a female ash? And what do you know about my blood?"

I was more than ready for these answers, and I damn well hoped Carter had them.

Chapter 11

Ryder, Kyle, and Sam were lingering closer now. No one wanted to miss his answer. Carter hesitated at first, and then more than one emotion crossed his face. The strongest was sadness and confusion.

Dammit! He didn't know.

He held both hands up to me, as if trying to appease the resting bitch face I was rocking. "I'm sorry, Charlie, I wish I knew how this happened to you. I have never fathered any other children, and know of no living direct offspring from Originals." His eyes narrowed and I was under a shrewd sort of surveillance. "What's special about your blood?"

He had obviously picked up on that little slip. My eyes flicked to Ryder, and he gave a slight shake of his head. Okay, we were still on the "trust no one" road. As I turned back to Carter, my mind already trying to figure out what to say to cover my tracks, my eyes brushed over Sam.

His features were more pinched than usual, and he was fidgeting, which was so unlike his normal behavior. What the hell was he hiding?

I was totally going to jump on his ass soon, and not in any sort of fun way. I would literally hold him down until he spilled. More and more I was trusting the silent and deadly enforcer, but until he fessed up to whatever secret held him so tightly, there would always be some suspicion in my mind.

Giving him squinty eyes, I let out a huff of air before turning back to Carter. He was still waiting for my special blood explanation. "Uh, I was really just hoping you'd know why the Quorum keeps ordering tests on my blood. They said I'm not showing the blood of an ash. They're probably trying to figure out why my blood is indicative of an Original still being alive."

I leaned closer to him, my gaze locked on. "How are you still alive?"

He let loose with that deep laughter again, the sort of laughter which makes you want to join in. "A story for another time, unfortunately. There are spies all over the city and we have already lingered for too long." He held his hand out to my mom and she didn't hesitate for a moment. "I'm going to keep her safe, Charlie, I promise you that. I will figure out a way to get in contact with you, no matter where you end up. Stay with your enforcers. They're a solid team and I trust them to have your back."

Oh yeah, I had no doubts he'd been spying on me even after I made it into the Hive.

The tears which were lingering on my mother's thick lashes finally fell. She stepped closer, wrapping her arms tightly around me. "I love you, Charlene Anne Bennett, never forget that. Please keep yourself safe." Her voice broke, and I found myself losing control. I literally buried my head into my mom's shoulder and bawled my eyes out. I just kept thinking that this might be the last time her arms were around me.

While I had no doubts that Carter would do everything in his power to keep her safe, I wasn't so sure of my own ability to survive this coming unease. Every vamp was going to be gunning for me soon. I could just feel it. Even with the sexy six at my back, it would be a miracle if we all survived.

Shit! I was not thinking like that. We would figure it out, or at least go down fighting.

When I managed to compose myself, I pulled back, brushing one hand across my mom's bangs, pushing them off her face. "I love you too, Mom, so much. I will see you again … very soon."

I made a mental promise to do everything I could to see her again. This was a promise I had no idea if I could keep, but I was going to try my very best.

Carter reached out and brushed a fingertip along my cheek. It was gentle, and the gesture had me fighting hard not to lose it again. I'd never had a father-figure in my life. Joanna Bennett had never been on a single date that I knew of, which was something I'd always attributed to her unwavering love for army dude. Now I knew better. It was all about this vampire and I totally understood why. A few moments with him and I could already tell I'd really missed something by not knowing Carter Atwater, Original of the fourth house.

All of the anger I held toward my father, for his abandonment of us, melted away. I could see the bigger picture now, and it was enough to know that he cared, that he had been watching out for us over the years. On impulse, I stood on tiptoes and just managed to reach his cheek to kiss it. He was a mammoth of a man, something straight out of the history books.

"Take care of her. She's everything to me,"

His eyes were molten silver as he nodded. "I'll contact you, Charlie."

Then he stepped back, gathered Joanna into his arms, and started moving. He was fast, and within seconds they were gone. I swallowed a few times, trying to sort myself out. There was no time for falling apart now, we had shit to do. I needed to cure the little girl and then all of us were getting the hell out of the Hive. I was hoping all of us included Tessa, but my gut told me different.

Life recently was all about kicking Charlie in the teeth. Tessa was a vampire, Mom was in hiding with my Viking father, and the Hive was going to try to kill me soon. Pretty sure I needed to find someone to trade destinies with. Mine was faulty.

Ryder's arms closed around me and all of sudden I was a mess of tears again. What was with all the waterworks tonight?

"I'm not tough," I wailed, as I gripped his shirt in both of my hands. "I don't want to handle this shit. I want to go home, build a nice fort out of blankets, and crawl into it with a good book."

"Charlie can read?" I heard Kyle mutter. "Swear to God, when I asked her to flick through the enforcer handbook she threw it in my face."

Ryder's arms tightened around me and I could feel his chest shaking with laughter. Holy shit. Here I was pouring out my worries and fears and the assholes were laughing at me. I leaned back and punched him clean into his hard chest. *Ouch.* Okay, that was not supposed to hurt me so much.

The silver in Ryder's eyes was dancing as he cupped my face with both hands. "Charlie, sweetheart, you are tougher than you think. And you're not alone … never alone. We can do this together, all of us. Whatever the Hive throws at us, we'll deal with."

I wrinkled my nose at him. "You've changed your tune. Usually you're all doom and gloom."

He cracked a broad smile and white teeth dazzled me. "You bring out the worst of my protective instincts, but I'm working on that. I'm going to focus on you as an equal member of my team. The reason my core enforcers work so well is that we are a single unit, we have each other's backs. Complete trust. You can't handle this shit alone, but together we can handle anything."

Complete Trust. Hah! Except for our little Sam. Keeping his secrets.

The dark, mysterious enforcer met my squinty eyes and gave me a nod. "Soon," he mouthed at me, and blinking a few times in shock I returned that nod. Seems he was going to finally let us in.

Turning around, I let my gaze linger on the path that Carter and my mom had just taken through the park. I let out an exaggerated sigh. "At least I know she's going to be out of Portland, no longer available for any of the Charlie haters to use as a weapon against me."

There were nods all around. It was one of the few positive pieces of information we had received in the past few weeks. Kyle started ushering us out of the area then, no more time to linger. There were only a few hours till dawn and we had shit to do. Plus, I still had to try and find my brainwashed, pod-person bestie tonight.

As soon as we exited the Humvee in the garage back at the Hive, my stomach dropped. The Quorum was standing inside, clearly waiting for us. I scanned across their group but Lucas was not there. Shit! My hand automatically went to my gun, but Ryder nudged me.

"Is there a problem?" he asked them, sounding completely unconcerned.

Allistair, aka fugly, sneered, holding out a hand, palm open. "You're all under investigation. Please hand in your badges. You're suspended from leaving the Hive until further notice."

Sam's eyes were blazing with rage. Kyle was keeping a poker face. And Ryder's jaw was just slightly clenched as he pulled his card from his pocket.

The lead enforcer's tone was low and deadly. "Over thirty years of service and this is how you treat me?"

A few of the Quorum members' faces fell at Ryder's remark, but Allistair shrugged. "If you could take simple orders this wouldn't be happening, but ever since you started fucking Charlie you've changed."

The words had barely left Allistair's mouth before Ryder's right arm came out of nowhere, connecting with the vampire's jaw. The crack of shattering bone ricocheted off the cement garage walls.

Ryder moved forward to pulverize him further, but two Quorum members zoomed into action, latching onto him, pulling his arms back and twisting them until near breaking point. Sam and Kyle were already moving to intervene, but Ryder shook his head.

"Throw him in the pit!" one of the Quorum members shouted.

Shit!

"Ryder!" I stepped forward, but he just nailed me with a hard look. His lips didn't move but his eyes said everything. The last thing we needed was all of us in the pit.

Allistair stood, holding what looked like a completely shattered jaw in one hand, and stalked over to Sam. He held out his free hand.

"Give me your laptop! Now!" His shout was garbled but understandable and it pleased me to see he was wincing in pain.

The aforementioned laptop was tucked under Sam's arm. "Sure thing, boss," he said.

In a move so fast I doubt most would have noticed or heard, Sam tilted his head over the side of the device and murmured, "Midnight."

I wondered for a second if I'd even heard it, but knew there had to be a reason the tech-inclined enforcer would hand over that computer so casually.

The Quorum members took an extended second to bestow us with dirty looks, and I resisted the urge to flip them all off. With a swish, they left then, taking off with the computer, Ryder, and our access cards. My eyes remained locked on their retreating backs, and I noticed they all shifted around

Ryder, keeping him deep in the center of the group—no way to snag him out of their evil grasps.

My heart was racing. How had everything gone downhill so quickly? Seriously, WTAF just happened?

"Sam, your laptop," I whispered, anything to take my mind off Ryder.

He dropped a comforting hand on my shoulder. "Has just been wiped of all information."

Well, hot damn. I'd been right about "midnight." Had to hand it to the silent enforcer, he was shaping up to be the smartest one of an already elite squad of dudes.

Kyle let out a muffled shout, his fists clenched as he focused on the doorway they had just taken Ryder through. "They're going to beat the shit out of him for what he did to Allistair."

My stomach dropped. I hadn't thought of that. I assumed he'd just be locked up for a while so they could prove their dominance.

Sam moved into action then, striding across the garage. "This moves up our timeline, Charlie. Talk to Tessa soon."

I'd forgotten all about my bestie, but Sam was totally right. I had to talk to her ASAP because I needed to retrieve my boyfriend and my new ash family, and then get us all out of this hellhole.

After reaching my apartment, we walked in to find Oliver, Markus, Jared, and Jayden sitting in the living room, playing cards and waiting for us.

Oliver stood. "Where were you guys? The Quorum put us on suspension, took our badges."

Kyle growled, "Us too, and Ryder is in the pit."

Jared let a few interesting cusswords fly. Wow! Australians had seriously dirty mouths. Definitely had to visit there one day.

Jayden strode across to me. "Hey, girl. While you were gone Tessa came looking for you and she said they've closed off the roof track for 'repairs.'" He finger quoted around the last word.

Those assholes. Goddamn vampires were shutting off any avenue we had for privacy. They were tightening the net around us and we were running out of time to do anything about it.

"I really need to see Tessa," I said, all casual-like. I did not want the vampires to hear my desperation.

My eyes met Jayden's, pleading with him. Come on, you clever BAFF, think of something.

A spark lit up Jayden's eyes. The black blazed at me and his eyebrows were practically at his hairline. "Alright, I need to get ready for my shift at the feeding center. I wonder if Tessa will start feeding from humans soon." He wiggled those eyebrows at me a few times.

Yes! That's it.

"She probably will. She's always loved all things vampire and can't wait to suck on a human. Speaking of … when's my appointment today?"

Okay, so I didn't really have enough time to be smooth.

Jayden grinned at me. Damn guy loved this playacting shit. "In two hours."

I returned that grin. Jayden would get Tessa to meet me in our feeding room in two hours. It was time to start praying she would agree to leave with me.

I sat in room number seven bopping my feet. Jayden had called to tell Tessa that her scheduled feeder was here, so now it was just a wait to see if she'd show up. Kyle and Oliver were standing guard outside of the feeding center, monitoring who was entering but trying not to be obvious about it. As the door handle jiggled I shot to my feet, throat tightening in anticipation.

The door swung open, revealing my bestie. She was all red lipstick and smiles. She looked healthy, perfect, and happy, happier than I'd seen her in a long time. To match the lipstick, she had on a red corset, teamed with skinny jeans and red peek-a-boo pumps. She was a knockout.

"Tess!" I crashed into her. "I'm so sorry I had to run off. My mom was in trouble."

She pulled away. "Is Jo okay?"

I nodded, before quickly giving her the cover story, in case there were listening devices in here too. "Yeah, she wasn't at work when I got there. I finally got a hold of her and she was halfway to California. She's decided to head to the beach for a little holiday. Get some sun before winter hits in full force."

"Awesome!" Tessa said, and already I could see my mom was forgotten as she bounced and grinned at me. And why was she holding her hands behind her back like that?

"Did you drink an energy drink again?" I asked in a joking way. "You know that stuff makes you annoyingly happy." There was no way her weird behavior was about an overdose of caffeine. Not to mention she wouldn't want to drink anything but blood now.

Tessa practically shrieked: "I'm engaged!"

She shoved her left hand in my face to reveal a huge diamond rock.

"Oh my God, Charlie, it was so romantic. I was getting a manicure at this shop at 2 am. Did you know they open the shops up for the vampires at night and we're allowed to shop and all of that?"

My mouth was hanging open and I could only gape at the huge diamond on her hand. "Tessa! I ... he ... you're..."

She squealed, seeming to take my stuttering as some sort of excited statement. "So, as I was saying, I was getting the manicure with Nadine, this new vamp friend of mine, and suddenly Blake hands the manicurist something and says to make sure to finish my manicure with this. I almost died when the lady put the ring on my finger. I knew immediately the diamond was at least three carats. Three, Charlie! Then Blake got down on one knee and proposed!"

No, no, no. "Tessa!" I was seriously pissed. It was as if she'd lost her mind, like literally pulverized the thing when she decided to jump into bed with Blake. "You can't get engaged. You're twenty-one years old and this guy nearly killed you changing you into a vampire freak-show."

Tessa's face hardened. "Why are you being such a bitch, Charlie? Seriously, you're just jealous! Your guy took forever to even kiss you and you're jealous that Blake isn't afraid of commitment."

I totally wanted to club her over the head and hide her in a suitcase under my bed until we could get the hell out of here, but she could, and probably would, kick my ass.

I had to change tactics, because my bitching crazily at her was not working.

"Okay ... this is coming out wrong, Tess." I leaned in closer and murmured my next few words. "My life is in danger and I can't really give specifics, but I need to tell you something."

Her face had softened a little. Taking this as an encouragement I leaned right up close to her ear.

"I'm leaving the Hive, and if you want to keep our family together, like you always proclaimed when you talked of being turned, you're going to have to come with me." I sucked in a deep breath. "If I don't leave soon, I'm dead."

As I pulled back, her face showed genuine concern. "Charlie what's going on? Blake knows people. He can help you."

I gritted my teeth. "No one can help me. You don't understand everything and..." I pointed my finger to the ceiling and swung it around in a circle. Tessa's eyes rose and she followed my gaze around the room. I wasn't sure she fully understood what I was trying to tell her about us being spied on, but she didn't push me further. She gave a sigh and looked at her new shiny ring.

There were a few tense moments. I wanted to reach out and shake an answer out of her. What was she even thinking about here? Finally she lifted those silver eyes and gave me a sad look.

"I'm going to stay here. Blake will take care of me."

My heart split in two and tears filled my eyes. I had officially been replaced. She would rather be with Blake instead of going with me.

I gave it one last shot. "Think about it for another minute. Not only do I want us to be together, I can't leave you here knowing they might use you to get to me,"

Tessa shook her head. "Charlie, I'm not going anywhere and neither are you. We'll figure this out. I love it here. I feel like I finally belong."

My chest began to shake with emotion. "I love you," I managed to say, before turning into a puddle of tears. Somehow I made it out of the door and into the hallway.

"Charlie!" Tessa yelled, but I ran, bursting out of the feeding center front door. Oliver and Kyle fell in behind me as I sprinted past. Once I made it back to my apartment, I slammed my bedroom door hard, threw myself on the bed and shoved my face into a pillow.

I screamed for as long as I could into my pillow, only stopping when my head shook and I had no breath left. Everything was out of control and I hated it. Helplessness was one of the worst emotions. Powerlessness too. Because I knew that it was bad to leave Tessa here, but she controlled her own life and choices, no matter how terrible they were.

Folding my body tighter around the pillow, I cursed soundly into it, even digging up a few of my favorites from the enforcers. And yet I didn't feel any better. For the millionth time I cursed the Hive. Seriously ... fuck this place. My entire life had been turned upside down because I was born different. But it shouldn't be this way, I was still human—well, some of me was.

I understood the vampire virus scared the humans, especially with so many dying from it, but ash weren't contagious. It was bullshit that we were subjected to this lifestyle. It was also bullshit that vampires abused their place of power and treated us like second-class citizens. I looked down at my shaking hands. Running through these veins was a cure, a way to end all of this.

I rolled over on the bed and fought to control my breathing, focusing on the plain white ceiling. Life was weird. You grew up as a kid with big dreams. Like wanting to be a famous actress or an NBA star, then in high school you scaled those dreams down as you ended up waiting tables with some acting on the side, or hopes to play college ball.

By the time you were in college you decided to just pick a safe major and end up in accounting or marketing. Why did that happen? Why were dreams slowly whittled away until there was nothing much left but the mundane existence of get up, go to work, come home and then die. That was life.

Well, fuck that. No longer was I content to be an accountant. Life purpose had fallen into my lap, and I could feel the rightness of my convictions. I was going to take this entire system and shake it up. By the time I was done with the world of vampires and Hives, I hoped nothing would remain as it was now. Ash should be free and vampires shouldn't even exist.

The realization that I could change things, that I was meant to, lifted a huge weight I had been carrying since I found out I was an ash, cleared away some of the agony I faced regarding Tessa and the little girl who was changed, and all the children who had suffered. One day there would be no more suffering, no more families torn asunder.

There was a soft knock at my door. I sat up, clearing my throat and wiping my face. "Come in," I said, my voice steady.

It was Kyle and Lucas. Lucas had wide eyes and a clenched jaw. Something was wrong. Of course it was. That was pretty much the story of our lives.

"What is it? What happened?" Adrenalin flooded me, my heart beating out a rapid rhythm. If Ryder was hurt, I was going postal on everyone.

Lucas crossed the room, quickly grabbing me under the armpits and yanking me out of bed.

"Hey!" Kyle said, moving across the room in a smooth stride, gun raised toward the former Quorum member.

Lucas stopped him. "I would never hurt her."

In a flash, he hauled me into the bathroom and turned the shower on full blast. I barely had time to suck in a breath before we were both under the freezing cold spray, fully-clothed.

I'm going to be honest here. When I first met Lucas, I might have had one or two fantasies that involved him ... but being fully clothed in an Antarctic shower with him ... was not one of them.

I met his feral gaze. "What the crap, dude?"

Kyle had followed us into the room still holding his gun, but his trigger finger was relaxed. He was giving Lucas a chance to prove his intentions before he shot him. Before Lucas could answer me, music blasted out of the radio in my room and Sam joined us in the bathroom. Again, not time for those early day's fantasies. Plus, I was a one ash woman now. Ryder was everything I wanted, and as soon as I figured out what crazy pill Lucas was on, I was going to the pit to get my man.

Lucas' voice was a low growl. "I finally figured out what the hell is up with your blood. All of the tests ... dammit! The puzzle has finally been pieced together. I can't believe you would hide that from me."

My heart skyrocketed, and then fell when I saw the look of hurt on his face. Now it made sense, the shower, the music—my apartment was bugged. Lucas clearly had decided he wouldn't rat me out with this information, or he wouldn't be working so hard to cover the conversation now.

Water pounded on my back as I leaned in closer. "Do you blame me, Lucas? You're a powerful vampire and I'm the fucking cure. I'm the one who could take away all of your power and make you weak again."

Lucas shook his head. "You could make me human again, make me *feel* again." His voice could barely be heard over the music and water.

Kyle's gun was at his side now. "Who else knows?"

Lucas waved his hand at the enforcer. "No one. Pure luck of course. If you had told me the truth, I would have stopped all testing. As it was, the vampire scientist who had been dealing with Charlie's blood went a little crazy when she found out. She was supposed to call me the second she got results but didn't. Luckily, I had a feeling I should check on her and caught her right before she was about to alert all the Quorum members. Let's just say she won't be around to break my trust again."

My stomach rolled at the casual way he spoke of "disappearing" someone, but part of me was grateful.

Lucas reached out and touched my face in a tender way. Kyle cleared his throat.

"You need to leave the Hive. Now," Lucas said to me, and judging by the look on his face he was sporting a major Nutella-flavored unicorn crush.

I shook my head. "Not without Ryder." I felt sick at the thought of him in that dingy room, without light, or food, enduring God knows what. Damn! We had to get him out.

"Yes, Ryder. Her boyfriend," Kyle snapped out.

Lucas smiled. "Yes, I'm aware she's taken. Still, Charlie needs to leave now and he can follow later."

Sam shook his head. "No, we have a code. We do not leave a man behind. Ever."

Lucas turned his angry, swirly eyes on the two enforcers. "Do you have any idea how powerful Charlie is? In a world torn apart by a virus that kills a high percentage of those infected and changes the other percentage to bloodsucking monsters, she's the way out. They will either kill her, experiment on her, or torture her by repeatedly draining her blood."

Sam stood to his full height now, looking absolutely deadly. "Yes, we know all of this. Give me one reason why I should let you live now that you have knowledge of her abilities."

Holy shit. I knew Sam had my back, but wow. Threatening to kill a vampire—one strong enough to be a Quorum member—took huge, platinum covered balls.

Lucas only grinned, looking completely unworried. He turned back to me. "You're in good hands. I'll help you get Ryder out of the pit and then you must run. I only ask one thing in return."

Please don't say kiss me or some weird shit like that.

"Anything," I replied, because if it was for Ryder, I truly would do anything.

Lucas' entire face changed then, desperation in his eyes. "Cure me," he said.

My mouth dropped open.

"No," Kyle said.

"I'll do it," I said. Sam let out a very animal like growl. "But not today. We're going to need someone on the inside, especially with Tess here. Are you okay with staying vamp for a little while longer? Until this war plays itself out?"

He sucked in a few deep breaths, and finally nodded. "Yes, you're going to need my help. I'll figure out a way to communicate with you once you're gone. We can do much together."

He was right, but now wasn't the time to make those plans. We had to deal with the immediate threats. Moving as close as he could get, Sam and Kyle leaning their bulk into the shower with us, the vampire began laying out the plan for getting Ryder out of the pit and us out of the Hive's prison gates.

All of us listened intently, throwing forward arguments on the logistics of his plan. Finally, we were all in agreement. It was a good plan, and I really hoped it was going to work.

Lucas brushed a hand across my cheek. "You have a responsibility now, Charlie, to make a change. There is so much you don't know. I wish there was time to show you."

I was confused. "Show me what?"

Lucas' eyes glittered at me. "Ash aren't privy to the inner world of our kind. Tessa will soon find out the vampires have built their kingdom on a bed of deceit, blackmail, and murder."

Goosebumps broke out on my arms, and I swallowed. He was a hell of a scary storyteller, and I was thinking of those files in the room. How much more ugliness could there be?

Lucas waved his hand at Sam. "With your computer skills, you could find out what I'm talking about. You just have to search in the right places."

Sam and I exchanged a look, and I knew he was thinking about that information he found on that message board, about Sanctum. I could practically see the thoughts churning through his mind. No doubt, next chance he was at a secure computer, he was going to have another attempt at finding the dirt on the Hive, following these bread trails from Lucas.

Wrapping my arms tightly around myself, I fought off the shakes, which were partly to do with the freezing water and partly with fear. My world was about to be turned on its head, and no way was I ready for it to happen.

Leaning forward, Lucas kissed my cheek. "Be safe, Charlie. I couldn't save my wife but … I will save you."

My eyes felt hot and damp. But before I could say anything or thank him, he was already out of the shower and gone from the room, leaving the three of us in a heavy, and uneasy silence. I wasn't sure about the boys, but my thoughts were nothing short of tumultuous. I was not ready for this. No way at all.

Chapter 12

After Lucas left, the boys and I got to work on our new plan. Kyle lifted his walkie-talkie. "Shift change. Oliver, Jared, and Markus to Charlie's apartment."

We were on point now. Time to put the "Ryder rescue and escape from Hive plan" into motion. First step, we needed all hands on deck. There were so many different elements to the success of this plan, and if even one got messed up, it could screw the entire thing sideways.

Pushing through the boys, I threw both of them a towel. They were only a little damp in places but I needed to change. Stepping up to my closet, I pulled out clubbing gear. If I was going to play this part, I was going to do it right.

Waiting until Kyle and Sam had left, the boys closing the door behind them, I stripped off my soaked clothing and shimmied myself into new underwear and a short black dress, a dress I had been waiting for the perfect moment to wear.

I'd had this piece handcrafted by an ash who specialized in concealed weaponry. The material was soft, flowing, but still tight in the right places. I could run, climb, and kick ass in this thing without a problem. There were even little sewn-in booty shorts so I didn't crotch flash anyone while laying a smackdown.

I added black tights and calf-high black boots, which had small side inserts for a few knives. I strapped on the thigh holster, and as I dropped the dress down I was more than pleased to see that it was invisible under the dress. That dressmaker ash was a freaking genius.

A few moments in the bathroom for dark makeup and sexy, tousled hair. We didn't want anyone to think we were anything but party people tonight—stupid, drunk, and out-of-control.

By the time I stepped into the living area, six males were standing around, hulking out the place. I gave a bit of a wolf-whistle. "Well, don't you boys clean up nice. I'm totally looking forward to a night of fun. I need a break from all the stress in my life."

I was slipping into my role, hoping like hell that whomever was listening on the other side of the bugs in here was relaying this shit word for word. It pissed me off so bad that we were under constant surveillance and had to watch everything we said. Thank God we'd be long gone from here soon.

Jayden stepped out from the shadows and threaded his arm through mine. "I dressed them up. Poor things can't seem to get out of enforcer black." He kissed me soundly on the cheek. "And don't you look gorgeous. Unlike them, you should wear this little black dress much more often."

I grinned, my eyes shifting across the enforcers as I took much more notice of their clothing this time. Hot dayum, Jayden had done a fantastic job as the stylist tonight.

Jared was in a fitted, olive-green shirt. It clung to his honed muscles and brought out the real blond Aussie surfer thing he had going on. Markus wore green also, but it was a different shade, much lighter, and his beard was neatly trimmed, a perfect man-bun on top. He looked extra-bulked and tall tonight, his combat boots topping him out near six and half feet. Oliver was all Latino lover. He had on a dark gray dress shirt, and slacks, and I knew Jayden had drooled the entire time he was picking out that outfit. Sam was still pretty much in black, although I caught a peak of a white cotton shirt beneath his leather jacket. He was epitome of tall, dark and mysterious. The last of the sexy six, Kyle, wore a blue shirt which brought out the lighter highlights in his dirty-blond tousle of hair. As our eyes clashed, I could see how unhappy he was. Like me, he was not taking this thing with Ryder well. But we were going to sort it out tonight.

Our mood was falsely jovial as we made our way to the karaoke lounge. The Hive was pumping tonight, and there seemed to be a great mix of ash and vampires around. I liked that. More victims for us. In a sad way, I was really looking forward to the next hour. I was not only going to let loose in the club, but I was getting my Ryder back. Bastards had messed with the wrong unicorn ash.

I threw my head back and started to dance as I entered the room. The music was blaring, and as we stepped further into the dark room, the beat enveloped me. All of us headed straight to the bar. The plan was in motion, and the next thirty minutes were the most important. We had to be seen drinking. A lot.

There were ash behind the bar, even though vampire females were prowling the floor taking orders. Kyle leaned in and ordered our first round of shots, the special vampire moonshine ones, and also a chaser beer for each of us. The moonshine was potent; it would knock me on my ass, but I wasn't planning on actually drinking it. The second the shot glasses and bottles were in front of us, we gathered our drinks closer. I grabbed my beer first, pretending just to take a sip, before discreetly gulping down half the bottle.

"Ready?" Kyle grinned, flashing those perfect teeth at me. I gave him a wink in return.

The seven of us lifted the clear glasses and took the shot. I made a face, managing to keep the disgusting contents in my mouth, before lifting the bottle and spitting it into the beer.

I shuddered a little. Hopefully these shots weren't so potent that I'd still get drunk from just having it in my mouth, because I was pretty sure I could spit fire right now. We continued this for thirty minutes, ordering beers and shots like they were going out of fashion. The bit of alcohol I was getting was enough to loosen me up, and then it was easy to start acting drunk. We were drawing attention, the enforcers around me were both feared and revered amongst the ash, even tolerated by the vampires, sort of. Not to mention the rumors were running wild about why our security clearance had been revoked and where Ryder was. Vamps were gossiping bitches.

When a new song came on—this group of karaoke wannabes were a lot better than the last—I let out a shriek and grabbed Kyle's hand, dragging him away from the bar and toward the dance floor.

"Wheee!" I squealed, pulling him into the fray, smashing against people as we went. I flailed my arms in a ridiculous version of dancing, even managing a couple of leg kicks which knocked down more than one vampire around me.

Kyle threw back his head and laughed. Somehow he'd managed to bury his anger deep enough to pretend with me. Both of us kept this up, creating more than a little ruckus on the dance floor. Kyle reached out and captured both of my hands, spinning me around. Ash and vamps were diving out of our way, but we made sure to extend our reach and still bump a lot of them. Aim of the game: annoyance. And we were on fire.

Finally, we nudged the wrong vampire. Knew it couldn't be long before their arrogance kicked in and someone decided to put us stupid ash in our place. I anticipated the shove, but because I was supposed to be drunk as a skunk, I pretended to trip and I hit the ground hard. Kyle roared above me, in a pissed off cave-ash type of way. Then it was on.

The vampire I had nudged was now locked into a brawl with Kyle. I allowed myself one quick glance to the far wall and saw Lucas enjoying some blood wine before I jumped up and threw myself into the fight. Forcing my movements to remain staggered and clumsy, I swung around and cracked the vampire, who had Kyle in a headlock, in the back.

I let out a crazy sort of giggle. Everyone had to continue to believe we were hammered. One of the ash bartenders leapt over the bar and came at me full force.

"Break it up!" he yelled, reaching for me.

Sorry, buddy, you're kinda cute, but you're going down. I gave him a strong upper cut to the jaw and he flew back as I let out another fake cackle of drunken laughter. Another bartender flew over the bar, but Sam tripped him before he reached the dance floor.

Suddenly Lucas was stalking towards us with two meaty vampires at his side. I fell to the ground still laughing, making sure everyone got a good view of my bootyshorts. Drunk chicks did stupid shit like that all the time. I should know because ... Tessa.

I gave a silent cheer as Kyle flipped the vampire over his shoulder and slammed him on the ground. The enforcer grabbed at his mouth and began to laugh as well.

Lucas shouted loud enough for all to hear: "Throw these idiots in the pit. They're completely intoxicated."

The vampire that Kyle had attacked stood to his full height now and glared at us. Suddenly meaty vampire #1 had my arms behind my back. I pretended to wobble and sway as he dragged me out of there with Kyle at my side.

"Screw you," Kyle slurred as meaty #2 jabbed him hard in the back. Kyle and I let our heads drop and our words mumble as we shuffled our feet along to the elevator.

We were dragged over to the special red elevator, meaty #1 and #2 using their security clearance to call it up. Entering the elevator, I met Kyle's eyes for a split second, and knew he was ready to rock and roll.

It had killed Sam and the rest of the crew to stay back and allow us to get our asses kicked, but the plan required just me and Kyle to get into the pit. The others were off doing their part now. My eyes flicked between the two meaty asshats. If I was being honest, I was a little nervous about taking my meathead down. I had never fought a full-blown vampire before. But we needed their access cards since ours were confiscated.

Kyle straightened, and it was time to put part two of the plan in motion.

"Dood, I gutta piss," Kyle slurred.

I nodded, slouching and swaying at the same time. "Just go … just let it go."

Meaty #2 freaked, pushing Kyle away from him, which released the enforcer's hands from behind his back.

"You will not piss in this elevator!"

Kyle, now hands free, grabbed at his zipper. "I can't stop, dude, I'm too … too…"

He fumbled, getting the zipper down before reaching inside of his pants. I seriously wanted to laugh my ass off at how horrified both meaties looked right then, but I needed to use this distraction to my advantage. I pretended to fall forward, and was relieved when my hands were released.

Elevator fight in 3 … 2 … 1…

Slipping my hands into my boot I yanked out a blade. At the same time Kyle pulled one from a secret pocket right near his junk. Brave dude.

All fake drunkenness gone, we had the complete element of surprise. Gripping the knife tightly, I sprang up and whammed the hilt up into meaty #1's nose, hearing the satisfying crunch of bone. As he leaned forward to grab his face I came down hard with the butt of my heavy blade and cracked at the base of the skull. The entire two-step maneuver had been fast and smooth. The sexy six would be proud of me. Those sergeant hardasses had been drilling this type of knock-out move into me over and over in training. Nice to know the boys riding my ass in the least sexy way was actually paying off.

Meaty #1 fell and I looked up just in time to see Kyle snap meaty #2's neck. Okay, so I guess if you caught them off guard, fighting a vamp wasn't so bad. Kyle gave me a fist bump and then I returned my knife to my boot, thankful I hadn't had to use the pointy end. The elevator was three floors from reaching the Pit so I quickly slipped my hand inside my dress and came up with two stainless steel razor-wire zip ties.

Kyle raised his eyebrow. "Damn, girl."

I winked, handing him one of the ties. We both made quick work of strapping the meaties' hands behind their backs. Then, as the elevator dinged and the doors started to open, Kyle smoothed his hair and I checked myself for blood.

Before stepping out, I pulled the button to pause the elevator. We were definitely going to need to make a quick escape. Then we quickly dragged the meat twins out and deposited them off to the side of the main entrance.

Leaving them, we crossed the dank, underground area. I started praying Lucas had come through for us. Without him, the rest of the plan would sink. Moving toward the bright reception spot, we approached the old-looking guard, Marty, who basically lived down here and knew everything about this place.

My blood turned to ice when another figure stepped into the light and I realized Marty was talking to a member of the Quorum. A female. She was one of the more silent members but I remembered her making rude jokes when they drew my blood last. She was on my bitch list.

There was nowhere for Kyle and me to hide, and since the sound of our footsteps had already echoed through the tunnel, we were immediately spotted. As she took a step toward us, her eyes blazed in anger.

Shit. Not part of the plan. Marty was supposed to be alone and Sam was supposed to have wired a large sum of money into his human family's bank account to ensure his cooperation. Lucas said Marty hated being relegated down here to the bowels of the Hive, hidden away. He had plenty of beef with vampires and therefore made the perfect ally.

With no other option, Kyle set off at a sprint, charging the Quorum member. Marty didn't even hesitate to jump out of the way, so I was guessing he was still in on the plan. I pulled my knife out again and charged down the narrow and dark hall right behind Kyle.

Quorum bitch stood there dumbfounded, her jaw slack. The last thing she'd expected was that we'd attack her—lowly ash should only bow to vamps.

She took a step back, recovering enough to sneer at us. "You wouldn't!"

Kyle slammed into her. They hit the ground as he threw out an elbow, cracking her in the throat. I used my height advantage to leap over them, landing on the other side of the grappling pair, turning back to try and find a way to help my friend.

The Quorum member was nailing Kyle—who was on top—with her red talon claws. The moment she had a good grip on his biceps, she threw him so hard into the air his back cracked into the ceiling. Oh hell to the no, bitch!

She didn't even see me coming. My hand flew down hard, jamming the knife into her eye. A scream ripped from her as Kyle landed on all fours next to her. He stumbled a little from the fall, but recovered in an instant to dive across her and wrap his hands around her neck. She missed his movements, distracted by the blade still lodged in her eye.

As he choked her out, I leaned down, full of rage, and whispered in her ear, "Welcome to the culling."

Kyle snapped her neck. I knew enough about vampires to know this would only keep her down for a little while. She would heal in a few hours. And we so didn't have time to kill the bitch. Plus, our escape would already have enough of the vamp world gunning for us. No need to increase our list of offences.

My eyes were surely blazing as I straightened and locked Marty in my gaze. He was still flat against the wall, looking very pale and shaky. Before I could start demanding, the vamp extended his hand. Cradled in his palm was a set of keys. "Ryder's in cell one-thirty-eight. Always respected him. Was a pleasure to work with."

Marty was turning out to be one of the least stupid and evil of the vamps.

Kyle took the key and nodded at him. "Shit's going to get rough around here. Do you have anyone you can stay with?" The enforcer didn't want repercussions of our actions befalling the poor vampire that the Hive thought was too old to do anything but sit in the pit guarding criminals.

Marty nodded. "My granddaughter has a cabin on Mount Hood."

Kyle clapped him on the shoulder. "Take care."

We wasted no more time, both of us dashing through the halls. I tried my best to ignore the screams and pleas which could be heard through so many of the doors. I wondered for a brief moment how many prisoners were actually in here, and what the ratio of ash to vampires was. Bet the ash were on the higher end; they were always a target. Though maybe they just killed ash when they screwed up too badly. *Grr.* I really had to stop thinking about that. Ryder was the priority.

I let Kyle lead us to cell one-thirty-eight. It took about eight minutes of winding through the underground prison system. Holy shit balls, I'd had no idea there were so many cells down here—they could seriously hold thousands. When we finally reached the right section and door, I lifted a shaking hand to the lock. It took me more than a few attempts but I managed to click it across. Kyle slammed a flat palm against the metal frame and my breath caught as we looked into the small, dingy, damp-scented room.

"Ryder," I said in a rush, my feet moving before I could think twice. I closed the distance, dropping to his side, the key falling from my hand as I reached for him lying stomach down on the cold, dirty floor. He was naked from the waist up and his back was a mass of red welts, as if he'd just been whipped or something. WTAF?

I swung my head around to find Kyle's furious face above mine. "He needs blood. They've starved him and that's why he's not healing," he said, letting out an enraged snarl. With a whoosh of air he was gone. Whoa, he was totally going to kill someone right now. Hopefully he remembered to grab some blood too.

Turning back to Ryder, I was startled to see his head had shifted to the side and his eyes were now open.

"Charlie?" His words were hoarse, and I could see him swallowing hard as if trying to find some moisture. "You can't be here ... too dangerous."

He started to push himself up, fatigue and pain racking his features. I flapped around for a bit, trying to find a place to put my hands that wouldn't hurt him, before finally managing to slip in under his arms to help him into a sitting position.

I leaned in closer, my heart hurting to see him like this. Of course, he was still a big toughie, trying to stand up in case anyone came for us. I held him down, leaning in to whisper. "Kyle's gone to find you some blood, then we have to get out of here. The Quorum is coming for me, for all of us, and it's not safe here any longer. Once you can walk, we have to cure the little girl, and then get the hell out of Dodge."

His eyes were a big swirl of silver as they examined my face, and I couldn't stop myself from leaning forward and resting my forehead against his. "Shit, I'm so glad to see you alive, even though the vampires need to all die for throwing you into this asshole pit."

Ryder breathed deeply against my cheek. "Been worried about you. Knew the boys would have your back, but the

Quorum ... tortured me ... wanted to know everything about you."

Dammit. They were totally coming after me and targeting all of my loved ones in the process. I tried to keep my anger from bubbling over. There was no time for the major meltdown, hissy-fit I wanted to throw. Ryder and I both reacted at the scraping sound from behind us. I was up and crouched in front of him, another knife from my boot in my hand, when Kyle dashed around the corner.

"Got the blood," he said, lifting two bottles up. "Marty was gone, but there is a little fridge beneath his desk. Lucky he drinks the same as Ryder."

Kyle must have noticed then that his best friend was partially up off the floor. He dived down to kneel beside him. "Fuck, man!"

Somehow everything this dude needed to say was in those two words, his fear, worry, pain, anger, relief—two goddamn words.

Ryder's arm was steady as he took the first bottle and downed it in seconds. He'd be extra thirsty with his body trying to heal those injuries. Blood really was a miracle cure for us.

The change started instantly. Already his tawny color was returning, strength clear in his body. The second bottle disappeared just as fast, and Ryder was able to stand without any assistance from us. Kyle reached over his head and pulled his shirt off. He was wearing a white muscle tee underneath. He handed the button dress shirt to Ryder.

"Throw this on. We have to get out of here. I'm not sure how much longer we have. Quorum bitch was still out when I got the blood, but she could come around at any point."

Ryder nodded, and barely even winced as he slid into the blue shirt. It was a little tight around the chest and arms but it would do for now. Wasting no more time, we took off through the pit. Ryder seemed to be gaining strength in leaps and bounds. Reaching out, he captured my hand, his eyes expressing a plethora of emotions.

"Thank you for rescuing me."

Damn, I wanted to kiss him so bad, even smelling like dirty-ass pit floor. I loved that he didn't carry on about me putting myself in danger to come down here, or go all caveman. He just thanked me with sincerity and respect.

"You too, bud." He turned to Kyle for a split second before his focus was back on me.

"We aren't rescued yet. Let's get the hell out of here before there's a thousand vamps gunning for our ass," Kyle said.

Shit! Gun … right. Might be time to switch out the knives for a weapon that could actually put a bloodsucker down. I slipped the blade into my boot and yanked out the pistol, even while on the run. That was how badass my clothes and accessories were. If I had time, I would have had that ash make me fifty of these outfits. One in every damn color.

We made it through the pit and back to Marty's desk without anyone stopping us. Quorum bitch was still on the floor; the elevator was still open and waiting for us. I wondered how Marty had gotten out—maybe Kyle had called it back down when he got the blood. Either way, I hoped it was a sign that luck was on our side.

We passed the still unconscious meaties and dashed inside. As soon as the doors closed we were zooming up. Kyle immediately turned to fill Ryder in on the rest of the plan.

"So by now Oliver and Jayden should be at the first safe point. They took one of the vehicles loaded up with the blood and supplies. Jared is in the other car, waiting outside of the grounds for the rest of us. Markus and Sam were going to stage the breakout for the little girl, so all that's left is for Charlie to cure her, then we can get her ferried away to the one of the compounds. Sam has a contact in line to pick her up."

Sam had been working his ass off making sure the plan with the child went off without a hitch. Just like with me, she had struck a real nerve with the silent enforcer.

"How did they get out of the compound without their access cards?" Ryder asked. "And where do we find the girl now?" The lead enforcer's eyes shifted toward the elevator panel. We were almost at the top.

"Sam rigged them to open without setting off the alarm. We timed their departure for guard shift change. Since we were in the pit, we have no idea if they made it out without alerting the vamps. Hopefully they did though. We had to get the cars out, otherwise we'll be screwed trying to escape on foot."

It hurt my heart to think about leaving here without Tessa. I wanted so badly to try and find her one last time, tell her that I loved her, but I couldn't risk the rest of my family because of her stubborn single-mindedness. I just had to hope Blake and Lucas would keep her safe, especially since something told me that when the Quorum found out I'd escaped, they would be all over my friends like a bad rash.

Ryder interrupted my morbid thoughts. "You didn't tell me where we find the girl."

"She should be stashed in that laundry room which opens to the outside. We figured it was the easiest place to escape from with her. Sam left us a trail to follow. There's supposed to be a space in the fence line which will be free from alarms."

Ryder gave a chuckle as the elevator dinged to let us know we were at the top. "What would we do without Sam?"

Kyle also laughed. "Funny thing is, he has really pulled out all of his skills since Charlie arrived. Methinks he has a little soft spot for our unicorn ash."

Ryder nodded, and looked at me. "Who doesn't?"

I batted my eyelashes at him. "If Kyle weren't here and we weren't running for our lives, I would totally—"

The elevator dinged again, cutting me off, and the boys laughed. Comic relief was like my nervous tic. As the doors to the ground level opened, we sobered immediately.

Uh oh. We had a big problem. Four hulking vamps were waiting for us, and a ton of people were running in the background.

"Plan B!" I shouted, simultaneously smashing the close and down buttons.

The four vamps rushed at the closing doors, but they had been just too far away to make it before we were cut off.

"Shit!" Ryder said, and since he didn't swear much I knew we were extra screwed.

As the steel box made its rapid descent, Kyle looked at Ryder. "We haven't been rock climbing in forever."

Ryder shook his head. "No, it's too dangerous."

Kyle leaned around us to pull the stop button. "I don't see any other way. This elevator only goes to two places—ground and pit. They're clearly waiting for us on ground. It's just lucky these shaft systems all connect between the different elevators."

Ryder took this moment to fully check me out, from my hair down to my feet. "Can you climb in those boots, Charlie?"

I put a hand on my hip, giving him my sassiest look.

Kyle grinned. "That's a yes."

Ryder exhaled loudly, lacing his hands together and forming a step. Kyle moved closer and inserted his foot into the handhold and pushed off hard. This pit elevator was larger than most, with ceilings almost fifteen feet high. The enforcer managed to knock out the ceiling access panel. It clattered to the side, leaving a large gaping hole in the ceiling. As Kyle landed, he wasted no time stepping into Ryder's hands again.

This time the lead enforcer crouched low and with an impressive display of strength, launched his best friend up through the hole. With a whoosh of air, Kyle disappeared, his mess of dirty-blond hair appearing seconds later as he stared down at us from the top of the metal box. He crooked a finger at me and I knew that meant it was my turn.

FYI, plan B sucked. This was like stupid shit they did in the movies that ended badly for everyone.

"Charlie…" Ryder motioned for me to jump up. Never one to expose my weakness, I swallowed hard and shoved my left boot in his hands. With far more power than I expected, he tossed me up into the air. My shriek got lodged in my throat as I forced my eyes to remain open, which was a big help as I grasped onto Kyle's outstretched hands. The enforcer's strong arms easily held my weight and he dragged me up. I chanced a quick glance down, knowing my booty-shorts-clad butt was all up in Ryder's face.

"Enjoying the view?" I called down to him as Kyle finished pulling me through the hole. I lost sight of my dark-haired enforcer when Kyle shifted me across to balance on the metal slats beside him. He then turned back to lean through the hole.

I could hear Ryder chuckling. Then somehow he made the leap up to grasp onto Kyle's forearms. Dude could jump like a freaking NBA superstar. It was moments like these that I realized how incredibly sexy and strong these boys were. Of course, Kyle most likely had a hernia now after pulling big-ass Ryder up, but at least he could be secure in how sexy and strong he looked.

"What now?"

I was pretty sure the muted siren had just started to blare. The Quorum would be figuring out how to break into the elevator system soon.

Ryder motioned for us to follow him as he moved across to the large cables which were keeping us from plunging to our death. "The sirens mean lockdown," he said "All members of the Hive will be urged to go to their living quarters. All doors will be sealed, all hallways monitored by cameras, and the people hunting us will most likely have shoot to kill orders."

"Awesome," I said, heavy on the sarcasm.

A loud rumble rocked the floor, and I used the cables to anchor myself as another elevator passed next to us. I tried really hard not to squeal, but holy scary.

Once the metal box passed and we could talk again, Ryder said, "That's the other system, which goes the full length of the Hive. We need to make our way across to it."

Kyle gestured to his wristwatch. "Sam put a tracker on me, so wherever we end up the boys will be there."

Ryder's face was now firmly looking like that of a man with a plan. "Alright, follow me."

Chapter 13

Ryder's brilliant plan was uncomfortable as hell. After almost dying from scaling our way across elevators and up cables and into the spaces between the Hive floors, we ended up cramped in the A/C duct, army-crawling on our elbows through the first floor to try and find the laundry shaft and get the kid. Jumping from the top of the elevator to scale a ten foot wall which led into the duct was pretty much the most badass and scariest thing I've done yet.

In the shaft, we had spaced ourselves twenty feet apart, Ryder in front of me and Kyle behind. That way we wouldn't overweigh the metal ducting and crash through it. I kept my eyes trained forward, focusing on Ryder's beefy shoulders skimming the side walls as he barely fit through.

I tried to calm myself again but nothing was working. Pretty much from the first moment we'd crawled in here my heart had started racing, breath stuttering. I'd learned a new thing today: I had a very real fear of being in small metal spaces.

I was distracted from my newfound claustrophobia by Ryder pausing ahead. From back here it looked like he had reached a grate. Despite the distance between us, his whisper was clear.

"This is it, the supply closet across from where the girl should be, right near the exit."

I relayed the message to Kyle, neither of us moving as we waited for Ryder to do his thing up there. Luckily the Hive was an industrial-style building and the ducting and grates were large, although Ryder still looked like he had to wiggle to fit as he dropped down into the room. I moved then, closing in on the open grate. My head popped over the side to see a dimly-lit supply closet below. Ryder was the only one in the room, and I felt immediate relief to know I'd soon be out of the confined space. Moving across the opening, I lowered my legs down first; strong hands gripped my thighs and I let myself drop into Ryder's waiting arms. We ended up face to face, his dark and silver eyes looking all warm and swirly.

Kyle cleared his throat, and with reluctance I stepped out of Ryder's arms, letting him focus on guiding his friend out of the vent. The three of us were then cramped in the six by six feet space, and as Ryder flicked on the lights I saw the shelves were packed with enforcer supplies—flashlights, glowsticks, walkie-talkies, and a bunch of other shit I had no idea about. Ryder grabbed a set of walkies and matched the channels before handing one to me. It was small, maybe three inches, so I clipped it on my boot. Kyle stashed a few supplies in his pockets, before turning to his best friend.

"For over thirty years, this has been our home." His voice was full of emotion, and it hit me then that most of the sexy six were old, some even grandpa old. Pushing those thoughts away, I slipped my hand into Kyle's and squeezed.

"Thirty years of cullings and ash murders. It's time for a change," I said to him.

Kyle managed a tight smile. "It is." He squeezed my hand back.

I looked up to see Ryder watching me with an intense gaze. "We're lucky you came into our lives, Charlie."

I smiled, wrinkling my nose at him. "That means a lot coming from the guy who called me 'forty-six' for two weeks."

Ryder chuckled. "Yeah, I'll own that. Okay, focusing again. Time to glue yourself to me. We need to save the little girl and ditch this place."

Kyle nodded. "Sam will see our location, and with a bit of luck he's waiting outside the exit door as we speak."

We gave a three-way fist bump, the low sound of emergency sirens the background music to our breakout song. My stomach tightened with anxiety as I drew my gun and Ryder put his hand on the doorknob.

"Luckily, this is one of the few monitored doors. They don't lock down unimportant rooms, so we will be able to get out. Hopefully Sam has exit ready for us." He twisted the knob, and sure enough it clicked right open. "Kyle and I will go first to take down any threats," he said as he stepped out, Kyle right behind him.

I followed a second later, striding out into a small hall, gun held up in a ready pose. This storage room really had been the perfect room to drop out of the vents. We were directly across from the laundry chute, which was where we hoped to find the girl waiting for us. Just down the hall was the exit door to the Hive, about four meters from us.

I continued acknowledging our luck right up until Ryder opened the laundry door. It was empty. Shit! Had the Quorum gotten to the girl already? Ryder and Kyle wasted no time. They were already moving rapidly toward the exit, I guess to see if there was any sign of our team or the girl.

Ryder glanced back to make sure I was following, giving me a smile as I closed the gap between us. The door clicked open easily, so Sam had definitely lifted some of the lockdown, which hopefully meant everything else was still going right. The two enforcers disappeared out into the darkness beyond. As I neared the exit myself, I was relieved to see and hear the very familiar rumble of a Hummer.

A broad smile broke across my face to see Sam's dark beauty. He was in the vehicle, laptop on his lap. Sitting beside him was the little girl, and I wondered if they had somehow known we were in trouble and had gotten her out just in case.

Jared, who must have been patrolling, ducked into my line of sight. He opened the back door for Ryder and Kyle, since they were already out of the building and a fair bit in front of me. I was just about to make my own exit when the Australian enforcer's face turned a sickly white color.

"Charlie, behind you!"

I didn't even have time to turn before a familiar jolt of electricity brought me to my knees. Straight away, my mind went fuzzy and black dots danced across my vision. *Don't pass out, don't pass out!* If I lost consciousness, I was dead. I managed to focus long enough to see the stark fear on Ryder's face. All of the enforcers were out of the car now, coming straight for me, but they were too far away. My uncooperative body was yanked backwards and the exit door slammed shut, buzzing as it closed. The vamps had overridden Sam, which resulted in a full and complete lockdown on this section of the Hive now too.

"Charlie!" I heard Ryder's muffled voice, followed by pops and hard slamming sounds against metal. Bullets. The attack was no use though, the Hive was specifically built to withstand this sort of violence.

I didn't want to turn away from the door, away from Ryder, but I really had no choice. I faced my attackers, meaty #1 and #2, both of them looking extra pleased that they had me back in their clutches. Right behind them stood Allistair.

Well, *shit*.

My hands clenched into fists, the aftershocks of electricity still dancing on my skin. Focusing on fugly, I noticed a remote control type device in his right hand and an electric stick in his left.

"For an ash, Sam is quite good with computers, but this door won't be opening again," Allistair said, holding up the remote. Behind me, the heavy pounding on the door continued.

I weighed my options here: try to fight three really pissed-off vampires while my body was still weak from the shock, or buy time until I had strength? I had no weapons close by, the gun had been lost when the electricity hit me. Crap.

"Alright you got me," I conceded, holding my hands up.

Meaty #1 and #2 surged forward and hauled me up by the armpits, starting to drag me down the hall. The Hive had a real deserted feel to it now; the sirens still blared.

I focused on Allistair. He was definitely the leader of this little squad. Guess it was a good sign that he hadn't killed me outright, but what the hell was his plan now? And why wasn't this crazy asshole on mandatory lockdown like the rest of the Quorum? I tried not to panic as each step took me further away from my family. Ryder and the boys would be going crazy, but I hoped they at least got the girl to safety before trying to rescue me. Yeah right.

The pace picked up, my feet skimming the ground as I was hauled around two corners and into a small medical room where a woman was waiting in a white lab coat.

Shit. Double shit.

Allistair got up in my face then, eyes pulsing silver. "What is it that's so special about you?" he asked, his eyes locked hard on the vein in my neck.

"I can tie a cherry stem into a knot with my tongue," I said calmly. "It's a one of a kind skill." His hand shot around and smacked me across the face.

Jesus Christ! Slapping hurt a lot worse than I thought. Ow! Despite the agonizing pain of what felt a lot like a broken jaw, I did not flinch or cry out. The only sign of my hurt was watery eyes as I stared him down.

"Take as much blood as you need to figure her secret out," he said to the lab woman. His bent nose stood out starkly in the overly-bright fluorescents here. His skin looked a little thin and drawn also. I wondered if he was due to feed. That could explain his current crankiness. Oh, and the fact that he was a grade-A asshole.

The female vampire nodded. She strong-armed me onto the table, attempting to strap me down, and I fought her the best I could, but with my head ringing and her extra vampy strength, she eventually managed to secure my arms and legs.

It was so much harder than I expected to keep my cool, calm, and collected face. Four vamps against one ash unicorn. I was not liking those odds.

Putting on my best badass enforcer face, I narrowed both eyes at Allistair. "If you haven't figured out my big bad secret by now, then why hire the Sanctum to capture me?"

Might as well information gather while I was stuck here.

Allistair crossed his arms, glaring at me. "First day you arrived on our doorstep I voted to lock you up in the pit and drain you of blood, plasma, and spinal cord fluid over and over until you were eventually dead, but it was vetoed."

Nausea churned my stomach.

"So I thought if I could make it look like a third party wanted you, when you were kidnapped, no one would blame me. That way I could do my experiments in private. The only reason I haven't killed you is because I know you're born of an Original and I expect your blood to give me some sort of powerful boost."

Ah hah. The reason the vampires wanted me alive. Well, this creepster at least.

An enjoyable thought brought a smile to my face. "Why don't you just take a drink and find out." I exposed my neck. *Please do us all a favor and drink so you can become a weak human and I can kill you*, I was mentally saying. Allistair's eyes locked in on my neck, a longing filling his silver eyes.

Before he could move though, the medical vampire strapped a band across my biceps, and starting jabbing at my veins. "I would advise against that. We still don't know enough about her." The rough bitch finally managed to find some blood, after making a mangled mess of my arm, and in a quick succession she filled two tubes before inserting a third.

Before Allistair could gloat more, the door flew open and a smoke canister filled the room. Within seconds the place was filled with an acrid and densely white smoke. I coughed, my eyes burning; it was impossible to see more than six inches in front of me.

I heard a scuffle of feet, and lifting my head I tried to see what was going on. Thankfully, before I could freak too much, the straps holding me down were released and the needle removed from my vein.

Strong arms wrapped around my shoulders and I was being hauled up over my bed and into someone's arms. I started to fight, and only stopped when we made it through the doorway and into the deserted hall. Lucas was holding me. At his side was Blake and Tessa. My head spun as the door to the medical room slammed shut. Blake quickly screwed in some bolts and a metal panel to keep it closed. Dude must have power tools tucked into his damn pants or something.

The Cabbage Patch Doll looking vamp turned to face me. "That should buy you ten minutes," he said, as Lucas set me down.

I swallowed hard. "Thanks."

Just like before with Kyle's two words, my one said so much more. Basically I'd just said: "You mother fucker, you changed my best friend into a vampire and then proposed to her and didn't tell me. I hate you. But thanks for saving my ass."

My glare-off was interrupted by Tessa. She body-slammed into me with a big hug. "Lucas told me everything and I want to help," she whispered.

My heart picked up a beat at her response. "Oh thank God! Let's go," I said, pulling her hand to follow Lucas, but she stayed cemented.

"Oh no, Charlie. I want to help you from inside the Hive with Lucas and Blake…"

My eyes shot to her boyfriend. Blake had really done a number on Tessa. She was head over heels for this guy. Still, despite recent questionable decisions, my friend wasn't a complete idiot, so maybe I was being too hard on him.

I squeezed her hand. "When we were twelve, we promised to buy houses right next to each other, to knock down the back fence and share a backyard." The memory had tears glistening in my eyes. Tessa's eyes began to leak as well.

"That's not going to happen in a world like this," she murmured.

She was right. The best we would get now was a meet-up at the feeding room.

"We're too exposed," Lucas prompted. "We have to go."

Tessa pulled me in for another bone-crushing hug and I whispered in her ear. "If you and Blake ever want a human life together, I can help you with that."

Pulling back, I saw shock on her face. She probably didn't fully understand what I was saying, but it was enough that she knew the option was there.

Lucas had my arm now, and Blake swooped in to pull Tessa the other way. As we were dragged in opposite directions, our eyes remained locked.

Tessa smiled, her beautiful, familiar grin. "Stay alive, bitch, and try not to dress like a boy so often."

I laughed and sobbed at the same time. "Don't get married without me."

She nodded and that was it. We were no longer in sight of each other. Lucas let me go, allowing me to walk on my own.

I fought to suck back my tears. It was so much harder than usual; there was no easy way to deal with leaving my oldest friend, a piece of who I was, to live her own life without me. Heartbreak didn't even begin to describe my feelings.

Trying not to slow our pace, I reached into my boot and pulled out the walkie-talkie. Pressing the button, I hoped to reach my boys. "It's me. Are you guys okay?"

After a short burst of silence, Ryder's voice came over the speaker: "Jesus, Charlie! I've been going crazy. I didn't want to use the walkies in case they heard and took it from you."

"I'm okay. They took some of my blood but I got out." We were in the stairwell now on the first floor. "Is this line secure?"

"Yes, for now." Was his reply.

Lucas pulled the little black device from my hand. "Sam!" he said tersely.

"I'm here," Sam came back.

"Can you open the south entrance stairwell door on the ground level?"

My eyes were pinned to the exit sign hanging over the door.

The walkie crackled and Sam sounded resigned. "No, I've been blocked. I can no longer access any of the Hive controls."

Lucas cussed and his eyes met mine. "I have a crazy idea, Charlie. Are you with me?"

You know, a year ago I loved crazy ideas, because they mostly involved Tessa daring me to down a bottle of tequila. Now … not so much.

"I'll be honest, I've had enough crazy to last me a lifetime."

Lucas gave me a resigned grin, before sighing and taking my hand. "It's the only way," he said, sounding almost like he was trying to convince himself.

Walking up one flight of stairs to the second level, he brought me to a door I had never noticed before. Opening it revealed a golden elevator door. For reals? How many secret Batman lair elevators were in this place?

"Special Quorum elevator," he said. "I doubt they have had time to revoke my fingerprint clearance with the strikes going on."

He pressed his thumb to a button and it glowed green. The door slid open.

The Hive was definitely filled with secrets. "Strikes?"

He didn't answer as we entered the elevator. I blinked a few times as he hit the button for the roof. *How could we escape from the roof?*

"Since Ryder and his core enforcer team have been suspended, the other ash enforcers have gone on strike. They refuse to take orders from anyone but Ryder. It's keeping the Quorum awfully busy."

My throat tightened with emotion and I felt horrible that we would be leaving all of these helpless ash behind. Hopefully I'd live long enough to try and change their circumstances.

The Quorum's private elevator was a speed demon, and in what felt like seconds it was opening up to a secluded section of the roof, an area I had never been before.

I turned to Lucas. "Where is the helicopter?"

Because surely he had one waiting for me? There was no other reasonable explanation for taking us up to the very place it was impossible to escape from. A veritable trap if we were discovered.

Lucas grabbed my arm and steered me out onto the roof, hurrying us across to the edge. He grabbed the walkie from me and radioed the boys. "I'm on the roof with Charlie. Security will have seen us by now. She's going to have to jump."

I gasped. The vamp had flipped his lid—lost his freakin' marbles. Dude was officially crazy.

"Lucas, are you insane? I'm not jumping off a sixty story building! My body will turn into pudding. I don't want to be pudding. I hate pudding. It's weird and jiggly and tastes like crap."

Ryder's voice came over the speaker. "Charlie you're not just any ash. You're Carter's daughter."

Levitation. Shit. Didn't he know super powers didn't work like that? You didn't get to use them on the spot to save your life; it was too much pressure. The odds were I would become a legend—you know, a dead superhero. A door slamming drew my attention behind us to where two vampires were stalking towards us.

Lucas gave me a tight hug.

"Come with me," I begged. "They'll kill you."

He shook his head and laughed. "I'm one of the richest vampires in this Hive. I own the deed to this land, with a clause that if I'm murdered the land goes to the humans. They won't kill me, but I will spend some time in the pit."

Shit.

"I'm going to be back for you and Tessa," I said to him.

He nodded and squeezed my hand before running to confront the vampires, throwing himself at them.

Ryder's voice came over the speaker. "Charlie? What's happening up there?"

"I'm on my way," I said to him as my legs began to shake. Sixty stories was a long-ass way down. I could already hear my ankles snapping.

"Look to your right. Aim for that building which is about twenty stories high. It's the vampire parking garage. We're on the top floor waiting to pick you up."

Okay, well forty stories to drop was a little better than sixty. And seriously. WTF, the vampires got their own parking garage? The ash weren't even allowed cars! Grr. I shook that thought from my mind and focused on the building. It was far as fuck, right across the other side of the Hive grounds. Maybe ten times farther than I jumped when I'd saved Jayden in the culling. Looking behind me, I saw

Lucas kicking ass, but becoming overwhelmed by numbers as more vamps arrived.

"Bitch, you can do this," my BAFF said through the radio, strong and clear.

I smiled, and with a deep breath, I jogged to the far end of the space.

I squeezed the walkie-talkie button. "Ryder?"

"Yes?" He sounded worried.

"I love you." Because I hadn't officially said it yet and there was a ninety percent chance this ended with me as pudding.

His voice came back strong: "I love you too, you know that. Do. Not. Die. That's an official order."

Hah! Bossy ash.

Dropping the walkie-talkie to the ground, I rolled my neck. *Here goes nothing.*

I took off in a run-like-your-ass-is-on-fire sprint, sailing past Lucas and the vampires he was grappling with. My heart was beating hella fast and my brain was screaming at me to stop, but I pushed my muscles faster. If I was going to make that jump, I needed speed. Coming near the edge, I did the most insane thing of my life…

I jumped.

"Shiiiiiit!" I screamed, sailing high into the air, higher than humanly possible. My instincts kicked in then, the heat unfurling from my center again as my body glided through the air. It wasn't the most graceful of levitation, but it was going to do the job. Tucking my legs up, with my arms out, I prepared to land as the rooftop came into view. Holy shit I was totally going to make it!

As I sailed into it like a cannonball, I caught sight of a Humvee and one other car on the roof. Tapping into more of the heat, I forced my body to glide rather than plummet as I began my descent. I found that if I straightened my legs, it slowed my fall a little. Holy fuck! I was legit flying. All too soon the cement lot crashed into my legs and there was a distinct crack as I rolled before skidding to a stop. Flying I was okay at, landing not so much.

My left leg was definitely broken ... but no pudding.

I was alive!

Suddenly Ryder was there scooping me up in his arms and shaking his head. "Are you okay?" His voice was gruff as he tenderly rubbed his thumb over my ankle.

I winced. "My ankle is broken but I'll be fine."

He shook his head in disbelief. "You're amazing, Charlie."

I didn't have time to respond before the sound of gunfire erupted.

"Let's roll!" Sam shouted, pounding on the hood of the Humvee.

Ryder crossed the parking lot to the vehicle in a dozen quick strides and placed me in the back, reaching across and yanking up a duffle bag to prop my leg up. Even with the limb as secure as he could make it, I knew it was still gonna hurt as we tore out of here.

The second the door shut and Ryder was in the front seat we were off. Scanning the car, I tried not to bust up laughing at Jayden sitting on Oliver's lap and the little girl sitting on Kyle's. Seems they had ditched the second car at some point and all joined forces to come back and save me, which was so sweet, but it did mean we were packed into the Hummer like sardines. Sensing me, the little girl turned and peered at me with those unnerving silver eyes.

"Hi," she said, and I waved at her, taking a deep breath and trying not to hurl. Sam was driving in circles down the parking garage to the main level. Markus reached across and helped to stabilize my leg, which was both painful and relieving at the same time. Hurry up, ash genetics, work your magic.

Jayden's leaned over the seat and grasped my hand, squeezing. As I squeezed back, I was so grateful that I was leaving the Hive with my BAFF. I missed Tessa but she had chosen her path, and I still had Jayden.

"Snipers on the roof," Markus said to Sam, who nodded but didn't lose an ounce of focus as he continued to racecar-drive our asses around the tight turns.

We were out of the parking garage now and speeding across the street to the far gate that the shipping trucks used. My guess was that this exit was less guarded than the others. Bullets snapped the ground as Sam swerved the Humvee.

"Hold on," Sam yelled as he plowed through the gates. With a heavy crash, they flung wide open and that was it—we were out of the Hive. The entire car gave a collective gasp of relief.

"Come here, I want to talk to you," I said to the little girl. What was her name again? Katelynn, right. As she turned her attention to me, I patted my lap.

Kyle helped her climb over the seat and she sat next to me in the back.

"Can you keep a secret, Katelynn?" I asked her, even though I knew that in a week's time the entire Hive would know what I was. I just knew that the blood the Quorum took this time would lead them to the knowledge that I was the cure.

She nodded, leaning in to me.

I showed her my arm and the blue veins that streaked it. "My blood can cure vampirism and I can make you human again."

Her mouth made a small O shape as she continued staring at my arm.

"Really?" Her voice was so small and I couldn't even deal with how wrong it felt seeing her like this—seeing the way the virus stole an innocent little life.

I nodded. "You just take a drink and then it will start to change you back, so you can live with your family and have a long and happy life."

She licked her lips. "Will it hurt you?"

I shook my head and offered my arm. She winced for a moment, clearly grossed out at the thought of biting flesh, but in the end she latched onto my arm and began to drink. The vampire in the club who'd drank from me had fed for about twenty seconds, so I assumed that would be enough for her too.

After thirty seconds, I lightly pulled her off. Her eyes were glassy, her mouth dripping with blood. She looked like she wanted to bite me again, but regained her composure.

"Your blood!" she squeaked. "It tastes like cotton candy."

Of course it did. Stupid unicorn blood. The rest of the car's occupants, who had been wrapped in a tense silence, laughed then. Staring out the window, I noticed that Sam was taking us down a dirt road and into a deeply forested neighborhood. The sun was coming up, and that meant no vampires would be driving around looking for us today. Markus began to duct tape towels up against the back windows to keep the girl in darkness. The sun would still give her one hell of a rash, weakening her, until she was cured. Kyle draped a blanket over her as Sam drove deeper into the forest. We were taking back roads up Mount Hood.

"We're almost to the drop-off point," Sam announced, and I saw he had pulled the Humvee up a long private driveway and into a gated compound. There were humans waiting at the gate with semiautomatic rifles.

"Who are these people?" I asked.

Ryder turned around and met my eyes. "Ash sympathizers. Rare people that believe ash shouldn't be punished for what their parents did, that they should be allowed to mingle with society. Some of them had ash children, or a friend who did."

Most humans hated ash. I don't know why, they just did. It was nice to know there were a few out there who got what we went through, who cared.

Sam pulled the Humvee into a dark garage and I saw two oddly familiar faces there. It took me a few moments to place where I remembered them from. My eyes dropped down to the blanket covering Katelynn. *Right!*

They had been on the news when all hell broke loose. They were her parents. The garage closed then, enclosing us in darkness. Kyle and Markus held their guns close, with the safety off. Ryder popped out of the car and opened the back door, pulling the blankets off the girl. As she sat up, she surprised me with a hug.

Did her skin already look a little less pale? Her eyes a bit less silver?

"Thanks," she whispered, and then jumped out into her parents' arms.

Ryder addressed her family and the few surrounding sympathizers. "She's been inoculated with the cure and will be human within the next few weeks. Don't ask me how, I can't tell you. Until then, you must take precautions with the sun, and she might need some final blood to help her heal."

He dropped a bag from our precious supply into one of the humans' hands.

Katelynn's parents looked at Ryder in shock and broke down into tears. The mother wailed, clutching her daughter closely. Tears sprang up in my eyes as I realized what a difference my blood had made in this girl's life. Never again could I just sit on the sidelines and hide. I had to figure out a way to take who and what I was and use it for the greater good.

I wasn't used to humans looking at us with anything other than contempt. Most of these sympathizers just looked utterly baffled, but there was no hatred.

"There's a cure?" rang out from more than one of them.

Ryder nodded, but his expression did not soften. He would not reveal my secret, and we'd be long gone by the time the humans could quiz Katelynn. "No more questions. Thank you for arranging this meet-up with the girl's family."

Despite the fact they looked like they wanted to protest, the humans just gave us lingering stares before turning and retreating. The garage door opened and Ryder shut the back hatch, getting into the car, and we were gone, heading down the long driveway and back out onto the road to Mount Hood.

Ryder turned to the driver. "Okay, Sam, I have trusted you this far, but now I need to know where we're going."

Sam gripped the wheel, staring out onto the main road. "We drive to Bend, take a private plane from there to north Canada, and then charter a helicopter to our final destination."

Ryder frowned. "And where is our final destination?"

Sam met Ryder's eyes for a moment, but then shook his head.

"I can't tell you, brother. You'll just have to trust me a little while longer."

Jayden caught my eye and we both scowled. Sam wouldn't be leading us into a trap, would he? But Ryder nodded. Clearly he trusted Sam with his life. With all of our lives.

After a three-hour drive, my ass was asleep. My leg was partially healed and we had already gone through fourteen bottles of blood. As we pulled up to the small airport in Bend, Oregon, I was getting an uncomfortable and heavy feeling in my stomach about Sam's secrecy. Were we all just expected to follow him out of the country into Canada with no other details and a dwindling supply of blood? Apparently so.

There was a small white plane waiting in a massive hanger. The boys began loading our supplies into the cargo holds while Ryder came to help me get inside.

"Who's flying this thing?" I asked.

"I am," Sam said, as he took my other arm and helped me up into the plane.

I raised an eyebrow. "You're a pilot?"

"Yes," he said, in his limited word usage way.

In such close proximity to Sam, with beams of sunlight filtering across the space, I could see he had the lightest smattering of freckles across his nose. Just another thing I hadn't known about him. After getting me up the small steps and into the plane, I was deposited into one of the large tan leather seats scattered about the main cabin. There were about ten chairs in total, so it was not a very large area.

I grabbed Sam's hand before he could leave.

"I'm a girl with daddy issues, Sam, so I don't trust easily. Why aren't you telling us where we're headed?" My pulse was racing as I prayed this didn't turn into a big confrontation.

Sam looked sadly at me and kneeled down, coming close. "I have no way of knowing if we are being overheard. What if the Quorum sewed listening chips into our clothing? Our duffle bags?"

My stomach rolled at the thought. Oh God. Were they on their way here now? I wanted to rip my clothes off and check the seams or something.

"There are some things in life worth risking everything for. I'm willing to risk all of you not trusting me or being mad at me if it means I can keep this secret destination safe."

Ryder's hand grasped Sam's shoulder. "You've never steered me wrong before. I trust you."

I squeezed Sam's hand as the rest of the boys began to file into the small plane. "I trust you too, Sam."

I realized that was totally the truth. These boys were my family now, and if you couldn't trust family you were screwed. Sam nodded and went into the cockpit. Ryder kissed my forehead before leaving so he could slide into the co-pilot chair beside Sam.

Jayden plopped down in the seat next to me and leaned over on my armrest and whispered, "Sam's a pilot? Good lord, that boy is sexy." Jayden fanned himself and I smiled. Resting my head on my BAFF's strong shoulder, I drifted off to sleep.

Chapter 14

The jerking of the plane jolted me awake. As I twisted my head to catch Jayden's eye, he made an exaggerated movement of wiping my drool off his shoulder.

"You're lucky you're cute, because I don't even let Oliver drool on me."

I brushed a hand across my mouth, which admittedly had a bit of drool at the corners, before reaching out and smacking his arm. "Shut up. What's going on?"

Looking out the window, we had landed in a mountainous, green, and totally scenic place. Must be Canada. The small tarmac we were rolling down seemed to be leading straight into a private plane hangar.

Sam smoothly guided us inside and then Ryder jumped out to close the huge hanger doors. It was darker inside now, but that didn't stop me from pressing my face to the window. Through the small opening I caught glimpses of a large industrial space. Movement drew my attention as a beautiful woman with long strawberry blond hair strode across from where she must have been waiting against the far wall.

Craning my neck to see more, I saw a line of plastic shopping bags along the wall.

After finishing all of his flight things, Sam exited the open-doored cockpit and spoke to all of us.

"Let's move. We need to be in and out of here quickly."

I rolled my ankle in a circle and was amazed that it barely hurt. Standing up and testing it out, I was able to walk on it with only a slight limp.

Ryder, who was waiting at the bottom of the stairs, reached out for me and helped me down. We then strode around the front of the jet and I let out a stifled gasp as Sam crossed the space to the woman and she threw her arms around him. He pulled her close, even lifting her up off the ground. Whoa ... Sam was never openly affectionate.

Kyle was grinning widely. "I knew it. There were no fishing trips," he whispered to me. "He totally has a love nest."

All of us were transfixed as Sam spoke in hushed tones with the girl and she nodded, hugging him again and then leaving. He turned and crossed back to us. Jared and the guys had already started unloading our stuff, but Sam stopped them with a single shake of his head.

"Leave it," he said.

We all froze, waiting for him to clue us in on what was happening.

He pointed to the blood cases. "Drink up. It will have to last you the rest of our trip, because we're taking nothing else with us."

Jayden's mouth popped open. "My clothes?" He looked mortally offended at the idea of leaving his designer outfits behind.

Sam shrugged. "Will be incinerated."

"Monster," Jayden whispered, his entire face crumpling as Oliver rubbed his shoulders.

Ryder gave Sam a discerning look then, no doubt trying to figure out what the hell was going on.

Sam, ignoring our glares, began to undress. His hand waved at the line of shopping bags. "My friend has bought us new clothes. Nothing from the Hive goes to our new location."

I raised an eyebrow. Damn, this was one paranoid dude, with a very detailed escape plan. Ryder caught me taking a quick peek at Sam's shirtless form—seriously, it was purely professional interest because he was always so covered up, even in the weights room. Ryder quirked one side of his mouth before pulling his own shirt off.

Sam was forgotten as I allowed my eyes to slowly roam down Ryder's chiseled abs and tan smooth skin. Good Lord, he was a piece of work.

Everyone was in varying stages of undress now, and Jayden's wide eyes met mine.

"This is what I imagine heaven is like," he said.

I wondered if that would make the enforcers uncomfortable. Most men would have been, but they just laughed and shook their heads.

Sam, who was dressed now, went around distributing clothes to all of us. Grabbing my pile, I turned to face the plane. I ripped the tags off the new clothing, then wasted no time peeling my shirt and bra off, and dropping my black dress, exposing my booty shorts and thigh holster for my weapon. The sound of skin smacking skin jolted me as I was reaching for my new shirt.

"Shit, Ryder, I wasn't looking. It was an accident," Jared said.

Chuckling, I quickly shimmied into the new clothes. Sports bra and plain black underwear, jeans and a cotton shirt. A little large, but would do the job for now. Turning around, I saw Ryder had Jared in a headlock, but they were both smiling.

Boys, they never really grew up.

The rest of the enforcers needed to get some action soon or Ryder and Oliver were going to be the envy of everyone.

"Drink up," Sam said, passing each of us three bottles of our preferred blood type. We chugged until we were sickeningly full.

Then, following the lead of our silent secret keeper, he led us into a long hallway and into another smaller hanger. There was an open-roofed section, and on a platform rested a large silver-bladed helicopter.

Dammit, this was so not cool. I was a bit of a control freak, had been since school. I was always the one in charge of the group projects, the one telling everyone what to do. So it was hard for me to just file into this helicopter, no questions asked, and let Sam fly us off to God knows where. My favorite ass-kicking boots had been replaced with Walmart flip flops, my sexy push up bra with a cheap sports bra. We had literally just left all our earthly possessions behind.

Not to mention I'd never been in a helicopter, and the sight of those massive blades, which Sam now had whirling in a dizzying motion, did not fill me with happy rainbow thoughts.

That was the thing with limited options. I really did not have any other choices but to get my butt in there and hope we all survived.

The ride to our destination was loud and we couldn't really communicate. I was burning with questions for Sam. Was this just another stopover or would this metal bird take us to our final destination? How the hell were we going to feed ourselves now that we had no stores of blood? We had left our weapons behind, so what happened if we were attacked again?

He was going to give me answers soon or I was going to torture them out of him. Jayden could go at his eyebrows. That was definitely a form of torture.

Despite my fears, I eventually started to enjoy the helicopter ride. We traveled over the most beautiful and picturesque land I'd ever seen. Green upon green, wild and untamed, which slowly morphed out into a world of endless ice and snow. I tried not to be a wuss, but I shivered in my seat at the vast and isolated wilderness.

Where were we? Canada? Alaska?

I hadn't seen a human or a house for a long time. Finally some sort of structure came into view, and as the helicopter began to descend I realized this series of buildings was made of shipping containers. This had to be our destination. Wherever we were, it was damn cold; snow was thickly blanketed over the ground. I eyed my flip flops with dismay. Yes, ash were less sensitive to hot and cold, but snow in flip flops ... hell to the no.

After the helicopter landed, I leaned across Ryder to see the buildings better. A series of massive shipping containers were stacked high and in a square formation, which had created a good sized space. A logo on the side of the building furthered my confusion.

Alaskan Scientific Research Facility. Well, at least I knew where we were now.

When the helicopter blades had completely stopped, we all unbuckled and I ducked low as I jumped out. Once I was clear of those deadly blades, I stalked right up to Sam. Every exposed part of my body was already chilled and covered in bumps. I fought off the shivers. Holy shit it was cold, like the coldest I'd ever felt in my life.

That didn't stop my attitude from emerging in full force. "Okay, we're here, in Walmart flip flops, with no listening devices. Now tell me..." My chattering teeth lessened some of the stern nature of my voice. "What is this place? Why have you brought us here to the middle of nowhere?"

Sam's face, which was always confident and sure, faltered. He blinked a few times as if trying to figure out what to tell me. "I ... we ... there's..."

My stomach dropped. Oh God, was it a trap? Sam might not speak much, but the dude never stuttered like this.

The other guys were around us too, everyone waiting for an answer. Suddenly the door to the building slammed open, the crack echoing across the uninhabited wilderness. An absolutely gorgeous, tall and bespectacled blond woman leapt down the steps and ran towards us. She was fully outfitted for the weather, wearing a large blue puffy jacket.

"Sam!" she yelled, waving both hands at him.

Her focus was laser-like on the enforcer, but as I shifted to see her better, she flicked her gaze across to meet my eyes. In that moment both of us froze to the spot.

No way! My breath came out in panicked bursts as I stepped closer to her to be sure.

The heavy black edging of her glasses perfectly framed the silver in her eyes, which wasn't as bright as mine, but it was there.

Sam, who seemed to have regained his composure, stepped toward the blonde. "Charlie, this is Becca, the other unicorn."

Holy eff me! I wasn't the only female ash.

***

Stayed tuned for the final installment of the Hive Trilogy. Annihilate is due for release mid-late 2016!

Acknowledgements

Jaymin Eve – I always thank my family, and this is because they deserve it more than anyone else. Thank you for the hugs, and kisses. Thank you for the love and understanding. It is such a blessing to be able to stay at home and see my little girls grow each day. Thank you, Trav, for supporting and sacrificing for me and our family. I love you guys so much <3

Also a massive thanks as always must go to my betas Andi and Marice. You two are legit superheroes. Have I told you that lately? I couldn't do this without your support, friendship and clever eye for detail. Big hugs!

To my editor Lee and cover designer Tamara. Thank you both for finessing and beautifying this story. Thank you, Lee, for understanding that I just have to say "right now" and "a little" and not yelling at me when you have to take them out of the story a hundred times. Thank you Tamara for your amazing eye and talent for cover design. You're the best and I'm so grateful to have found you.

Thank you to all of the readers who have stuck with me, especially those in my Nerd Herd, Ash Enforcer group and Release Team. I absolutely love seeing your posts and enthusiasm for books and the worlds we create. I'd be sad to open FB and not see an awesome meme (or ten) to start my day. Leia and I appreciate every review, comment, email and message. We know we couldn't do this without all of you, and we are so grateful. Thank you! Thank you!

Lastly to Leia. Fate was at play when we met. Our friendship was meant to be, aligned in the stars. I know I have a friend for life, and I can't wait for all of our future book endeavors. <3 you BAFF!

Leia Stone – A huge thank you to my mom who helps to watch my twin tornadoes so that I can write these books for you all. To my husband who is my biggest fan and supporter, I love you babe! To every reader that has ever written to me saying, "please don't stop writing, I love your books." This is really all for you. I am so grateful to have such amazing and loyal readers. Priscilla and Bridgett my amazing betas, I love you girls. Thank you to our amazing Ash Enforcers who love Charlie as much as we do and post hilarious unicorn memes to prove it.

Lastly, Jaymin Eve, we were sisters in a past life and I love how seamless our creative process is. Thanks for being an amazing writing partner, friend and fellow mom. I look forward to our many many creative projects in the future. Eve Stone forever <3

Books from Leia Stone

Matefinder Trilogy (Optioned for film)
Matefinder: Book 1
Devi: Book 2
Balance: Book 3

Hive Trilogy
Ash: Book 1
Anarchy: Book 2
Annihilate: Book 3 (2016 release)

Stay in touch with Leia: www.facebook.com/leia.stone/
Mailing list: http://goo.gl/0EX98P

Books from Jaymin Eve

A Walker Saga - YA Paranormal Romance series (complete)
First World - #1
Spurn - #2
Crais - #3
Regali - #4
Nephilius - #5
Dronish - #6
Earth - #7

Supernatural Prison Trilogy - NA Urban Fantasy series
Dragon Marked - #1
Dragon Mystics - #2
Dragon Mated - #3

Sinclair Stories
Songbird - Standalone Contemporary Romance

Hive Trilogy
Ash - #1
Anarchy - #2

Stay in touch with Jaymin:
www.facebook.com/JayminEve.Author
Website: www.jaymineve.com
Mailing list: http://eepurl.com/bQw8Kf

Printed in Great Britain
by Amazon

THE PALE-EYED MAGE

THE DARK AMULET BOOK I

JENNIFER EALEY

Copyright (C) 2020 Jennifer Ealey

Layout design and Copyright (C) 2019 by Next Chapter

Published 2019 by Shadow City – A Next Chapter Imprint

Edited by Wendy Ealey

Cover art by Cover Mint

This book is a work of fiction. Names, characters, places, and incidents are the product of the author's imagination or are used fictitiously. Any resemblance to actual events, locales, or persons, living or dead, is purely coincidental.

All rights reserved. No part of this book may be reproduced or transmitted in any form or by any means, electronic or mechanical, including photocopying, recording, or by any information storage and retrieval system, without the author's permission.

PART I